The Death of Innocence

The Death of Innocence

Michael Houtchen

Seventh StarShadow

Copyright © 2020 by Michael Houtchen

All rights reserved. No portion of this book may be copied or transmitted in any form, electronic or otherwise, without express written consent of the publisher or author.

Cover design: Stephen Zimmer

Cover design in this book copyright © 2020 Stephen Zimmer & Seventh Star Press, LLC.

Editor: Holly Phillippe

Published by Seventh StarShadow

ISBN: 978-1-948042-98-7

Seventh StarShadow is an imprint of Seventh Star Press

www.seventhstarpress.com

info@seventhstarpress.com

Printed in the United States of America

First Edition

ACKNOWLEDGMENTS

I want to thank, as always, Stephanie, my muse, who also happens to be my wife, for all her encouragement. A special thanks to Charlotte 'M'. Yes, the same Charlotte as in the book. I can't forget FJ for his input. And finally, and definitely not the least, my publisher, Seventh StarShadow, especially Holly and Stephen.

Dedication

To my children: Eric, Nathan, Erik, Katie, and Samantha.

Chapter 1

"Mike, how does it feel being a bottom dweller?" Ray laughed, throwing in his cards.

"That was only the first hand," Mike shot back. "You know as well as I, the scores in *Hand and Foot* can change in a heartbeat."

"What's the score again?" Charlotte asked, as she started arranging the cards to be shuffled.

"Really, Charlotte?" Mike replied.

Charlotte laughed.

Mike stared at the thin white scar running across Charlotte's left check. The surgeons had done a great job re-constructing her cheekbones, and Charlotte could cover the scar with makeup, but she chooses not to. This was her *Red Badge of Courage*. It's hard to believe it had been a little over ten months since Charlotte had been beaten and kidnapped by terrorists, who were looking for a lost hydrogen bomb off the coast of Tybee Island, Georgia. It's harder to believe that it was this small group of "card playing senior citizens" who rescued her and saved the citizens of Savannah. No one would ever know, because the government hushed it up, which was alright with Mike. Things could have gone really bad that week and would have put an end to their card playing, not to mention the millions that would have died if the bomb had detonated. Mike hadn't said anything, but there had been times during the last ten months he'd noticed Charlotte staring off into space. He wanted to ask her if she was reliving those events, but he didn't have the nerve.

"I'd like to hear the score again," Stephanie laughed.

For a moment, Mike stared at her. "My own wife. The mother of my children. Even you?" Everyone, including Mike, laughed this time. Margaret started to say something, but Mike stopped her with a raised pointer finger.

"Here's the damn score again," Mike said, giving in. "Stephanie is ahead with 1940 (she raised both arms in triumph), Margaret is next at 1425, Charlotte is third with 1205, Ray is 900, and I'm 890."

"You didn't answer my question. How does it feel being a bottom dweller," Ray chimed in.

"You're only ten points ahead of me," Mike exclaimed. "The worm will turn before this game's over."

"Doubt it."

"I wish FJ was here," Mike stated flatly.

"Why's that?" Ray asked.

"I could be catching his shit as well."

Everyone laughed.

"Where is FJ, anyway," Stephanie asked, getting some small plastic bowls and a big container of Peanut M&Ms out of the pantry.

"He didn't say," Ray replied. "Said he had a big date tonight ... No, that's not right ... He said he had two big dates tonight."

"What does that mean, two big dates?"

"With FJ, who knows," Mike laughed. "Everything's big when you're a dwarf."

"That's not funny," Stephanie said.

"Yes, it's funny," Ray laughed. "If he were here, FJ would agree. You know as well as I – FJ doesn't like being called a little person. He was born with dwarfism, and he's not ashamed of it. Besides, he gives Mike hell about having only eight fingers, and you don't hear Mike complaining about being handicapped. Oh, pardon me, physically challenged."

"You guys shouldn't be making fun of Mike either."

"I'm right here," Mike interrupted. "And we're not making fun of each other. We're only kidding. We kid each other because we're brothers from different mothers, or at least we act like it. We mean no harm, and Lord knows, we would never make fun of a stranger who's physically challenged. And Lord help the person

2

who makes fun of one of us while the others are around." At that moment Ray's phone rang.

Looking at the Caller-ID, Ray didn't recognize the number. It was nine o'clock, and Ray didn't like getting calls in the evening from unknown numbers. He thought about not answering. He was torn. It was probably one of those tele-marketing calls everyone hates. One of those were someone is asking to speak to Bonnie. Who is this Bonnie, and why does everyone want to speak to her? What would they do if Bonnie actually answered? *But it could be important.* He was, after all, the Sheriff of Franklin, Kentucky.

"Hello."

"Ray, this is George, George Watson."

"What's up, George?"

I hope you're not looking for Bonnie.

"I hate bothering you, but I'd like for you to look at something."

"Can it wait till tomorrow?"

"No, the M.E. wants to move the body."

"Body?" Ray asked, pushing away from the table. Those around the table froze at the word "body."

"We shouldn't talk about it over the phone," George replied.

"Agreed. Where are you?" Ray asked.

"We're at an abandoned house out in the middle of nowhere, on Phillips Lane, about two miles off Highway 585, where the 585 and I-65 overpass intersect. You can't miss us. There's ... Let's see ... two firetrucks, an ambulance, the M.E.'s van, and my patrol car."

"I'll be there in twenty."

"What was that about?" Margaret asked, as Ray put his cellphone back in his shirt pocket.

"That was George. He—"

"I caught the George part, but George who?"

"George Watson."

"Oh, that George. What's he up to?"

"He wants me to look at a body."

"I caught that as well. Who?"

"Wouldn't say. Not over the phone, anyway."

"Was someone murdered?" Charlotte asked.

"He didn't say. Could be anything."

"That's horrible," Stephanie said. "Where is he?"

"Out on Phillips Lane, near the interstate. Off Highway 585. I'd say, about twenty minutes from here."

"So, why's he calling you?" Mike asked. "That's outside the city limits and not in your jurisdiction."

"He knows that. Maybe he needs help identifying the body."

"And that couldn't wait till morning?"

"I guess he also wants me to see the crime scene."

"Crime scene?" Charlotte asked. "So, somebody was murdered."

"He didn't say. Okay, people, we shouldn't jump to conclusions. I don't know any more than any one of you, and I won't know if I don't get out there."

"Then why are you standing here talking to us?" Margaret remarked.

Chapter 2

It wasn't hard finding the abandoned house, out in the middle of nowhere. Rolling hills, croplands, pastures, and patches of woods too small to be called a forest, would normally be pitch black this time of night, but not tonight. You could see flashing blue, red, and white lights a mile away. It looked like a scene out of *Close Encounters of the Third Kind*. The band *Walk the Moon's song "Shut up and Dance"* was playing on the radio when Ray pulled onto the dirt drive leading up to the house.

Ray parked beside George's car, got out and stood staring at the multi-colored lights bouncing off the somewhat white, abandoned vine covered house. Ray didn't like the look or smell of abandoned houses, and if you believed all the horror films, bad things happen in abandoned houses. He prayed there wasn't a basement. Worse things happen in the basements of abandoned houses. George Watson was standing on the front porch, staring down at Ray.

George was in his mid-thirties, really tall and really thin. He wore his clothes baggy, because he couldn't find any that would easily fit his frame. His clothes made him look like a country bumpkin, but don't let the look fool you. He was sharp as a tack and Ray's friend.

"Ten," George said.

"What?" Ray asked, carefully climbing the rickety stairs.

"You said it would take you twenty minutes to get out here, and it only took ten. Somebody must have been speeding."

"It's one of the perks of being a cop," Ray laughed, shaking George's hand. "Did you get a new phone number?"

"No. Why?"

5

"Your name didn't come up on Caller-ID. Just a number."

"That's my personal number. The deputy phone accidentally got dropped and is in the shop."

"George, why am I here at this ungodly hour?"

"What? Did I interrupt your card playing?"

Ray smiled and pitched him a finger.

"Come on, Ray," George laughed. "I'll show you why you're out here at this ungodly hour."

George stopped in the doorway and turned back to Ray. "Ray, this is not going to be good," George said, in his serious voice. Ray frowned, not liking where this was going.

Several battery-powered lamps were flooding the room. Ray could see several state CSI techs going about their business taking pictures, dusting for prints, putting small things in envelopes, and larger things in paper bags. "In here," George said, motioning with his hand. George led Ray into a side room which smelled of mold, vomit, and urine. Wallpaper clung to the walls in shreds. Spider webs filled the ceiling corners. As far as Ray was concerned, they could stay in the corners. Fine dust, stirred up by the techs, could be seen floating in the flood-lamp beams. Used condoms, cigarette butts, and discarded beer cans were being bagged and tagged. The only furniture in the room was a couple of broken dining room chairs and the dining room table. All normal stuff for abandoned houses. The one thing that shouldn't have been there was lying face down, beside the table, in a pool of blood. Ray stopped, letting his senses adjust to the horror: abandoned house, spider webs, trash, dust, smells, and a dead body. Ray quickly made the sign-of-the-cross. The M.E., kneeling beside the deceased, rose when she saw Ray.

"Hi, Nicole," Ray said.

"Hey Ray," Nicole came back. "I wanted to take the deceased back to the office, but George asked me to wait till you got here. Please, don't take long. It's getting late, and it'll be close to midnight before we get her booked in."

Nicole Goetz had been the county's medical examiner for thirty-plus years. Because of her age and weight, she was starting to slow down. Ray knew, there would come a day very soon when Nicole would seriously have to think about retiring. Ray dreaded that day. As far as he was concerned, she was the best in her field. Nicole looked like the little old grandmother everyone envisions, with a flowery print dress, knee high stockings, curly white hair, wrinkles everywhere, and small granny specs. Don't let her looks fool you. She had seen her share of death. She had never married. As she put it, "I'm single. I love it. I am woman. Hear me roar. You better listen for my roar, or you're libel to get your ass bit off." She loved playing Texas Hold'em, smoking cigars, and drinking Jack Daniels straight up. She could cuss like a sailor, when provoked. She was Ray's kind of woman.

Ray turned his attention to the deceased. He could see the body was that of a young woman with long blond hair. Five-foot-five, there about. Caucasian. Petite. She was wearing a white cotton shirt, blue jeans, and white tennis shoes. Bloody red blotches stained the back of her white shirt, each stain about two inches in diameter, no doubt, created by some type of blade. Ray didn't count, but there had to be over a dozen.

That many wounds meant only one thing, he thought. It was a crime of passion.

Ray walked around to the woman's head and knelt to get a good look at her face. A strand of hair was blocking his view. Carefully taking his little finger, Ray moved the strand out of the way.

Jerking upright and without warning, Ray fled the room. Nicole and George looked at each other, shaking their heads. This was hard, and they knew it. Dodging CSI Techs, Ray hurriedly made his way through the living room, to the front door and out onto the porch. Off to the side, out of everyone's way, he stood there staring out into the darkness, sucking air, trying not to hyperventilate, or puke. He kept reminding himself, this was not his first rodeo, not his first dead body. Tears started welling in his eyes. "Jesus," he sighed. It was then Ray felt a hand on his shoulder.

"Ray, you okay?" George asked.

Ray shook his head.

"Shit, no."

"I'm sorry, but I warned you, it wasn't going to be good."

"You know who she is, don't you?" Ray asked.

"Yes. I'm afraid I do."

"George, she's my Godchild."

"I know that too. I'm sorry."

"Then why in the hell did you bring me all the way out here?"

"I'm getting ready to head back into Franklin and break the news to her parents, but you should tell them, because you're her dad's best friend." For a moment, Ray stood there, staring at George.

"You're right, George. It would be better if they heard it from me."

"When they find out, how do you think they will take it?" George asked.

"How do you think? At first, they will be devastated. Then their pain will turn to rage and they will want revenge."

"That's what I thought. That's why I called you. Ray, you better stop her father, before something happens."

"I don't know if I can."

Chapter 3

Ray with a flashlight in hand, gave the abandoned house and grounds a good once over, before leaving. Besides the main driveway, there was another entrance coming from a side road. It curved around the back of the house, to a broken-down storage shed. The shed was nothing more than a pile of rotting timbers.

By the time Ray re-entered the city limits of Franklin, it was well past midnight. He thought about waiting until a more decent hour before heading over to FJ's, but this kind of news couldn't wait. What if someone else heard about the death and headed out to FJ's, to console him? They wouldn't know the correct words to say, to keep him from losing it. No, FJ had to hear it from him. Hopefully, he'd find the words to keep FJ from going ballistic.

Ray slammed on the brakes. *Jesus.* The light at the intersection of West Cedar and McLendon had caught him. Ray sat there, cursing and slamming the steering wheel. Then it dawned on him. He was the fricking Sheriff of Franklin, Kentucky, and he was on official business. *Piss on it.* Reaching down, he flipped on the red and blue flashers, but stopped short of turning on the siren. There was no use in waking up the good people of Franklin. He was a better neighbor than that. Looking in the rearview mirror, he noticed no one approaching, nor was there anyone on McLendon to the right. It felt good being sheriff. At this moment, it felt good running a red light.

FJ lived in a Gulf Stream, on a small lot on Macedonia Road, off Highway 31W, just south of Franklin, and Ray knew it would take about twenty minutes to get out there. As Ray drove, his mind wandered to when he first met Milton Frederick Johnston.

9

Twenty-five years ago, late one night, at a bar on the outskirts of Franklin, some drunks were about to do a number on Frederick, but Sheriff Ray Harris had stepped in and broke it up. Whenever Frederick was in town, the two would get together. It didn't take long for them to become close friends. Twenty-five years ago seemed like yesterday. After twenty-five years, a person's body gets lumpy, old, and slow, but not a person's memories.

Frederick was born with achondroplasia, a common form of dwarfism, with a normal-sized head and torso, but shortened limbs. He used to brag that what was in his pants more than made up for his shorter arms and legs. Abandoned by his mother because of his "ailment," Frederick ran away from several foster homes, before finally ending up in a traveling circus. At first, he was in a troupe of clowns and adults laughingly pointed him out to their children. "Look at the midget," they would shout. In truth, the word midget refers to a very short person, but with normal proportions. Frederick preferred to be called what he was, a dwarf. Frederick advanced through the circus ranks, first as a clown, then an acrobat, followed by an escape artist, and finally a knife thrower.

Circus pay was crap. Most of the time, not even minimum wage. After covering expenses, the rest of the evenings "take", was divided up equally among the performers. Big cities, big takes. Small towns, shitty takes. Luckily, the circus furnished smokes, lodging, and beer. Frederick started investing his money in stocks, bonds, and real estate, without telling his girlfriend Zoe (a.k.a The Girl on the Flying Trapeze). He knew unless he invested his money carefully, he wouldn't have a pot to pee in when he retired, if he got to retire, especially now since he had a daughter to think of. Frederick and Zoe Payne had partied in a hay field late one night in the middle of June, smoking pot and doing shots of tequila straight out of the bottle. It had been a scorcher for June, and to help combat the heat they decided to take their clothes off. Nine months later, a baby girl was born. Zoe swore up and down the baby was Frederick's, and Frederick liked the idea of being a dad. Zoe named their daughter Betty, not after any family members, but after Zoe's favorite cartoon character, Betty Boop.

10

Betty grew up in the circus tending livestock and the ferocious wild animals. She watered and fed Dorothy the forty-year-old Indian elephant who had arthritis and could barely walk, Sammy the blind and toothless African lion, the dozen or so miniature ponies, a troop of dachshunds from Hell, and an uncountable number of exotic birds and monkeys. Betty was home schooled. Circus schooled would be closer to the truth. She could spy a pickpocket a mile away. She knew all the sideshow barker's scams and would turn them over to the owners. Her parents taught her people came to the circus to have fun and forget their worries for a few hours, not to be taken advantage of. Betty loved her life. And why not? Wasn't it what all kids wanted to do? Run off and join the circus? That's what her parents had done. She was living the dream. Her mother loved her dream as well. Always traveling, seeing new sights, new smells, new foods, and new people. It never got old. Her father wasn't as pleased.

Frederick had changed, since becoming a father. It was alright for him when he was younger. That was a different time. Back then, people were different; kinder, more trustworthy — not today. No, the circus was no place to raise a daughter. Fred had seen how men stared at his daughter. Hell, he used to lust after other women with the same look, the same thoughts. The only problem with leaving the circus– Frederick knew no other trade, no other skills. There would come a day when the choice would be taken out of his hands.

They say time knows no bounds, and it's true. Betty grew into a beautiful young woman. She took after her mother; with long raven hair, slim body, ivory skin, and her mother's height of five-six. People stared as the two women passed them on the street, holding the hands of the little person walking between them like he was their child, their child with a beard.

They say love knows no bounds, and it's true. One evening at the Franklin Kentucky Fairgrounds, Betty noticed a handsome young man staring at her. Mr. Thomas Hall, twenty-years old, and a pig farmer by trade, it turned out was her one and only, according to him. All week he followed Betty around making goo-goo eyes

11

at her. Finally, Betty confronted him and asked him his intentions. He came right out and said she was the most beautiful woman he had ever laid his eyes on, and someday she would be his wife. Betty laughed so hard she peed her pants, but by the end of the week, they had run off to Nashville and got married. Mother and father of the bride weren't happy. Mother and father of the groom weren't happy.

Frederick and Zoe preached to Betty that she was too young and naive to get married. Too late, Betty explained, she was already married. Frederick stood there with his stubby hands behind his back, staring up at his new son-in-law, who stood over twice Frederick's height. Frederick was having trouble containing himself, and the words he wanted to use were words that would make a sailor blush. Tom's parents were more logical and asked how this marriage was going to work. Betty traveled with a circus, while Tom lived in Franklin raising hogs. Betty said they'd been thinking about that all week and that she had the perfect solution. She would stay in Franklin with her husband. Frederick exploded in a cursing spree. Pluto, the circus strong-man, heard every word and blushed. He had once been a sailor.

"No," Frederick screamed. "Not just no, but hell no."

Chapter 4

Ray would rather suck raw eggs, than do what he had to right now. Ray's tires crushed in gravel as he brought the patrol car, to a stop in front of FJ's trailer. It was pitch black with the only apparent light coming from the back end of the trailer, which Ray knew was FJ's bedroom. Ray sat there a moment, before getting out of the car. He could do this, he told himself. He had to do this. He had to do this for FJ.

It was deathly quiet and still. Because of what could happen after FJ was told of his grandchild's death, it appeared the moon was hiding behind a cloud, and the wind was holding its breath. FJ's '94 Honda Odyssey was gone, but a red T-Bird sat in its place. Walking over in the dark, Ray shined his flashlight into the driver's side and noticed the car was set up for average size people. FJ's Honda had a booster seat installed to get him high enough to be able to see over the dash. Very long pedal blocks were also added, to allow FJ to reach the brakes and throttle. The Odyssey was the only car FJ was legally allowed to drive. Ray wondered who owned this car.

Ray's knuckles rapped on the aluminum door. For a minute, nothing. *Come on, FJ.* Rapping on the door again brought no response. *Jesus, FJ. Open the fricking door.* Slamming on the door with the flat of his hand, Ray was rewarded with, "Keep your damn pants on."

"FJ, its Ray."

"Keep your damn pants on Ray." The door opened a crack. "What is it, Ray? Something happen to Margaret?"

"No. But we need to talk."

"You have cancer?" FJ asked without opening the door any further.

"What in the hell does that mean?"

FJ stared at him, waiting for an answer.

"You're kidding. (FJ stared) Okay, no. I don't have cancer."

"Syphilis?"

"What?"

"Syphilis?"

"No."

"Gonorrhea?"

"Damnit, FJ. No."

"No STD's at all?"

"No."

"So, you're telling me, it doesn't hurt when you pee?"

Ray shook his head.

"Take two aspirins and come back tomorrow," FJ said, closing the door.

Ray stood there a moment staring at the aluminum door.

"What the ..."

Ray started playing the door like a drum with both hands.

"Come on, Frederick. It's important."

FJ opened wide the door.

"You only call me Frederick when something really bad happens. You said Margaret was okay. Mike and Stephanie, okay?"

Ray nodded.

"Has something happened to Charlotte? She hasn't been kidnapped by terrorists again and needs my rescuing, has she?"

Ray shook his head this time.

"Okay," FJ said sadly, turning away from the door. "Come on in,"

Stepping into FJ's trailer, one enters straight into the living room. Across the room from the front door and off to the right, was the bathroom and laundry. To the left, the kitchen and dining area. A short hallway ran off to the right, to the only bedroom. At the moment, the only thing that caught Ray's eyes was FJ. He was standing there naked as a Jay-bird. At that moment, Ray had an epiphany. Why was it always Jay-birds? The last time Ray looked; all birds were naked. Why not Crows? Naked as a Crow? Why not Ducks. How about Cardinals or Robins? Naked as a Robin sounds good.

"Jesus," Ray exclaimed. "FJ, get some clothes on."

FJ grabbed a pillow off the couch and covered his crotch. A giggle came from the bedroom.

"You have company? A girl?" Ray asked.

FJ raised two fingers and smiled.

"Two girls?"

FJ's smile got bigger.

"They need to leave," Ray said sternly.

"Oh, come on Ray."

"Frederick, they need to leave. Now."

"Come on, girls. The sheriff says you have to leave."

The first girl that came out of the bedroom was a full-busted redhead, wearing only a pair of red panties with white letters W-K-U across the crotch. She had to be over six-foot-tall and like most redheads, covered in freckles. Her messed up hair brushed the small trailer's ceiling. Probably a college girl from Western Kentucky University. The second girl looks like the other, same build, same height, same dress, but was blond. FJ noticed Ray staring at their height.

"They're both on Western's volleyball team."

"Ladies," Ray said, "you need to get dressed and head on back to Bowling Green."

Noticing they were half-nude, both girls covered their breasts with a hand and forearm. Ray noticed the redhead had a white spot of something on the corner of her mouth. He pointed, too afraid to ask what. Taking the tip of his finger, FJ wiped the spot off, looked at it, smelled it, and put it in his mouth.

"Jesus," Ray exclaimed, turning away.

"It's Cool Whip," the redhead laughed. "We emptied a large tub of Cool Whip on each other and then we -"

"Stop right there," Ray said, holding his hand up.

"You really a sheriff?" the blond asked. Ray nodded.

"You have a gun?" the redhead asked.

Ray patted the holster on his belt.

"You two need to get out of here," he said, pointing toward the front door.

"We need to take Mr. Dinklage ... Peter back to his car. It's at Tony's Bar in Bowling Green," the redhead said, putting her free hand on FJ's shoulder.

"I'll get Mr. Dinklage back to his car," Ray said, pointing at the door again.

"And remember girls," FJ said with a finger across his lips. "Not a word that I'm here in Franklin slumming."

"No, Peter. Not a word." They both giggled at the same time.

"When will we see you again?" the blond asked.

"I come to Tony's now and then."

"We'll be looking for you," the redhead laughed.

After they had gone, Ray took a seat on the couch.

"So, you told them you were Peter Dinklage, the actor? You do that all the time. When are you going to get it through your head, that's illegal?"

"I thought it was only illegal to pretend you're a priest, police office, or a doctor, maybe a lawyer," FJ said, standing there naked as a Robin. "Besides, they approached me. 'Are you the little person who plays the little person on *Game of Thrones?*' the redhead asks. I tell the redhead; he's not playing a little person on the show because he is a little person. Everyone in the bar laughs. Then someone in the back yells out, 'You're Peter Dinklage.' Then I held my hands up and said, 'You caught me.' Then everybody's happy. I certainly was, until you showed up."

"Okay. I know, as well as you," Ray laughed, "just because you wear your hair and beard just like the actor on the show, it doesn't give you the right to pretend to be him, even if you do look like him ... Sort of."

"Sort of?"

"You can't go around signing autographs using his name. I know that's most definitely illegal."

"Ray, why are you here?"

"Go get some clothes on first."

FJ disappeared into the bedroom and left Ray sitting on the couch. Ray looked over at the refrigerator and wondered if FJ had any raw eggs. He didn't know what he was going to say, and he dreaded what was coming. A cabinet with all FJ's electrical devices stood beneath a wall-mounted flat-screen. On top of the cabinet was a couple of 8x10's. Ray stood and walked over. He stood there a moment looking at one of the photos. It was of two young people, Betty and Thomas. *The week of their wedding,* he thought. They seemed happy.

The day Betty left the circus, FJ retired. The circus owner wasn't pleased. Zoe wasn't either. "How are we going to live?" she exclaimed. It was then FJ told her about the money he'd been investing. She went ape-shit. Why had he kept that from her? Didn't he trust her? How could he? If he loved her, he should have told her. What other secrets was he hiding? She screamed and stomped her foot. It would be a cold day in Hell if he thought she was going to leave the circus. It must not have been a cold day in Hell, because the next day when the circus train pulled out, Zoe was on it. It was an early morning departure, and a cold fog hung over the tracks. FJ and Betty stood on the Franklin Station platform, watching as the train pulled out to parts unknown. They wondered if they would ever again see Zoe Payne, a.k.a. The girl on the flying trapeze.

Sadly, Ray picked up the other 8x10. A beautiful young girl smiled back at him. She was sixteen. Memories from last year floated through Ray's mind. Memories of another girl who was also sixteen when she died. A young girl named Sara Sinclair. A young girl who was murdered on Tybee Island. At that moment, FJ came walking out of the bedroom.

"She's all grown up," FJ said, when he noticed Ray looking at the photo. Ray nodded.

"FJ, that's what I'm here to talk about."

FJ must not have heard, because he continued. "That picture was taken last week. It was her sixteenth birthday." Ray nodded again.

"I know. I was there. FJ, we–"

"I know you were Ray. Her Godfather needs to be at all her birthdays. I think it's a federal law."

"FJ–"

"I'm not sure. Could be a state law. You remember when she was born?" FJ asked. "Of course you do. You and Margaret were there. I remember looking down at her, and I told Betty, 'The baby looks so innocent.' And, that's when Betty said, 'Pop that will be her name. Innocence.' Ray, it was the proudest day of my life; the day I got to name my granddaughter."

"Damnit, Fredrick," Ray said, placing the photo back on the cabinet face down. "We need to talk."

Chapter 5

"Okay Ray," FJ said, as he climbed onto the sofa. "Let's talk."

Ray sat down beside FJ. He couldn't look into his friend's eyes. It was too hard. All he could do was stare at the ceiling.

"Well, Ray. You wanted to talk."

"I don't know how to begin," Ray whispered. "It's about–"

"My God, something's happened to Betty? Or Tom?"

"No, Frederick."

"Why do you keep calling me by my given name?"

"Where did Foster Care come up with that name? When you got older, did they give you the opportunity to change your name? What would you have named yourself? And, you never told us, but how many families did you live with before you finally escaped to the circus? Three? Four?"

"Ray, are you here to talk about my name and upbringing, or is there something else? You going to spit it out, or do we have to play twenty questions?"

"Innocence is dead," Ray blurted out. It wasn't his finest moment.

FJ sat there staring at Ray as if Ray were speaking Klingon. The words just didn't make sense.

"Ray, what are you trying to say?"

"I'm sorry, FJ. Innocence is dead."

Finally, the words sunk in.

"Oh my God," FJ exclaimed, sliding off the sofa. "When?"

"I don't know the exact time; earlier tonight or sometime late yesterday. Hell, I don't know when. Her body was found outside my jurisdiction."

19

"Her body was found? What in the hell, does that mean?"

"FJ, I can't give you details, if I don't know details. If I were to guess –"

"How did she die?"

Ray sat there, staring.

"Was she murdered?"

Again, Ray just sat there staring.

"You can't say, or you don't know?"

"A little of both."

"Who murdered her?" FJ questioned.

Ray shook his head.

"Who found her, then?"

"George Watson didn't say."

"George, the County Mountie?"

"George called me to come out and identify her body. He thought it would be better if you heard it from me. He's breaking the news to Betty and Tom."

FJ walked over and picked up the photo Ray had placed face down on the cabinet. His back was to Ray, but Ray could hear sobs. Ray wanted to say something, but he didn't know what to say. What can you say at a moment like this? What words would ease the pain? Sometimes, no words are the best words. Ray wanted to embrace his old friend, showing him some kind of support, but Ray's legs were too weak to stand. Time stalled. How much time? Who knows? A few minutes for sure, but for Ray, it felt like it had been hours.

"So, Innocence died sometime this evening or yesterday," FJ said, breaking the silence and restarting time. "But you're not sure. You're not saying if she was murdered or not. But I'm guessing she was murdered because you haven't disagreed. You don't even know who found her."

Ray frowned. "I am sorry; I don't know much."

FJ turned to face Ray. "You don't know. You don't know. You don't know. You don't know a damn thing. Ray, what good are you?"

For Ray, time stalled again. *FJ's right. What good am I?* A knock on the door jumpstarted time.

Standing, Ray opened the door. It was Betty and Tom. Betty gave Ray a quick hug and went to her dad. Dropping to her knees, she embraced her father.

"Oh, Pop," she sobbed. "She's dead."

They swayed and cried on each other's shoulder. Ray's eyes were welling up, as he stood there holding Tom's hand.

"We didn't see Fred's car outside," Tom whispered to Ray. "Thought for a moment he wasn't here. But we saw your patrol car and decided to come on in."

"I forgot all about FJ's car," Ray admitted. "Tom, you may need to run him up to Bowling Green and pick it up. He left it at Tony's Bar and Grill."

"That's not a problem. Ray, how much do you know about what happened to Innocence?"

"Probably nothing more than what George already told you. I'm sorry, Tom."

"I know you are. What happens next?"

"Yes, Ray, what happens next?" Betty asked, looking up at him.

"George should have told you all this. He's in charge. But, in a death like this, there will have to be an autopsy. The M.E., Nicole Goetz, is good. She'll–"

"What do you mean, in a death like this?" Betty interrupted.

"What George is not telling you," Ray snapped, "is Innocence was murdered."

"Ray! George said she's dead, and they're going to perform an autopsy to determine why. Ray, was she murdered?" Betty asked, looking up at Ray.

"I've said too much," Ray admitted.

"Don't expect Ray to answer," FJ snapped, looking down at the floor. "He doesn't know jack shit."

"Dad, that's not fair. Ray said he's not in charge. If he knew anything, I'm sure he would tell us."

"Would you, Ray? Would you tell us?" FJ asked, this time looking straight at Ray.

21

"I would tell you if I could."

"If you could? That's bullshit," FJ exclaimed. "You've been a family friend for years, and all you can say, 'If I could.' Ray, you need to leave."

"Dad!"

"Ray, I don't want you in my house."

"Fred, that's awful stern," Tom stated.

"Stay out of this, Tom."

"No, FJ's right," Ray said, nodding his head. "I need to leave. I'm not doing any good here. If I hear anything I can tell, you'll be the first to know. George will get with you sometime soon, probably tomorrow, and make arrangements. He'll do you good."

Betty stood and embraced Ray. "I'm sorry, Ray," she whispered. "I know how much you loved Innocence. You are family Ray. You have always been family. You will always be family. You know that." With tears floating from his eyes, Ray nodded. Ray turned and nodded to Tom. For a moment, he stared at FJ. Then he turned and left.

Chapter 6

Ray stopped the cruiser at the entrance to FJ's lot, laid his head on the steering wheel, and cried his heart out. He couldn't remember the last time he cried this hard. *Hell, I didn't cry this hard when mom or dad died.* Images of Innocence lying there on the dusty floor flashed through his mind. Images, clothed in shadows of what could have happened to her, haunted him. His brain hurt. FJ was right. What good was he? He didn't know jack shit, but that was going to change. Innocence didn't die in the city limits, so the case didn't fall in his lap. But that wouldn't stop him from conducting his own investigation, even if it meant stepping on some people's toes, even if it meant losing his badge. Betty and Tom deserved that. FJ deserved that. He deserved that. More important, Innocence deserved that. His cell phone rang. The Caller-ID said it was Margaret.

"What's going on, Ray? You haven't called, and it's been hours."

"I'm sorry, Margaret. But I've been tied up. I'm on my way home right now, and I'll fill you in when I get there."

"Where are you now?"

"I'm leaving FJ's."

"Has something happened to FJ?"

"No, Margaret ... Margaret, there's something else I need to do right now. I need to make another stop before I get home. I could be a while. Please, don't wait up."

"Ray, you've been up all night. You're seventy years old, and you're not a spring chicken anymore. You've got a weak heart and high blood pressure. All this stress is physically weighing on you.

You're libel to fall asleep driving."

"I'm not going to drop dead from a heart attack if that's what you really mean, nor am I going to fall asleep at the wheel. Margaret, I'll be home in an hour, no later."

The Simpson County Coroner's office was just down the street from the Franklin Police Department. At this hour, Cedar Street was deserted, so Ray cruised slowly by the two-story building looking for any sign of life. Nicole's car was parked out front instead of in the back, and there were no lights burning in any of the rooms facing the street. But that didn't mean Nicole wasn't in there. Most of the real work took place in the back. Parking on the street, Ray got out and approached the front door.

Ray knew the front door into the building was always locked, no matter what time of day. No one could gain access without first identifying themselves and stating their business. Standing in the spotlight shining from above the entrance, Ray pressed a button which read, "Press me." Simple enough. Somewhere in the building an alarm sounded, a few seconds later Nicole's voice came over a small speaker mounted beside the door. "Hello, Ray. You're out awful late, or is it early?"

Ray waved at the small camera mounted above the door.

"I guess, late. You got a minute, Nicole?"

"Give me a few."

Ray looked up and down the street. Still, no one was out and about. Too early. He craved a cigarette right now. He had quit smoking ten years ago, but there wasn't a day that went by, that he didn't want one. Ray gave the street another look-see. It wouldn't be long before Johnny Martindale would be dropping off the morning paper at the local stores. The sound of the door unlocking drew Ray's attention. "Nicole–"

"Before you get started Ray," Nicole said, standing in the doorway, holding the door open with her left hand, "you know I'm not supposed to talk to anyone, not even you, about Innocence. How would you feel if I talked to someone about one of your cases?"

"Nicole, I understand, but I need something, anything. My mind is racing. It's killing me."

"Okay, Ray. You're not going to like this. We just began processing her, and it's late. We won't start the autopsy until in the morning, which is only a few hours from now, and I'll be damned if I'll perform an autopsy half asleep. So, I don't have anything to say right now."

"Did she die from the knife wounds?"

"Damnit, Ray. Didn't you hear anything I just said? I don't know. It could have been blunt force trauma."

"How can knife wounds contribute to blunt force trauma?"

"You didn't notice the back of her head?"

"No. I guess I was too busy looking at all the fricking holes in her back."

"Ray, someone took something to the back of her head. And before you ask, right now I don't know which one came first — the blow to the back of her head or the 'knife' wounds, and I won't know if they were knife wounds, until the autopsy. And that won't happen until sometime tomorrow morning. Now go home. Tomorrow, I want you to get with George Watson before you do anything else. If you bring me a signed statement from George allowing you to be a participant, or he calls me, then I'll fill you in when I find anything. Until then, my hands are tied. Ray, go home and get some sleep."

"At least she wasn't raped," Ray said, ignoring her words.

"Is that what's bothering you? Is that why you're here? Ray, I can't say. Not that I'm hiding anything, but I don't know, not right now at least."

"But she still had her clothes on."

"Rapist have been known, because of remorse or shame, to redress their victims."

"You're shitting me? Is that what happened here?"

Nicole took a big breath and slowly exhaled. "Ray, like I said, we won't know anything until after the autopsy, and that won't happen until tomorrow; I mean later today. Ray, please go home and get some rest."

A car, driving on the wrong side of the street, was slowly making its way down Cedar. It was Johnny Martindale delivering

25

the morning paper. He drove on the wrong side of the street so the driver's side would be closest to the front doors. This way it allowed him to throw the rolled-up paper from the driver's window. Ray knew it was against the law driving on the wrong side of the street, but he'd known Johnny since the day Johnny was born, and it was way too early in the morning for traffic to be out.

"I'm not sure I can get any sleep," Ray said to Nicole. "That's why I'm not home now." Ray nodded to Johnny, who waved back. "There's too much plowing through my mind right now. I keep seeing Innocence lying on the floor. Nicole, I've seen dead bodies before, but—"

"But not someone you love," Nicole interrupted. "Someone close to you, who was murdered. Someone whose life was snuffed out way to early. Ray, what you're going through is normal. Go home. Even if you can't sleep, try at least to rest. In the morning, get with your doctor. He can give you something to help you sleep."

Franklin is a small town, a really small town, and the drive home took only five minutes. Margaret was still up, waiting with a cup of coffee and a bottle of aspirins.

"About time," she said, handing Ray the cup and the bottle. "Talk to me."

For the next few hours, Ray went over everything that had happened since he left earlier last night. Except he left out the knife wounds. That information could be used to catch the killer. It was four in the morning when Ray crawled into bed. His head was throbbing.

Ray slept, but his dreams where full of demons. Flashes of abandoned houses and dead girl's eyes floated in and out of focus. The coppery smell of blood overflowed his sinuses. It hung in the air like a stain. Something told him it was a dream, but he couldn't wake up. He tried. God knows he tried. The closer he came to waking, the deeper he fell. He wanted to scream. He tried to scream. He opened his mouth, but nothing came out. Finally, exhaustion became his closest friend, and he gave in to its warmth and darkness. He woke in a cold sweat.

Ray swung his legs off the bed and sat there holding his

throbbing head. Looking at his watch, it was ten o'clock in the morning. He felt as bad as when he first went to bed. But he had to get up. He needed a shave and a shower. He needed a cup of strong coffee. He needed aspirins, and he needed to make two phone calls, one to FJ and the other to George to set up a meeting. Only one of the calls was answered.

Chapter 7

"Thanks for meeting with me George," Ray said, shaking hands.

"Well, you said you were paying, and I could pick the restaurant. How could I refuse?"

"You picked one of my favorites. Margaret and I come to the Cracker Barrel every Sunday after mass. I love their breakfast, especially the biscuits and gravy."

George looked at his watch. It was eleven o'clock. "Me too. You know, it doesn't have to be breakfast time to enjoy breakfast."

"I know exactly what you mean."

Once seated, both men ordered coffee. George selected the Old Timer's Breakfast. Ray ordered the Double Meat Breakfast.

"Ray, I'm sorry, but you look like shit. Hard night?"

Ray nodded. "You don't know how hard. George, I need something from you."

"I know. I talked with Nicole earlier today. She said you came over. Ray, I'm not sure I can let you get involved. You're too close to the deceased."

"George, if you don't let me help, I'm not sure I can handle Frederick."

"Is that the only reason?"

"Sure it is."

"Really?"

"No. Not really. George, I feel useless. I want to do something. I desperately need to do something."

"Jesus, Ray. You've put me in a hard place. You're a friend, and I want to help. Really I do. But I got a call this morning from the state HQ. How did they put it? They believe, this case

29

is beyond my meager talents. They said a County Constable is elected based on how popular he is, not on his skill set. Do you believe that horseshit? They're sending down some big shot from Frankfort this morning to take over the investigation. They said, if I follow instructions and keep out of the way, I could help. Ray, they want me to be their fricking flunky."

"I can understand where you're coming from," Ray said. "But, if you don't kiss ass, we won't know what's going on."

"Ray, you don't think I know that. That's why I went out and bought a case of Dr. Bronner's Organic lip balm."

Both men laughed.

"Look," Ray continued, leaning in. "This guy coming down from Frankfort doesn't know the where-abouts around here. He's going to need somebody's help, and it might as well be you. Together, you and I have a better chance of solving Innocence's murder then he does. What do you say? You, and me?"

George sat there a moment staring at his fried eggs.

"Count me in, Ray."

"So, there are things you know that I don't," Ray said with a big sigh of relief. If George had said no, Ray didn't know what he would have done. "I need to be brought up to speed. Was Innocence murdered at the house, or was her body dropped there? Why that house? Who discovered the body? Who was she seen with that day? Why would anyone want to kill her? How did she die? I mean, was it the wound to her head, or all the knife wounds?"

"I can answer some of those. Nicole said, from all the blood loss, it looked like Innocence was murdered at the house. She will better determine that after the autopsy. I think that answers your first question. Let's see. The house in question is the old MacGregor place. It's been abandoned for years. A lot of high school kids go out there to party. They drink, do drugs, and have sex."

"Innocence wasn't that kind of girl," Ray blurted out.

"Ray, I mean no disrespect, but are you sure? When was the last time you had a heart to heart with her? Hell, would she even tell you? Better yet, would she tell her parents? I'm going to have to ask them that."

Ray could feel his temper rising. "If she was having sex, then she was raped. Good God, she was only sixteen."

"You're right. The law says that's rape, but you know kids today. Maybe you don't. Kids are trying everything at her age. Ray, it's something we'll have to look at." Ray didn't like it but nodded his head anyway.

"So, who found the body," Ray asked, changing the subject.

"Billy Hayden. He called me around 7:30 or 7:40 last night. He was coming home from the store. It turns out, his wife is pregnant and craving bananas and pickles. How gross is that? My ex-wife used to fulfill her craving by dipping bar-b-que chips in mayonnaise. You talk about gross. It almost made me puke just watching her." Ray started tapping his fingers on the tabletop. "Anyway, as Billy drove by, he noticed a light burning through the cracks of one of the boarded-up windows.

"When the kid's party out there, they use lanterns or candles or both. If it was a candle, Billy didn't want the house to burn down, so he called me. There are times when I wish the old house would burn down. It would save me a lot of sleep from having to go out there. Hell, Billy called me out there a month ago, because a group of college kids had come down from Western and were having an orgy. I was told half the girls' volleyball team was there. Billy told me he thought he saw a young kid dart out the back door. If there was a kid there, that's serious shit. The kid was gone by the time I got there. I think someone from Franklin, who knew about the house, planned it all. That time, they left dozens of candles burning." Ray smiled. George continued.

"So, Billy enters the house, and he finds a candle burning. He also finds Innocence. It looks like she met someone out there."

"That's hard to believe," Ray confessed. "How did she know about that place, and who did she meet?"

"That's the question, isn't it?"

"Okay, who does she hang out with?" Ray asked.

"You would know better than I. And I won't know that till I've, we've, talked with her parents. By 'We,' I mean the big shot from Frankfort and me."

"That won't keep me from talking to Betty and Tom," Ray said. "Hell, Innocence was my Godchild after all. What was the motive?"

"The motive and how she died. I don't have the answer to either of those questions," George confessed. "Maybe Nicole will have the answer to the second question."

"When's the autopsy?" Ray asked.

"She should be doing it now. She wants to turn over the body to the family as soon as possible."

Thoughts of what Nicole was doing to Innocence's body, made the biscuits and gravy in Ray's stomach harden into concrete. To change the subject, Ray asked. "Who would want to kill Innocence?"

"If we had the answer to that question, I bet we would have the motive."

Chapter 8

As they had walked to their cars, George told Ray he was meeting the asshole from Frankfort at the ME's department in half an hour.

"I might be late," George said, sarcastically. "I could blame it on 'my meager talents.'"

Ray laughed, but secretly he liked the idea. That gave him plenty of time to meet with Betty and Tom. Maybe FJ was at their house. Before Ray left the Cracker Barrel's parking lot, he tried FJ's number. FJ didn't pick up. *Probably sees it's me on Caller-ID.* Next, he selected Betty's number from his list of contacts. She answered on the second ring.

"Hey, Ray," she said before he could say anything.

Probably sees it's me on Caller-ID.

"Hi, Betty. You got a minute?"

"Sure."

"Is FJ there?"

"No. He won't leave his trailer, and he doesn't want us to come over. Ray, he says he's okay, but I can tell he's drinking. You know what he's like when he's been drinking."

"Hell. Do you blame him? I'm not sure I would handle it any differently. Betty, can I come over? I'd like to ask you some questions."

"Sure, come on over. We've been wondering when you would."

"Is Tom home?"

"He's out in his workshop. We can't do anything until after the autopsy."

Ray felt the concrete biscuits and gravy in his stomach again.

33

"Great," He said, taking his mind off the autopsy. "Maybe both of you can help me out."

"Come on over."

"Maybe I'll swing past FJ's on my way over."

"Please don't. Not right now, at least. Give him some space. Ray, he's in a foul mood. Give him a day or two."

"I'll be over in a minute."

Betty was right. What he needed right now was answers, and that wouldn't come from a drunk.

Twenty years and five hog farms later, Tom and Betty Hall were doing quite well. For the first three years, the two scraped by, living next door to their one and only pig farm. Not anymore. Betty couldn't handle the pig smell and all the poop, tons, and tons of pig poop. It was everywhere. Handling poop was the company's number one expense. It had to be disposed of, so it wouldn't endanger the environment. Farmers had been fined and sentenced to long jail time, for secretly dumping pig poop in their local streams and rivers.

No matter how much you tried, poop was always on the bottom of your shoes. No matter how much you tried, you were always tracking it in. Betty swore, someday they would have a changing shack as a go-between, from the pig farms to the main house. Before you could come to the main house, you had to strip down in the shack, take a shower, and dress into clothes that had never been near a pig pen. And vice versa. Before you went to the farms, you had to stop at the go-between shack and change into poopy clothes. The main house had to be far enough away, miles in fact, from any pen to guarantee no smells. Thank heaven for Quail Ridge.

Betty and Tom built their house in Quail Ridge, just north of Franklin proper, one year before Innocence was born. To build a home on one of its three acre lots, the home's value had to be in the four-hundred to five-hundred thousand dollar range. Hogs are smelly and always covered in poop, but they make great hams, chops, sausage, and bacon.

When Innocence was old enough, her friends from school

would come over for pool parties, sleep overs, and birthday parties. Ashley McCoy became Innocence's best friend in the first grade. BFFs. Today, they were both junior varsity cheerleaders. If you saw Innocence, Ashley was around somewhere. Ashley was having a hard time, almost as hard as Betty and Tom. At the moment, Ashley was in Innocence's room, going through her photo albums. Early that morning, Ashley had called asking for a photo to remember Innocence by. *Like you don't have hundreds of selfies of you and Innocence already,* Betty had thought. When Ashley arrived, Betty had told her to run on up to Innocence's room and bring down some photo albums. She would need some pictures for a slideshow the funeral home would make. Betty would wait in the den.

Truth be known, Betty hadn't entered Innocence's room since George's visit, when she learned about her daughter's death. After George left, she went upstairs and stood by Innocence's bedroom door, but she couldn't cross the threshold. It was as if there was an invisible barrier blocking the doorway. She couldn't even bring herself to reach inside and turn the light on. She was afraid of what she would see, of what might grab her. She knew at some point; she would have to pick out something for the funeral from Innocence's closet. Maybe, she would run up to Bowling Green and find something new; something Innocence hadn't worn. Something Betty hadn't seen Innocence wearing before.

For sixteen years, Innocence had called this home. This was the only home Innocence knew. The only home she would ever know.

Today, the 3,000 square foot home was eerily silent. Tom was out back in his workshop, dealing with the pain by creating something beautiful in wood. Ashley was in Innocence's bedroom. Betty sat alone in the den, sipping on a rum and coke, staring at the walls. Overnight everything had changed. She hadn't told Tom yet, but she wasn't sure she could live in this house any longer. This house. She couldn't bring herself to call it home. It was not a home anymore. Shadows of Innocence were everywhere. They haunted her. No matter where she looked, she saw something that reminded her of her daughter. The smell of her daughter's hair hung thick in the hair. Betty knew it was only her mind playing tricks on her, but she could swear it was real. She knew she was on the verge of a nervous breakdown. After the funeral, she'll tell Tom; for her to keep her sanity, they'd have to move. *After the funeral.* Bending over, Betty covered her eyes with her hands and sobbed deeply. The doorbell rang, making her jump.

Placing her drink on the coffee table, Betty grabbed a couple of Kleenex and hurried off to answer the front door.

"Come on in Ray," Betty said, opening the door and dabbing her eyes.

"Betty, who mows your yard?"

"I don't know Ray. Tom has some service. Is it important?"

"No, not really. Just curious."

"Let's go to the den," Betty said, closing the door. Ray paused when a sound came from upstairs. "Ashley McCoy's in Innocence's room, looking through pictures," Betty said, placing her hand on Ray's arm. Ray knew the girls were close. He remembered seeing her at Innocence's birthday party last week.

"Have a seat," Betty said, as she walked to an intercom system mounted on the wall by the sliding doors leading out to the swimming pool. "I'll let Tom know you're here." Ray took a seat on the sofa. He noticed the drink on the coffee table. With Betty's back to him, Ray picked up the drink and took a sniff. There was a heavy smell of Bacardi. Ray quickly placed the glass back on the table, as close to the place he had picked it up.

"Tom," Betty said, pressing one of the buttons on the front panel, "Ray's here."

"Tell him, give me a minute to get the sawdust off, and I'll be right in."

Ray nodded.

"He heard you," Betty said, smiling.

Ray stood when Tom entered through the sliding door and shook his hand. "Have a seat, Ray," Tom said, pointing at the couch. "Would you like something to drink?" he asked, noticing the glass on the coffee table.

"Nothing right now. Thanks. I just ate breakfast with George

Watson."

"Betty said you have a few questions for us. But let me ask you one first. When are we going to get Innocence's body?"

"As soon as the autopsy is over," Ray replied. "Should be sometime this afternoon."

"That's what George said," Betty added. "But we were hoping it would be sooner."

"You don't want to hurry these things," Ray assured them. "You want the job done right."

"So, Ray, what questions do you have for us?"

Taking a small spiral notepad from his shirt-pocket, Ray flipped to the first empty page.

"Some of these questions may sound harsh, but they need to be asked. And I'm sorry, but George probably asked you the same questions already, and if he didn't, he will. So, no matter how hurtful, you'll have to answer them again. For your information, George and I don't want anyone to know we're working together."

"I understand. I heard about the cop from Frankfort," Tom assured him. "Go ahead and ask."

"Remember, some of these questions will hurt, but to get the full picture, they have to be asked. (Tom and Betty nodded) Innocence was found, out at the old MacGregor place."

"George told us that," Betty said. "We've never heard of the MacGregor's."

"Did George tell you what goes on out there?" Ray asked.

"Yes, he did."

"Was Innocence a party girl?" Ray asked.

"She had friends. They hung out together. They went to parties. Does that make her a party girl?" Betty asked.

"You know what Ray means," Tom said. "What he wants to know, was Innocence a slut?"

"Is that what you meant?" Betty asked, her eyes starting to fill up.

"Not in those words," Ray answered, giving Tom a stern look. "Jesus. This is tough. What I meant; did she like to drink? Did she have multiple boyfriends? Has she ever tried drugs? Was she into sex?"

"No. No. Hell, no. And I'll kill the bastard who ever touched her," Tom exclaimed. "Shit, she's only sixteen. Ray, she was a good girl."

"I know she was, Tom. But, as I said, these questions would be hurtful, but I had to ask. How was she doing in school?"

"AB honor roll. Cheerleader. She loved school."

"Did someone have a grudge against her?"

"What for? (Ray shrugged his shoulders) No, Ray, everyone liked Innocence."

"Did anyone have a grudge against either of you?"

"Do you think someone would hurt her, to get even for something we did?"

"Tom, I have to ask."

"No, Ray," Tom said, looking at Betty. "There's nothing like that going on."

"Did she have a boyfriend?"

Tom looked at Betty again and shrugged his shoulders.

"She went out on a couple of dates, but with different boys," Betty answered. "I don't think she had a steady."

"She was found at the MacGregor place late Friday. Do you have any idea why she would be out there at that time, and who she would be meeting?"

"None," Tom and Betty answered simultaneously.

Ray stood to be going but sat back down. "One other question. Did Innocence have a driver's license?"

"Yes," Tom answered. "I gave her a red Chevy Camaro the day she got her license. That was the day after her birthday party."

"I knew you were giving her a car, but I didn't know she already had her license. Where's the car now?"

"I don't know," Tom answered. "I assumed it was out at the MacGregor house."

"I didn't see it when I was out there," Ray said, rubbing his balding head. "It could have been towed in before I got there. Tom, where did she normally park?"

"In the garage, of course."

"Could we check?"

The three bays of the garage were occupied: Tom's car, Betty's van, and Innocence's red Chevy Camaro.

"Did she go out Friday night with anyone?" Ray asked, as he looked in the driver's side.

"Not that I'm aware of," Betty answered.

"Nor I," Tom added.

"When was the last time you saw her?"

"Yesterday morning. Right before she went to school," Betty answered. "She said Ashley was grounded, so she'd probably stay home and watch a movie or something."

"I told her I loved her yesterday morning, right before I went to work," Tom said sadly. At that moment, it dawned on him, that would be the last time he would ever tell his daughter he loved her. A tear ran down his cheek, and he turned away.

"Ray, is there anything else?" Betty asked, starting to choke up.

"I'll call George. He needs to tow Innocence's car in, and have his people go over it."

"Okay," Tom said, after getting his composure back. "Anything else?"

"I'm sorry, but yes. One more thing. Can I go through Innocence's room?"

"Is that really necessary?" Betty asked. "Oh, what's wrong with me? Of course, it's necessary."

"I might find something that could help."

"Sure," Betty said. "I think you know the way." She wasn't about to go upstairs.

"I know the way. I'll let you know when I'm leaving."

Chapter 9

Ray stood just outside the bedroom doorway watching Ashley McCoy lying on Innocence's bed, bobbing her head and looking through an album. *Strange kid,* he thought. It was then he noticed earbuds and smiled. It was a Déjà Vu moment. He remembered seeing Innocence lying just like that on her bed, her head bobbing and listening to music. Ashley was surrounded by Innocence's favorite stuffed animal–elephants.

"Ashley," Ray said softly. No response. "Ashley," He said a little louder. Giving up, he walked over and waved his hand in front of her face, making her jump. Jerking the earbuds free, and settling crossed-leg on the bed, she exclaimed, "Sheriff Harris, I didn't hear you come in."

"You wouldn't have heard the trumpets at the second coming," Ray laughed.

"Huh?" She asked, making a face.

"Never mind. Betty told me you were up here. I was wondering if I could ask you a couple of questions about Innocence."

"I guess," Ashley replied, rubbing a locket hanging around her neck. "But I'm not sure how much help I can be."

"That's a pretty locket you have there," Ray said.

"Thank you. Innocence has one just like it. We exchanged them last Christmas. Sheriff, what do you want to ask me?"

"Sometimes young people will tell their friends things they would never tell their parents," Ray told her. "You know what I mean?"

"I guess."

Ray noticed how similar Ashley was to Innocence. No wonder

41

he had the Déjà Vu moment a few minutes ago. Ashley's hair was the same color and style as Innocence's. Ashley wore the same type of clothes. From what little Ray had seen, Ashley had the same mannerisms. Then it occurred to him. Maybe it was the opposite. Maybe Innocence copied Ashley. Maybe it was a BFF thing.

"Did anyone have a grudge against Innocence?"

"I don't know what you mean."

"Did anyone bully her, hit her, send her threatening notes, make her cry?"

"No, not really. Not that I know. Nothing she ever told me ... A couple of the girls on the cheerleading squad used to make fun of her. It made me mad. I know it make Innocence sad, the way they treated her. I wanted to punch them."

Ray smiled.

"How did they make fun of her?"

"They used to oink at her in the hallways. (Ray frowned) Because her dad raised pigs."

"Really? They oinked at her?"

Ashley made several oinking sounds.

"Do these kids have names?"

Ashley sat there, staring at the flower pattern on the bedspread.

"Ashley, do they have names?"

"I don't want to get anyone in trouble."

"If they did something wrong, it's not you who's getting them into trouble. They're already in trouble. But you could find yourself in trouble, by not helping."

Ray took the names of two girls–Mary Austin and Janice Carson.

"Mary Austin, is she the daughter of Jessie Austin, the dentist?"

Ashley nodded.

"I don't recognize Janice Carson's name," he said. "Do you know who her family is?"

"I don't know, Sheriff. She's just a girl at school."

"That's okay. I'll find out ... Ashley, how popular was Innocence? Did she have a lot of friends? More important was anyone jealous of her?"

"No, Sheriff. Not really. She hung out with me, mostly."

"That's all?"

Ashley nodded.

"Ashley, what I'm trying to get at, did Innocence have a boyfriend? Someone close?"

"No, not really."

Why does she keep saying, not really?

"Now I'm confused," Ray confessed, rubbing his balding head. "Betty said she went out on a couple of dates." Ashley laughed.

"You call those dates? Sheriff, if I go to the movies with my brother, I wouldn't call that a date. Would you? She went out with Randy Bennett once and Danny Harper once. But they're just friends, and you asked if Innocence had a boyfriend."

"Okay. That's true, and Innocence would tell you if she had feelings, real feelings, for one of these boys?"

"Sure, she would. We're BFFs."

"One more question. Were you and Innocence together last night or the night before?"

"I see her every day at school, but since I got my report card Thursday, I've been grounded. I got two Ds. Can't leave the house till Monday when I go back to school."

Ray smiled.

"But, here you are, and it's Saturday."

"I know. Since Innocence's death, I got a pardon. I wish I were still grounded."

"Ashley, could you do me a favor?"

"Sure, Sheriff Harris."

"Can you give me the room for a few minutes? I need to look around. Sheriff stuff, you know."

Ray closed the door as soon as Ashley departed. Standing with his back against the door, and taking a deep breath, counter-clockwise he gave the room a once over. *Where to begin?*

The walls were painted in earth-tone colors, pleasant and inviting. A 3-foot x 5-foot black and white poster of Mark Ronson hung above the headboard of her bed. Ray didn't know the guy and would never have known his name if it hadn't been written in script

43

near the bottom.

I wonder who the hell he is and if that's his handwriting or some marketing ploy.

The single bed was covered with a dozen stuffed elephants, grazing on a flowery printed bedspread. *Flowery printed blanket, something I'm sure all sixteen-year-olds hate, but moms love — anything to keep mom happy.* Ray's eyes wandered from the bed to the dresser. From this distance, it looked sparse. He hadn't seen a lot of girl's dressers, but he envisioned the top overflowing with perfume bottles, makeup kits, hair spray cans, brushes, and combs. He would have to have a closer look. He would have to look in each drawer. He would have to invade her privacy. What would he do, what would he say to Betty, if he found porn or battery-operated toys? Yes, he knew she was only sixteen, she was his godchild, and she was innocent and perfect, but he had read too many police reports about teenagers today. He hadn't been born under a rock, as some people believed. Nor was he living under one. The worst thing would be if Betty found these things in Innocence's drawers. *If there's anything like that there, it will disappear before Betty has a chance to look.*

Leaving the dresser behind, Ray continued his visual tour around the room, stopping at the computer desk. Above the desk was another black and white poster, this time of a young Lesley Gore. Ray didn't need a signature to recognize her. She was popular back in his hay-day, back in the sixties. He loved all her songs, especially *"You Don't Own Me."* Toyota had used the song in one of their commercials, and Ray heard from one of his grandkids, it was used in the movie *Suicide Squad.* That he didn't know, and how his grandson described the movie, would probably never know. At the lower right-hand side of the poster was a note, "To Innocence from her BFF, Ashley." *Probably another birthday present.* On the desk was Innocence's laptop, which he prayed wasn't password protected. There would be a ton of data: photos, emails, and downloads. Beside the computer was several books stacked on top of each other. Hopefully, these would show what Innocence was into. Again, more drawers to go through. His phone dinged, with

44

a text message from George.

"Autopsy complete. Blood work sent off to Frankfort. Should take about a week before the Tox-Screen makes it back. Nicole has a theory on the cause of death. Me and Miss Frankfort are leaving to go over to Betty and Tom's in a few. If you're there, you might want to disappear. Miss Frankfort heard how close to the family you are. Nicole leaves for the day at 5:00 pm. She'll wait a little while. Then she's heading home."

"Thanks, George," Ray texted back. "Still here at Betty and Toms. Should be leaving in half an hour. Take your time coming over."

Beside the desk was her closet. The trifold doors were opened, and Ray could see clothes spilling out onto the floor. Each article of clothing would have to be inspected. This was more work than one person could do, but no one in his department was going through this room — no sir. No one under his authority was going to invade her privacy. He knew Frankfort would bring in a regiment of techs to comb the room, but he had no control over that. What if doing his examination, he found some incriminating evidence against Innocence? A reason someone would want to hurt her. Perhaps, even kill her. What if he found something that pointed to the killer? Would he leave it for Frankfort to find, or would he keep it under wraps? The right side of his brain said, take it and don't tell a soul. Solve the murder yourself. She was your Godchild. You'd prove to FJ – you're not worthless. The left side of his brain said, he had to leave it. Frankfort could process the data far quicker than he. *They do have more resources.* What was most important? His pride or finding the killer. At that moment, Ray didn't have the answer.

Ray found Ashley and Betty together in the den.

"I did a quick look through her dresser drawers." *Thank God, no porn or electric toys.* "And I didn't find anything that might help in solving the ... this." He caught himself about to say murder. "If either of you think of something that could help, call. (Both nodded) I'll show myself out." He paused in the doorway. "Did Innocence keep a diary?"

"Yes," Ashley answered quickly. "She used to read bits and pieces to me."

"Ray, do you think it could help?" Betty asked.

"Maybe. I was just curious if girls still did that stuff today, with all the electronic gadgets out there. And because I didn't find one in her room."

Chapter 10

Ray pulled his patrol car around back the M.E.'s office and parked beside Nicole's Honda. George's SUV was nowhere to be seen, which was good. The back door was set up like the front. Press a button and wait. A minute later, Nicole answered the door herself.

"Come on in Ray," she said, turning away. "I was expecting you."

Together they went down a darkened corridor and turned into the well-lit autopsy room. On a table, covered with a sheet, lay a body.

"Is that her?" Ray asked. Ray noticed his voice quivered on the word "her." Nicole nodded.

"You want to see her?" Nicole asked. Ray could only shake his head. Truthfully, he wanted to. He desperately needed too. He wanted to make sure this was not just a nightmare and that it wasn't somebody else's body they found; that Innocence was truly dead and that the throbbing in his head was for a reason.

"No," he answered sadly. "I'm not sure I could handle it."

Nicole took Ray by the arm.

"I understand," she said, softy. "Come over here by my desk and take a seat."

Once Ray was seated, Nicole opened a folder and took a deep breath. "Let's get right to it," she said. "It's getting late in the day, I'm tired, and I need a double shot of Jack. You know Ray, Innocence was my friend too. Hell, in Franklin if you didn't know someone, it's because you're an alien." Ray didn't laugh. Nicole got serious. "As I thought. The cause of death was from blunt force trauma, caused by a blow to the back of the head. The first

47

and second cervical vertebra, as well as the base of the skull and the brainstem, were crushed. Death was instantaneous. From the amount of blood found at the scene, Innocence was murdered in the dining room. The murder weapon was not found on site, which means the killer must have taken it. From the rounded shape of the wound, I would say something like a piece of pipe was used, or it could have been a baseball bat.

"The wounds in her back, all sixteen of them, thankfully, were post-mortem and not made by a knife. The wounds were too rounded, almost elliptical. I would say they were made by a pair of scissors."

"Scissors?"

"Yes. Pointy scissors. Closed pointy scissors. For the record, there wasn't a lot of blood loss from the back wounds, which indicates her heart had already stopped beating. In other cases like this, I would say it was a crime of passion. (Ray nodded) You asked me yesterday, was Innocence raped. Yes, and no."

"What does that even mean?" Ray asked.

"Innocence was sixteen, so sexual intercourse at her age is considered rape, and she did have sex. She—"

"So, she was raped."

"Please, let me continue. She did have sex, but it was not forced upon her. There was no vaginal trauma, no bleeding, no bruises, and no tearing of the vagina wall. I can't stress this enough; she was not forced.

"Also, there were no bruises found anywhere on her body. There was nothing under her fingernails. Ray, everything indicates she did not put up a fight, which means Innocence knew her killer."

"I think so too. Her car's in her garage. Nicole, she rode with her killer out to the house."

Ray sat there, looking at the cloth covered body.

Did your killer know he was going to kill you on the drive out?

"Nicole, are you sure she had sex?"

"Yes Ray, I'm sure."

"Was there DNA?"

"No. But I did find traces of OXO-9, which is a lubricant for condoms. Ray, the bottom line–she had sex, but it was consensual."

Ray dreaded asking the next question. "Was Innocence pregnant? That's a motive that's killed a lot of women."

"Innocence wasn't a woman. She was just a kid. But no, thankfully she wasn't pregnant."

"You're telling me she had sex, and then someone just up and killed her?"

"I'm not saying that at all. Based on how the OXO-9 has degraded, I would say she had consensual sex sometime late Thursday or early Friday morning. The stage of rigor mortis and her core temperature tells me she died sometime between four or seven Friday night. That works into the time frame Billy Hayden gave when he found her. The two events, her having sex and someone killing her, could be and possibly are, the results of two different people."

"Or, it could be some bipolar *Jekyll and Hyde* son-of-a-bitch," Ray added.

"Or, that could also be the case," Nicole admitted. "I sent samples of her blood to Western Kentucky University for a workup. They promised me a three-day turn-a-round. That's pretty damn quick. We'll see if she was using anything."

"Jesus, Nicole. You're making it sound like Innocence was a tramp."

"Damnit, Ray. I know Innocence as well as anybody. She was sweet and kind, but kids today are doing things we would never have tried or even thought of trying. There's more shit out there that seems innocent enough but will kill you in a heartbeat. Ray, I would run the same damn tests on the Pope."

"I'm sorry, Nicole. You're right," Ray said, staring at the tile floor.

Nicole thumbed through her papers. "Let's see. I noticed a few strands of hair were remove, probably as a keepsake. That would indicate the use of a pair of scissors. The same scissors that could have caused the wounds in her back. (Ray raised an eyebrow) Ray, many murderers take souvenirs – panties, jewelry, teeth, fingers, toes, and strands of hair."

"So, if I find a few loose strands of hair, I find the killer."
Nicole smiled.

"Not if you find them in a barber shop."

"Anything else, Nicole?"

"She had a taco for lunch."

Ray stared at her.

"That's about it, Ray?"

"When will you turn the body over to the parents?" Ray couldn't bring himself to say her name.

"I called Tom a few minutes before you got here. He said George and the Special Agent are out there right now, and he'll call Crafton's Funeral Home and see if they could pick her up in the morning. I told him they could pick her up any time, day or night."

"The night my dad died they picked him up at midnight," Ray said. "They're good as gold."

"Tom's still going to wait until morning."

Ray nodded.

"Nicole, I need to go home and try to put all this together."

"I don't envy you," Nicole said. "How's Frederick taking this?"

"I don't know. He hasn't answered my calls."

Chapter 11

FJ stared at the birthday picture of Innocence he took last week. He took a big gulp of gin, making a face. He had started with gin and tonic on ice, but had switched to gin straight up. His reasoning–He didn't want to fill up on the tonic, and the ice was taking up too much room in the glass.

Tom had run him to Bowling Green to pick up his van earlier in the day. Neither said a word on the way north. Each was lost in their thoughts. On the way home, FJ stopped off at a liquor store just off I-65, where he purchased three one-liter bottles of Bombay Sapphire and two six-packs of tonic.

On the floor beside him, one empty gin bottle lay on its side. "Poor dead soldier," FJ mumbled sadly. He spun the empty glass container like playing Spin the Bottle. With so much liquid, FJ's bladder was starting to scream and when FJ tried to stand, his legs wouldn't respond. It was as if his stubby legs belonged to someone else. Laughing, FJ tried to stand again. It was then he realized he couldn't rise from the floor. Even if his life depended on it, he couldn't rise from the damn floor. "Screw it," he said, as he pissed his pants. It was then FJ passed out.

***

As Ray pulled into his driveway, he noticed Mike and Stephanie's Odyssey parked behind Margaret's CRV and Charlotte's Nissan parked out on the street.

God, I hope they're not here to play cards tonight.

"We're in the dining room," Margaret yelled, as Ray walked

in the front door.

The whole gang was there, except FJ. Ray sat down at the head chair and let out a big sigh.

"Well, tell us all about it," Mike said, placing a large Jack and Coke in front of Ray.

"About what?" Ray asked before taking a long pull.

"About what? About your day, of course. You need to catch us up," Stephanie chimed in.

"Where do you want me to start?" Ray whispered.

"At the beginning would be nice," Charlotte suggested.

"I met with George this morning for breakfast at Cracker Barrel. I think George got the Old Timer's Breakfast. I got my usual, the Double Meat Breakfast."

"Too much info," Mike interrupted. "Only the important things. Please. It's getting late, and I'm not getting any younger."

"They brought in an agent from Frankfort," Ray continued, staring hard at Mike. "They don't feel George can handle such a high-profile case."

"I bet that pissed George off, royally," Mike commented.

"You know it did. Hell, it would me. Let's see. I spent half the afternoon with Betty and Tom."

"How're they taking it?" Charlotte asked.

"Better than I thought they would."

"We're planning on taking food over there tomorrow," Stephanie said. "We'll see if they need help planning the funeral."

"Innocence's friend," Ray continued, "Ashley, was there going through some of Innocence's photo albums. She seems like a nice kid. She reminds me of Innocence in her mannerisms, the way she dresses, the way she wears her hair ... I ran her off so I could go through Innocence's room."

"I bet that was fun," Mike said, sarcastically. "I mean going through her room, not running Ashley off. Did it help?"

"It always helps," Ray replied. "It showed me what we already knew. Innocence was a normal, sweet, and loving girl. I found nothing that said differently. What I didn't find was a diary, and Ashley said she kept one. (Ray took a pull off his Jack and Coke)

I left there and went over to Nicole's office. Innocence died from blunt force trauma caused by a blow to the back of the head. They're releasing her body tomorrow."

"Then they should have her obituary in Monday's paper," Stephanie added. "Which means, evening prayers Tuesday and her funeral Wednesday at Saint Mary's."

Ray agreed. He sat there a time sipping on his drink.

"So, that's all you can tell us?" Margaret asked.

"That about sums it up," Ray replied, finishing off his drink. "I'm pooped, and I'm sorry, but I really need a shower and some sleep." He wasn't going to talk about the scissor wounds, and no way in hell was he going to talk about Innocence's sex life.

"You haven't said anything about suspects, or why someone would want to kill her."

"Those are the two most important questions that need to be answered, and sadly, the two questions no one has answers for. God knows I wish I did. That would come close to bringing all this to an end."

"Would you tell us if you did have answers?" Margaret asked. For a moment, Ray sat there thinking of how to respond without pissing everyone off. Okay, pissing off friends wasn't that bad, but pissing off a wife was a different matter.

"Probably not. Something like this doesn't need to get out to the public, and right now, you guys are the public. Truthfully though, I don't have the answers."

"There's one thing you haven't talked about," Mike said.

"What's that?" *Please, please, don't ask about being raped.*

"You haven't said anything about FJ," Mike answered.

"I tried calling him several times today, but he's not answering. Hell, his cell doesn't even switch over to voicemail. Probably means, he's got me blocked."

"Betty says he's drinking. I bet he's passed out, or worse," Charlotte said sadly.

"What do you mean by worse?" Ray asked. "You mean, suicidal?"

Charlotte nodded.

53

"The little asshole may be a lot of things, but suicidal he's not."

"Ray, why don't you go over there?" Mike asked.

"He needs his space, and he needs some time. I plan on going over there sometime tomorrow afternoon, but I have some things I need to do in the morning."

"Like going to mass?" Margaret asked.

"She's right," Stephanie agreed. "We should all go."

"Ray," Margaret continued, "FJ, Betty, and Tom really need our prayers right now."

"As always, Margaret you're right," Ray said. Margaret nodded in agreement.

"We can all go to the eight o'clock mass," Ray suggested, "but just to let you all know, I have some people I need to interview afterwards."

"Who?" Margaret asked.

Ray sat there, staring at her.

"Oh, I get it," she said. "We're the public."

Chapter 12

Sunday Mass was beautifully tearful. Father Riney's homily focused on love–love of God, love of neighbor and love of Innocence. Betty and Tom fought back tears the entire time, while Margaret, Stephanie, and Charlotte constantly dabbed their eyes with Kleenex. If you were sitting near Ray and Mike, you would have heard sniffles. FJ didn't attend. FJ never attended mass. It wasn't that he didn't believe in God, but he blamed God for allowing him to be born a dwarf. Ray wondered if FJ would attend Innocence's funeral mass Wednesday. Surely, FJ would attend his own granddaughter's funeral. He'd better, or FJ was in for an ass kicking.

After mass, everyone wanted to go to Cracker Barrel for breakfast. It's what they had been doing every Sunday for years. One Sunday, for some reason they didn't go over to Cracker Barrel, and the Manager called Ray that afternoon, to make sure nothing serious had happened. Today Ray had more important things to do. Sherriff stuff. He told them as much, but they insisted he needed something in his stomach, or he'd get a headache.

"You guys go on. I'll grab a sausage biscuit at Hardee's," he promised.

"What's so important you would miss going to Cracker Barrel?" Margaret asked.

"I need to run over to the office and look up some addresses."

"Addresses for who?"

Ray just stared at her.

"Oh, the public thing again."

Of the list Ashley had given Ray, he was only able to come up with addresses for Mary Austin and Randy Bennett. He would stop

55

by the high school tomorrow and have a talk with Janice Carson and Danny Harper. Mary's mom was one of the two dentists in town. Randy Bennett's dad, Jim Bennett, owned half of Franklin, at least that's what all the gossipmongers say.

Ray parked on the street in front of the Austin's house. Walking up the sidewalk, he noticed how well the lawn care was. *I wonder who mows your lawn.* Taking a deep breath, Ray knocked on the Austin's front door. A couple of minutes passed, and Ray knocked again, this time a little harder. Again, no answer. It never occurred to him that the family wouldn't be home. As the odds would have it, they currently were at the Cracker Barrel having Sunday brunch, sitting at a table across from Margaret and the crew.

Mary, I'll see you tomorrow at school.

It was different at Randy Bennett's house. No sooner had Ray rang the doorbell, it was opened by a sweet little girl with blond hair and big blue eyes. She reminded Ray of little Cindy Lou Hoo from Dr. Seuss' *How the Grinch Stole Christmas.*

"Is your daddy or mommy home?" Ray asked in a soft, sweet, this is how you talk to an adorable little girl, type of voice. The child smiled up at him, then turned and screamed in a deep scratchy voice that made Ray cringe, "Dad, there's some old man at the door who wants to talk to you."

Oh, my God! Are you possessed? Ray thought.

"Thank you, Cindy," a middle-aged man said as he came to the door.

No fricking way.

"Yes, can I help you?" the man asked.

"I'm Sheriff Harris," Ray replied. "I–"

"I know who you are Sheriff," the man interrupted. "I voted for your opponent in the last election."

"That's nice, Mr. Bennett. I would like to speak to your son Randy, if he's home."

"You can call me Jim."

"Okay Jim, and you can call me Ray."

"Sheriff, what is it you want to talk to Randy about?"

"It's about Innocence Hall."

"Yes, I heard about her death. Very sad. But I don't see how Randy can help. I'm not even sure he knew her."

"If my information is correct, he took her on a date once."

"Oh, that I didn't know. Come in please, and I'll get him. He should be in his room. Here, have a seat," Jim said, indicating the sofa in their formal living room. Ray would call it formal for there was furniture here too expensive for anyone to sit on. Ray was surprised he hadn't been asked to take off his shoes before stepping on the room's beautiful oriental carpet. Oil paintings, not prints, covered the walls. Ray smiled. The painting of *Dogs Playing Poker* wasn't one of them.

Ray stood when Randy walked into the room and offered his hand, which Randy took. To Ray, it was like shaking a fish–limp and lifeless. Ray motioned to the couch. Randy seemed like a good kid. At least he looked the part. He wore his jet-black hair trimmed behind the ears. Dark rim glasses. The glasses made him look intelligent. He was wearing jeans and a Kentucky Wildcats t-shirt. He was taller than Ray and looked like he worked out. *Probably a jock.*

"I have a few questions for you about Innocence Hall."

"I don't know much about her," Randy said, taking a seat beside Ray.

"You went on a date with her." It was more of a question than a statement.

"We went up to Western to watch the Hilltoppers play, if you call that a date."

"What would you call it?" Ray asked.

"Sheriff, what are you insinuating?" Randy's father asked.

"It's simple, Jim. I'm asking Randy if he ever dated Innocence. I don't think that's too hard a question. Do you?"

Jim was about to reply when Randy jumped in.

"I called it a date, but Innocence didn't. She insisted. She just wanted to be friends, and if it led to something else, then so be it. She didn't want to rush it."

Rush it? Like sex? Ray thought.

"Rush it?" Ray asked.

"You know. Not getting serious to quick."

"Sounds like Innocence was a smart girl," Jim said.

"She was," Ray replied.

"She was beautiful," Randy whispered.

The three sat there silently; each caught up in a spell of their own thoughts. It was Randy that finally broke the spell.

"Sheriff, from the first day I saw her in school, I liked Innocence. She was bright and funny. She was on the cheerleading team, but she wasn't snobby like some of the other girls. She got along with everyone, that I saw."

"What do you mean, that you saw?"

"There were rumors some girls were making fun of her."

"How so?"

"I don't know. Just rumors. I never saw anything."

"Were any of the guys hitting on her?"

"Not that I'm aware of."

"What made you ask her out?"

"I'm on the basketball team, and I'd been seeing her during afterschool practice. I thought she'd been watching me. So, I got up the nerve and asked her to a game."

"That's it?"

Randy nodded.

Randy's answers seemed straight forward, but there was a nervousness in his voice. Randy was hiding something and was afraid to talk in front of his dad. Ray would bet a paycheck on that. Ray also wondered if Randy's dad recognized it. Randy and Innocence may have only been out on one date, but that didn't mean they haven't been seeing each other on the sly. The ultimate question was about Randy's sex life, but Randy wasn't going to spill the beans in front of dear old dad. He might tomorrow when Ray talked with the other kids at school. Ray knew it was illegal to talk with minors without their parents being present.

"Randy, you're a good kid," Ray stated, "but, is there anything, anything at all, that you can tell me about Innocence that could help in my investigation?"

"I'm sorry, Sheriff."

"That's alright. I'll be stopping by the high school tomorrow to talk with some other kids. Maybe, if you think of something between now and then, you can tell me tomorrow."

Randy nodded.

"Maybe I should be there as well," Jim said, looking at his son.

"There's no need dad," Randy assured him.

"He's right, Jim," Ray added.

"Randy, you don't know how some answers can be taken in the wrong way," Jim stressed, placing his hand on his son's shoulder. "Maybe, we should have our attorney there as well."

Oh crap, Ray thought. *You did recognize the nervousness.*

"Dad, I have nothing to hide."

For your sake kid, you better not, Ray thought.

Ray sat in his car, going over the interview in his head. Randy didn't have much to add. Only that he and Innocence were friends. He had asked her out on a date, sort of. She wanted their relationship to grow slowly, or that's just what's he saying. Hopefully, the other kids would be able to clear some things up in Randy's statements. Randy's nervousness was making Ray nervous.

Chapter 13

FJ's Honda Odyssey sat in its usual place outside FJ's trailer. Ray wondered if he were making a mistake coming here this soon, or if FJ would even let him in. *The time has come,* he thought and smiled. He remembered the first time he ever heard that saying. *The time has come.* Ray didn't remember the occasion, but he remembered FJ quoting it.

"The time has come," the Walrus said,
"To talk of many things:
Of shoes–and ships–and sealing-wax–
Of cabbages–and kings–
And why the sea is boiling hot–
And whether pigs have wings."

Ray thought it funny. FJ told him it was from *Through the Looking-Glass and What Alice Found There* by Lewis Carroll. FJ used to read the book to Innocence when she was little. So now, every time Ray heard the phrase, he thinks of the poem, he thinks of FJ, and he thinks of Innocence.

"The time has come," Ray whispered as he opened the car door.

Ray knocked several times on the door but got no response. *He could be in the bathroom.* Ray waited. He leaned against the door. He was tired. It seemed the case was going nowhere. *Maybe George was making progress.* Ray looked around the yard. *I wonder who mows your lawn.* He looked at his watch. *How long should*

61

I wait? Is he taking a one or a two? Ray knocked again. Still no response. *Must be a two.* He waited. He looked at his watch again. Charlotte's words from yesterday came back to him. Maybe FJ was suicidal. Alcohol could do that. Ray didn't buy it. Not FJ. But what if Charlotte's right? *Jesus.* Ray slammed on the door with the flat of his hand. No response. Ray tried the doorknob and found the door unlocked.

The room was dark, but Ray didn't need light to recognize the heavy smell of booze and urine. Shaking his head, he fumbled along the wall for a light switch. With a click, the room burst into light. There before him on the floor were two empty bottles of gin, several dark stains on the carpet, and FJ curled up in a ball on the sofa.

Stepping over the bottles and the stains, Ray placed two of his fingers alongside FJ's throat. He had a pulse. He also had a smell. A very bad smell.

"Jesus, FJ," Ray whispered.

He gave FJ a shake. Nothing. He shook him a little harder. FJ moaned. Shaking violently, Ray was rewarded with a "piss off."

"Wake up, FJ."

"Who in the hell, let you in?"

"Your door was unlocked."

"My bad."

"FJ, you need to wake up. You need to wake up now. We need to talk."

"The last time you said, 'we need to talk,' someone died. Who died this time?"

"No one, but we need to talk. Everybody's concerned about you."

"Go away. I'm fine."

"You don't smell fine."

With a moan, FJ rolled into a sitting position.

"Have you told me why you're here? (Ray shook his head) So, why are you here?" FJ asked through squinty eyes.

"We haven't heard from you in days."

"Have you found Innocence's killer?"

"We're working on it."

"So, Ray, tell me again. Why are you here, really?"

"To make sure you didn't do something stupid."

"Like what?"

"You know."

"What?"

"You know."

"Like kill myself?"

"That did cross Charlotte's mind." Ray hated throwing Charlotte under a bus, but it was better her than him. "FJ, we need to talk about what's going to happen in the next few days."

"Okay," FJ sighed. "But first, what's that horrible smell."

"That horrible smell is you. Please go take a shower, and for God sake, do something about your breath."

As FJ staggered to the bathroom, Ray knew there would be no discussion about FJ's actions during the last few days. Nothing would be said about FJ's outrage when Ray broke the news about Innocence's death. It would never come up about Ray being thrown out of FJ's trailer. All of that was behind them. Forgiven and forgotten. That's what they always did when there had been a situation. That's what families did when they love each other, and Ray and FJ were family, brothers from different mother's–and fathers.

***

A dark blue late model Audi Sedan slowly crept past the entrance to FJ's home. It paused only a moment to verify the Sheriff was at the Johnston's home. The driver wondered what they were discussing. The driver also wondered if the Sheriff, or the agent from Frankfort were any closer to determining who the killer was. The driver desperately needed to know. The driver made a U-turn and headed back toward Franklin. It was almost time for supper.

***

FJ came out of the bedroom wearing fresh clothes. He smelled better, but he still looked like crap. He paused a moment looking at the stains on the floor, before climbing up on the couch beside Ray.

"Bring me up to speed," he said, rubbing his eyes, "especially what's going to happen in the next couple of days."

Ray promised his friend he would tell him everything he could about the case, but Ray had to be careful not to disclose anything only the killer would know.

"It will come out in the ME's report, that the cause of death was blunt force trauma to the back of her head."

"Was it painful?"

"Nicole said her death was instantaneous."

"I suppose that's one good thing. Any closer to finding out who killed her?"

"No. Tomorrow I'm going over to the high school to interview some of her friends."

"You think that will help?"

"It can't hurt."

"You think I can come?"

"No, you can't."

"I understand." There was a long pause. "These friends have names?"

"Yes, but I can't give those out."

Another long pause.

"What happens in a couple of days?"

"The funeral."

"Oh, that."

"You will be there?"

"Why shouldn't I? She was my granddaughter."

"Good. I was worried."

"About what?"

"You're not much of a church goer."

"This is not going to church. This is going to a funeral."

"You're right. You need to talk with Betty. She has all the details, and besides, she's worried about you."

"Okay. I'll go over there when we're done here."

"She'd like that."

Ray stood to leave.

"Ray, is there anything else you can tell me?" FJ asked, taking Ray's arm.

I know what you're wanting, Ray thought.

"I'm sorry, but no," Ray replied.

Ray felt better when he pulled out of FJ's driveway. He was glad FJ hadn't directly asked if Innocence was raped. He didn't know how he would have answered that question. When Ray got home, there was a message from Margaret taped to the microwave.

"Stephanie and I are over at Betty's. Charlotte's meeting us there. There's leftover pork-chop casserole in the fridge. Put it in the microwave for two minutes on high. Be sure to put a paper towel over it. I don't know what time I will be home. We're helping Betty plan the funeral. George Watson called our landline and said the agent from Frankfort wants to meet with you tomorrow. You're to text him with a time. Ray, why did George call the landline and not your cell?"

Because he didn't want the agent to know we were friends and calling my cell would have given that away.

Chapter 14

Ray slept in this morning, if you could call it sleeping in. He tossed and turned all night. His sleep filled with the same nightmare, haunted houses and dead eyes. His head was pounding like it did yesterday. He had taken a couple of vacation days to fully focus on the case. Thankfully, his deputies were covering for him down at the station. Every officer in the precinct knew Innocence, and if a police station had a mascot, it would have been her.

Starving, Ray stopped by Hardees, grabbed a sausage, egg, and cheese biscuit, along with a coffee, and wolfed it down on the way to the school.

Ray parked his cruiser in the Franklin-Simpson High School visitor's parking lot. He had texted George before leaving home, about meeting him and the Frankfort agent at the police station, at one pm. Which meant, he had the rest of the morning to interview Innocence's classmates.

After walking through security, the guidance counselor, Mrs. Harriet Taylor, met him in the main office and showed him to a conference room with a small metal table, around which were six folding chairs.

"Sheriff Harris, we're so sorry to hear about Innocence's death," Mrs. Taylor said, taking his hand. "If there's anything we can do to help, please, please, let us know."

"Thank you, Mrs. Taylor. When I talked with you earlier this morning, I asked to meet with Mary Austin, Janice Carson, Randy Bennett, and Danny Harper. I hope they showed up for class today."

"I have no idea why they wouldn't, Sheriff. I have them and

their parents waiting for us in the library. Whenever you're ready, I'll bring them here, one at a time, for you to interview."

"Their parents are here?"

"Yes, of course. You can't meet with minors without at least one parent or their lawyer present. Surely you knew that."

"Of course, Mrs. Taylor. Everyone knows that."

"Just to let you know, Mr. Bennett brought his lawyer as well."

"That's great," Ray replied, sounding like Tony the Tiger.

"Very well then," Mrs. Taylor said, looking puzzled. "Who would you like to meet first?"

"If it's alright, I'd like to go to the library. I have something to say, and I just as well say it to the entire group. It will save me from having to repeat it to every family."

Mrs. Taylor led Ray down a side corridor into the school's library. Sitting around two study tables were the four students and their parents. You could tell which parent or parents belong to which student because they were huddled together in family groups. Ray recognized Randy Bennett and his father. The man with them he didn't recognize. *Must be the lawyer.* The rest were all new faces. To Ray's knowledge, he had never seen any of the students at Innocence's house, for any of her parties. About thirty feet away from the study tables stood Ashley McCoy and a couple of other girls. They were busy searching the library's online card-categories. Occasionally, Ashley would steal a glance at Ray.

"Good morning," Ray started, "and thank you for letting me take a little of your time. As you know or have guessed, I'm here about Innocence Hall's death."

"Then why are we here?" an African American girl asked, indicating her and her parents.

"Miss?"

"Janice Carson."

"Well Miss Carson, your name was given to me by someone who says you had ... issues with Innocence."

"What kind of issues?"

"We'll go over that when I conduct your interview."

"Who said I had issues?"

68

"That I'm sorry, is privileged. But again, we'll get to that when you and I talk in a few minutes. Ladies and gentlemen (Ray always wanted to say that), here's how we're going to handle the interviews this morning. I will call for each of you, and you and your parents, or parent will meet with me in a conference room. I will ask questions, and I will record your answers. Know, you're not under arrest, nor are you a suspect, so you're under no obligation to answer any of my questions (Here Ray was staring at the Bennett's lawyer), but your answers could help me find Innocence's killer. I cannot stress enough; you are not a suspect. Are we all clear on that? (Everyone nodded) Very well. So, Mary Austin, will you and your parents, please follow me back to the interrogation room."

As they turn to go, Mrs. Taylor was already standing out in the hallway, holding the library door open, as if she were leading them back to the room.

"Can I talk with you a minute?" Ray asked, taking Mrs. Taylor by the arm and pulling her away from the group. "Please wait here," he told Mary and her parents. When he was far enough away from prying ears, he leaned in.

"Where are you going?" he whispered to Mrs. Taylor.

"I am the guidance counselor, and I need to be in the meeting."

"Mrs. Taylor, as you so rightly told me a few minutes ago, minors need to have their parents, or at least one parent present, and or, their lawyer present for such meetings, but there's nothing that says anything about the guidance counselor being present. I'm sure you understand."

"Understood, Sheriff," she unhappily replied. "What can I do to help?"

"Well, Mrs. Taylor, you can stay in the library and make sure no one leaves, and no one steals a book."

Ray left Mrs. Taylor standing there, with her jaw almost hitting the floor.

"Have a seat, please," Ray said, as he closed the door to the meeting room. Taking a small device out of his pocket, he showed it to Mary and her parents. It was a small personal audio recorder.

"Mary, like I said, I will be recording our interview. Why?

First off, I'm horrible at taking notes. For some reason, no one can read my handwriting. (Mary smiled) Second, I will have the recording transposed, word for word, for the record. Is that okay with you?" Mary nodded. "Parents? (Both nodded) Okay, then."

Ray fumbled with the recorder and sat it on the table between him and Mary.

"It's ten-twenty in the morning, and I'm meeting at the Franklin-Simpson High School with Mary Austin and her parents, who names are?" Here Ray pointed at her father.

"Jim," her father said.

"Grace," her mother added.

Ray continued. "I'm meeting with Mary Austin and her parents, Jim and Grace Austin. So, let's begin. Mary, how well did you know Innocence Hall?"

"We're in a couple of classes together. Were. We were in a couple of classes together. Sorry."

"That's okay," Ray assured her. "It's hard to believe she's gone. So, she was in a couple of classes with you. How was that?"

"Fine, I guess. Classes are classes."

"Was there anywhere else?"

"We were on the cheerleading squad together."

"And how did that go?"

"Fine."

"Just fine?"

"Sure. Just fine."

Everything's fine with her.

"Mary, really?" Ray asked, leaning in and staring hard at Mary. He could see Mary was starting to fidget and was staring at her parents.

"Sheriff, are you trying to badger my daughter?" Jim asked.

"No. I'm trying to get to the bottom of all this. Mary, this is what I was told. You and a couple of girls were making fun of Innocence."

"Who told you that?" Mary asked.

"Were you making fun of her?" Ray demanded.

"Daddy," Mary whispered, seeking her daddy's help.

"I think we're through here," Jim said, placing his hand on Mary's shoulder.

"Very well. But, know this, I asked Mary here because I thought she could help me. Nothing more. But, since she refuses to answer my questions, she is now the prime suspect in the death of Innocence Hall." Mary started crying.

"Sheriff, please," her father begged. "Surely, we can clear this up?"

"It would help if Mary would answer my damn questions!" Ray shouted, slapping the metal desktop with the flat of his right hand, making all three Austin's jump. "Mary, did you or did you not make fun of Innocence Hall?"

"Yes," Mary whispered, staring down at her hands.

"I'm sorry, but I didn't hear you," Ray shouted.

"Yes," she said louder, this time looking straight at Ray.

"How did you make fun of Innocence?"

Mary sat there, staring at Ray.

"Mary, let me ask you again. How did you make fun of Innocence?"

"We used to oink at her."

"What did you just say?" Grace asked her daughter.

"We used to oink at her. Mommy, it was just for fun. Her dad raises pigs."

"For Christ sake," Grace said, looking disgusted at her daughter.

"Mary, what else did you do?" Ray asked, knowing he had broken her spirit.

"Nothing, I swear."

"Mary?"

"No, really, Sheriff. That's all I did. That's all Janice, and I did."

"Did any of the other girls do anything worse?"

"Not that I'm aware of."

"Mary, are you telling me everything?"

"Yes, Sheriff. Everything."

"Are you sure there aren't rumors floating around about her

death, or why she died?"

"Rumors? Sheriff, I don't understand."

"Rumors. You know. Was she into drugs or a gang? (Ray wondered if Franklin were big enough to have a gang) Any kind of things that could get you killed if something goes wrong?"

"No, Sheriff. I never heard anything about drugs or gangs. Innocence wasn't that kind of girl. She was nice. It was me and Janice who did wrong. Innocence didn't deserve it. I know that now, and I wish I could take it back. I'm so sorry. Mommy, I'm so sorry." Mary started crying again. Grace wrapped her arm around Mary and pulled her close.

"Baby, I know you are," Grace said, kissing Mary's forehead.

"Mary, I believe you when you say you're sorry," Ray said, softy. "I really do. So, I'm going to let you go home or back to class now. But one more question, please."

"Yes?"

"Where were you between four and seven last Friday?"

"Let's see. School let out at three-thirty. I wasn't feeling well, so I didn't stay for practice. I drove straight home."

"Yes, she got home at four o'clock," Grace agreed. "I was making cookies."

"Please, Mrs. Austin," Ray said, "I need Mary to tell me."

"I ate a couple of cookies. Did my homework. Checked my email. I messed around on the internet until supper. Supper would have been around; I don't know, six or six-thirty. It was six-thirty. Yes, I'm sure it was six-thirty."

"How can you be so sure?"

"Because *Who wants to be a Millionaire* was just coming on."

"That's right," Grace assured Ray. "We ate at six-thirty. We always eat together, so I had Mary turn off *Millionaire.* I know that's kind of old fashion, but we like to talk about things that happened during the day, and the TV would have been a distraction. We would have finished around seven or seven-fifteen."

"That's what I needed to hear," Ray said. "Mary, thank you for answering my questions, and if you think of anything else, you call me. I mean it. You call me."

"I will, Sheriff, I promise."

"Mary, would you return to the library and tell Janice, it's her turn?" Mary nodded.

As soon as Mary and her parents left, Ray thought about erasing the tape, but her interrogation needed to be transposed for the record. He wiggled the fingers on his right hand, wondering if any were broken. He now wished he hadn't been so damn dramatic in slapping the metal tabletop. It wouldn't happen again.

Chapter 15

Ray went over the same opening spill as he did with Mary Austin and soon got down to business. "It's ten-fifty. I'm meeting at the Franklin-Simpson High School with Janice Carson and her parents William and Doris Carson."

Janice looked nervous, but not as much as her mother, who was almost in tears. Janice's father stood behind his daughter with one hand on her shoulder, giving her support. He had an angry look about him. Ray guessed it was not so much his daughter's involvement in a murder investigation, as it was the family being involved in a murder investigation.

"Janice, how many classes did you and Innocence have together?" Ray asked.

"No classes, Sheriff. I saw Innocence only at cheerleading practice and during games."

"Did you have a grudge, or any ill will against Innocence?"

Janice seemed shocked.

"No. Sir. I–"

"Sheriff, you said someone told you Janice had 'issues' with Innocence Hall," William Carson said, interrupting. "Sir, I promise you, our daughter would never have issues with anyone. She is a good God-fearing child. She believes in the commandment to love thy neighbor as thyself. What you're asking is total nonsense?"

"Mr. Carson," Ray replied sternly, "whether the allegation is nonsense or not, will be determined during this interview, if you would let me continue. Now Janice, did you have 'issues' with Innocence?"

"No, Sheriff."

"Okay, let me ask you differently. Did you ever make fun of Innocence?"

Janice felt her father's hand biting into her shoulder. Janice looked at her mother, not knowing what to say.

"Go ahead, Janice," her mother said. "Tell the Sheriff what you told me yesterday."

"Yesterday?" Janice's father erupted. "What did she tell you yesterday? Maybe we need to call a lawyer, before this goes any further. Randy Bennett's dad brought a lawyer with him today."

Doris grabbed her husband's arm and shook her head. "Sheriff, when Janice found out about Innocence's death, she told me–"

"Please, Mrs. Carson," Ray interrupted softy, "I need to hear this from Janice herself."

Doris nodded. "Go ahead, Janice."

Janice's father crossed his arms, placing his right hand under his chin.

"When I found out about Innocence's death, I didn't know what to do. It's been eating at me since that day."

"What's been eating at you?" Ray asked softy.

"Mary and I used to make fun of Innocence. It wasn't anything serious, you know, just simple fun."

"And how did you make fun of her?"

Janice paused, too embarrassed to answer.

"Go ahead. It's okay," Ray assumed her.

"We used to oink at her."

"Why?"

"Because her dad raised pigs."

"Oh my God," William Carson exclaimed, looking away. "Is that all?"

"Is that all? Isn't that enough?" Ray shot back. He was beginning to dislike William Carson. No, it was beyond that. He most defiantly didn't like William Carson. "Mr. Carson, how does oinking at someone play into loving thy neighbor as thyself? How would you like it if someone made fun of your daughter?"

William opened his mouth to respond.

76

"He wouldn't like it," Doris Carson intervened.

"Sheriff, I feel so bad," Janice said with tears flowing from her eyes. "I don't know why Innocence was murdered. I don't know who did it. Even after I teased her, she seemed like she didn't pack a grudge. She was a good person."

"Did you ever hear anyone putting her down? (Janice shook her head) Did you ever see anyone picking on her? (Janice shook her head) Did you ever hear rumors she was doing bad things, illegal things?"

"No, Sheriff. Never. Innocence was just that, innocent. She probably was the most innocent person I have ever known. I'm not Catholic, and what little I know, I think she could have been a saint. I wished we could have been friends. She would have been a good friend. You think she could have forgiven me?" A tear appeared in the corner of Ray's eye.

"Knowing Innocence, I'm sure she already did," Ray answered, patting Janice's hand.

"Sheriff, are we done?" William asked.

"One more question. And Janice, it's one of those questions I've been asking everyone. Where were you between four and seven last Friday?"

"I met with Coach McClure after school. That was around three-forty or a quarter till. She wanted to go over a new cheer. After that, I went home. I don't know. I got there around five. Did my homework. Let's see. Got on Facebook. Sent some text messages. Those kinds of things. I do remember; Mom got home around six. After that, I talked with a friend on the phone. Her name's Shirley Schoettle. We talked from six to supper time, which was around six-thirty."

"You know we'll check your phone records?"

Janice nodded. "It'll show we were talking."

"Now I think we're done," Ray said, rising from his seat. "Janice, I'm sure you had nothing to do with her death, but if you remember anything that you feel can help us, you call me."

"I promise. Is there anything else?"

Ray stood there, thinking who he wanted to call back next.

Randy Bennett with his lawyer or Danny Harper.

"Janice, would you ask Danny Harper to come here?"

He'd let Randy's father squirm a bit longer.

"Mrs. Harper, please have a seat," Ray said, gesturing toward one of the metal chairs. "I'd like to get started. I've taped all the interviews so far. I hope that's alright with you."

Mrs. Harper nodded.

"Okay," Ray started, "Danny, what can you tell me about Innocence?"

"Not much. I see ... saw, her at the games, practices and in class."

"You had several classes with her?"

"No. Just math."

"Her mother told me; you took her on a date once."

"Yes. We went to see *Wonder Woman*."

"How was it?'

"It was great. The special effects were awesome."

"I don't mean the movie. I meant how was the date?"

"Oh, it was fun. Innocence was a person you could hang out with and just be yourself. She didn't put on airs, you know? (Ray nodded) I don't know. The date was fine, and she was fun."

"How much fun did you have with her?"

"I don't know what you mean?"

"How close did you get to her? (There was a blank look on Danny's face) Let me ask you this. When you took her home from the movie, did you kiss her?" Danny blushed.

"I gave her a peck on the cheek."

"A peck on the cheek? That's all?"

"Yes, sir."

"You never kissed her again?"

"No, sir."

"Are you being square with me?"

"Yes."

"How many times did you and Innocence have sex?" Ray blurted out, trying to catch Danny off guard.

"Huh? Never! I swear."

"On my God, Sheriff?" Mrs. Harper exclaimed. "You're truly not saying Danny had sex. He's a virgin." Danny looked up at the ceiling and smiled. Ignoring her, Ray continued.

"Come on, kid. You're good looking. She's good looking. You went out with her. Come on. Hormones kick in. I can understand. One thing leads to another."

"Sheriff," Danny's mom pleaded.

"You can talk to me," Ray continued. "Maybe, it would be easier if your mom waited outside."

"That sure as shit ain't going to happen," Mrs. Harper promised.

"That's okay, Mom," Danny said. "The Sheriff has to ask, and no, we did not have sex. Not that I didn't think about it. And Mom, don't go Titanic, but I'm not a virgin."

"Danny!" his mom exclaimed.

"I've had sex with a girl, once, but not with Innocence. Never with Innocence." Danny finished.

"Oh, my God," Danny's mom, exclaimed.

"And why not?" Ray asked. "Were you too good for her?"

"No. Just the opposite. She was too good for me."

"Boy, I don't know what to think about you," Ray said, wishing he had a cigarette right now.

"It's the truth, Sheriff. I have nothing to hide. I went out with Innocence. We had a good time, and I kissed her goodnight. That's all. I asked her out another time, but she said no."

"Why do you think she said no?"

"I don't know, Sheriff."

"Danny, where were you between four and seven last Friday?"

"Basketball practice."

"From four to seven?"

"No. From five to seven. I hung around school till it was time for practice. There're others that can attest to that."

"I will check it out."

"Go for it, Sheriff. As I said, I have nothing to hide."

"Okay. You're free to go. I may have other questions for you sometime." Danny nodded. "Would you send Randy back?"

"Sheriff, Innocence and I never had sex. She was cute and sweet, and I wished I could have gotten to know her better. I'm sorry she's dead."

Ray was choked up and could only smile and shake his head.

Chapter 16

Randy sat between his father and his lawyer, while Ray sat on the opposite side of the table. Randy's father, Jim, sat there with a smirk on his face. *This is not going to be easy,* Ray thought. The lawyer sat there looking like a snobby son-of-a-bitch in a thousand-dollar suit. *What do they say? What do you have when you find one lawyer on the bottom of the ocean? A good start.*

"You are?" Ray asked, indicating the lawyer.

"I'm the Bennett's lawyer, Harold King, of *King, King, and King.*

Three King's, Ray thought. *I bet you send out neat Christmas cards. I can see it now. If you want to sue somebody's ass ... Or ox. Come see us at–We Three Kings.*

"Randy, I know you and Innocence went out. You say, only once. Look. It's been a long morning, and I'm getting tired, so I'm going to cut to the chase. Did you have sex with Innocence Hall?"

"What?" Randy shouted, standing up.

"Sit down kid," Ray demanded, loudly.

"Randy don't answer that," Harold said louder. "As you know Sheriff, Innocence was a minor, and if my client had sex with her, that would constitute rape. Are you asking my client to incriminate himself? That's not going to happen today, Sheriff. Not today."

"Mr. King, I'm concerned more about who killed the girl."

"Then why ask about Randy having sex?"

"It could come down to motive."

"I don't get you."

"Come on. You're brighter than that. What if she was pregnant and threatened to tell her parents? Or worse, tell his parents. Everyone knows the Bennett's have money. Maybe, that's the reason she got pregnant, so she could get to the money. That's been the motive in many deaths."

"Was she pregnant?" Randy asked.

"Shut up, Randy," his dad exclaimed.

"He's right, Randy. It would be in your best interest to be quiet right now," his lawyer added. "Sheriff, was she pregnant?"

"We're waiting on the autopsy report. (Ray lied) What do you think, Randy? Was she pregnant? Did you and she go out to the house, to talk about becoming a sweet little family?Let's see. Randy, Innocence, and the baby makes three. Or, did she demand money to keep quiet? To get an abortion? Is that it?"

"I think that's uncalled for," Jim Bennett exclaimed.

"Randy, was Innocence going to spill the beans?" Ray continued.

"I don't know what you're talking about," Randy answered.

"You being a father would ruin your chances of getting a scholarship. Wouldn't it?"

"No. I mean, yes. I'm getting confused."

"So, did you murdered her to shut her up!"

"No."

"What did you use to kill her? I already know. (Ray lied) I just want to hear you say it."

"Enough of this," Mr. King shouted, standing up. "Is Randy being arrested for the girl's death? Yes or no?"

"She has a name," Ray bellowed.

"Is my client being arrested for the death of Innocence Hall?" King demanded.

Ray took a big breath to slow his heartbeat. "Not right now."

"Then we're free to go?"

"One last question. Randy, where were you between four and seven last Friday?"

Randy looked at his lawyer, who nodded.

"I was at ball practice."

"The whole time?"

"Most of the time."

"When did you leave?"

"I don't remember."

"Sheriff, I think we're done here," Mr. King said, turning toward the door. "If you have any other questions for Randy, you can ask them through me. Here's my card."

After the three had left, Ray looked at his watch. It was eleven-forty-five. It had been an hour and forty-five minutes since he started the interviews. No wonder his throat was dry and scratchy.

"After all this, what did you gain today?" Ray asked himself while rubbing his forehead. The headache was back, and he needed to put something on his stomach before he got sick. He had an hour and fifteen minutes, before he had to meet George at the police station.

Chapter 17

Ray got to his office thirty minutes early and spent most of the time doing catchup paperwork. From his lack of sleep and the now ever-present headache, which he named Dave, Ray craved a nap, even if for fifteen minutes. *What do they call that? Oh yeah, a powernap.* But that wasn't happening. His admin, Susan McCormick, stuck her head into his office.

"George and the Special Agent are here, Sheriff," Susan said.

"Thanks. Go ahead and show them in," Ray replied, searching his desk-drawer for a bottle of aspirin.

Susan McCormick was the office heirloom. She'd been around longer than anybody could remember. Rumor had it, Susan had been around since Franklin was incorporated into the state back in 1820. She was a full-figured African-American in her mid-something. Ray knew if he wanted to know her age, all he had to do was look in her folder. But where was the fun in that? She was the acting grandmother of the station. She knew everyone's birthdays, even though she never baked a cake. Here's an example:

Susan: Today is So-and-so's birthday.
Anybody: Really?
Susan: Yeah, somebody should have baked a cake.

George shook Ray's hand as soon as they entered and turned to make introductions.

"Sheriff, this is Special Agent, Jennifer Broxon. Frankfort sent her down to help."

To Ray, Special Agent Jennifer Broxon seemed awful young

85

to be a Special Agent. She couldn't be much older than twenty-five or twenty-six. She was of average height, but a little too thin for Ray's taste. *Like my taste matters.* She wore her sandy brown hair cut short, just above the ears. *Cute.* She wore very little makeup. The fact is–she didn't need makeup. *You have a pretty face.*

"I heard you were brought in on the case, Mrs. Broxon," Ray said, shaking her hand. Her grip was strong and firm. He liked her already.

"It's Miss, and please call me Jenny."

Ray knew she was a "Miss," George had texted him that much, but he didn't want her to know about their texting.

"Alright Jenny, have a seat," Ray said, pointing at the two chairs in front of his desk. "Would you like some water or coffee?"

"Coffee would be nice," Jenny replied. "A little creamer with a couple of sugars."

"I would like mine black with–"

"George," Ray interrupted, "as many breakfasts as we've had together, I think I know how you take your coffee." Walking over to the door, Ray yelled, "Susan, we'd like some coffee."

"So would I," Susan yelled back. "Make mine black, straight up."

Ray smiled at George and Jenny.

"Excuse me," he said, slipping out of the room.

A few minutes later, he came back balancing three cups of coffee on the back of a clipboard.

"Did you get Susan her cup?" George asked. Ray stared hard at him.

"Yes, he did," Susan yelled from her desk.

"So, Jenny, what do you think of Franklin?" Ray asked, popping four aspirins into his mouth and washing them down with a swig of coffee. "Most people get us confused with Franklin, Tennessee," he continued. "We're not as big as Franklin, Tennessee, but we've had some well-to-do names come from here. There's Anne Potts; she grew up here, she was in the *Ghostbusters* movies, coach Joker Phillips (Jenny shook her head) he was the University of Kentucky's football head coach back in 2010. Oh, there's Billy

Ray Cyrus, the singer. Billy Ray still owns property here, and every year when we have to send out tax statements, Susan volunteers to hand-deliver his."

"But Ray won't let me do it," Susan yelled from her desk.

"This is the first time I've been in Franklin proper," Jenny confessed, "but, I've seen the name on the interstate signs when heading to Nashville. From what I've seen, it's a pleasant little town."

"Where're you staying?"

"I'm at the Econo Lodge, just off I-65."

"That's a good place. I haven't heard anyone complain about staying there. One of its managers goes to our church," Ray said, making small talk. Dreading the big talk.

"Sheriff, we need to lay our cards on the table," Jenny said, setting her coffee cup on the corner of Ray's desk.

Oh Boy, here comes the big talk.

"Well, then, ladies first."

"We've made a few inquiries and interviews already," Jenny stated, "and your name keeps coming up as asking questions about the death. (George nodded in agreement) Ray, we know how close you were to the deceased, so I can understand your point-of-view, but the death occurred outside your jurisdiction. Which means you don't have a horse in this race."

"That's true, Jenny, but every person I've talked with lives within the city proper. Which is in my jurisdiction, and as such, I have the right to question any damn one I please. Pardon my French."

"I would feel the same," she admitted. "So, let's quit all this sneaking around bullshit and start helping each other. Pardon my French."

Yeah, I like this girl.

"Okay. Cards on the table. Again, ladies first," Ray said.

"I probably don't know any more, than what you already know," Jenny admitted. "So, I was hoping you could enlighten us."

Ray saw no reason keeping anything from either of them. Three heads could be better than one. So, for the next thirty minutes, Ray went over every interview.

"So, to sum it up," Ray said, taking a sip of his now cold coffee. "Janice Carson is a snob. She gets it from her parents. But if you break through her icy shell, she does have a heart. Girls like her think they have to be rude to be cool. Mary Austin, on the other hand, is a sweet girl. Her only problem is–she desperately wants to fit in, to be part of the cool crowd. So, she teamed up with Janice to make fun of Innocence. These two may be bitches, but they had nothing to do with Innocence's death. That's my opinion.

"Danny Harper is a good kid. Bottom line. After my interview, I felt he and Innocence would have made a cute couple. He did say he thought about having sex with Innocence. He's just a boy trying to become a man. We've all gone through it. I mean us men. (He said this looking at Jenny) I'm sure you talked with Nicole about the sex part. (Both nodded) But he swears they didn't, and for some silly ass reason, I believe him.

"Okay. Let's see who's left. Randy Bennett. (Ray sighed and rubbed his forehead. The aspirins hadn't quieted Dave.) Randy Bennett is also a snob. A snob who also happens to be a little prick. He knows he's cooler than shit, and he flaunts it. He loves to hide behind his daddy's money. He's the one who had sex with Innocence. I'd bet on it. But of course, he denies it. You should have seen him sweat. You should have seen how his dad and their lawyer acted. They know. Did he kill Innocence? That I don't know, but he's my number one suspect."

"We're meeting with all of them this afternoon," Jenny stated. "I'll take what you discerned to heart and watch for any incriminating responses. Good work, Sheriff. You know these people better than I. I'm afraid I have very little to add. Innocence's Tox-Screen indicated there was nothing in her system, no drugs, no alcohol."

"I didn't think we were getting the results back that quick," Ray said.

"Being a Special Agent has its perks. I placed a call to a friend in Bowling Green, who placed a call to a friend whose sister works in the state lab, and we got the results back this morning. Tomorrow,

I believe, is when the public can pay their respects to the family at the funeral home. (Ray nodded.) I think we need to keep a close eye on those attending. Sometimes, appearances tell a lot."

"Agreed," Ray added.

"Well then, Sheriff," Jenny said, rising from her seat, "I think this meeting is over for now. It's been a pleasure meeting you. Here's my card. Call or text me any time if you come up with new info. Being one of George's friend, I assume George has your number, your personal number? (Busted. Ray and George both nodded.) Good. If I come up with something, I'll call or text you."

"Perfect," Ray said, showing them to the main lobby.

"I like that girl," Susan said, taking a sip of coffee as they left.

So did I, Ray thought.

***

The dark blue late model Audi slowly crept passed the Sheriff's home, on the corner of Scotland Avenue and Cemetery Street. The driver had watched the Sheriff leave the Police Station at five o'clock and had followed him home. *What kind of information did you get from the cop from Frankfort? How did your interviews go? I wish I could have been a fly on the wall. I wonder, will any of you ever understand why the bitch had to die? Probably not.*

Chapter 18

Ray stood in the main lobby of the Crafton's Funeral Home decked out in his dress blues. Both hallways, the east, and the west were packed from the viewing area to the exits, on both ends of the building. According to Clayton Crafton, this was the biggest funeral they had ever processed. There had to be over five hundred people; close friends, neighbors, and classmates, all trying to pay their respects to Betty and Tom. Visitation was supposed to end at eight o'clock that evening, but Clayton assured them that wasn't going to happen. But they were not to worry, he would make sure to accommodate all visitors.

The funeral home had opened its doors to the family at two o'clock. For half an hour, the family had a private viewing with Innocence. Betty and Tom were there, of course, as was Tom's parents and FJ. Also included in the family group was Ray, Margaret, Charlotte, Mike, Stephanie, and Ashley. The room was packed with flowers and more flowers, religious statues, candles, crucifixes of all sizes, ornate rugs embroidered with Scripture or soothing words of comfort, wind-chimes, and steppingstones. All of which were gifts for the family. The overpowering fragrance of flowers filled the room. An instrumental version of *Amazing Grace* floated from ceiling mounted speakers.

Innocence was dressed in a beautiful, white-laced gown, that Betty and Stephanie had picked up in Bowling Green yesterday morning. Her long blond hair, parted down the middle, hung in long golden braids across both shoulders. A crown of small yellow daisies and baby's-breath encircled her brow. She looked like a flowerchild from the sixties. In her folded hands she held a

91

white and gold rosary, a gift from Mike and Stephanie. To Ray, she looked like Sleeping Beauty awaiting her prince charming, not the bloody and broken child he saw lying on a dusty, deserted floor five days ago. Ray suddenly felt weak in his legs and had to sit down before he fell.

He hobbled over to a couch and sat down at one end. A minute later, FJ wandered over and climbed up onto the couch at the other end. They sat there in silence, staring straight ahead at the casket, each lost in their thoughts. At two-thirty the funeral director opened the doors to the public, friends of the family, classmates, and teachers of Innocence poured into the room, filling the room almost immediately with sobs, hugs, I'm sorry to hear about your loss, she'll be missed, she looks beautiful, is there anything I, we, can do?

Now at three o'clock, Ray was stationed in the main lobby. From his vantage point, he could see the viewing area, and the large hall leading to it. Jenny was stationed halfway down the east wing. She could see from Ray to the east exit. George was midway between the main lobby and the west exit. They would see all the comings and goings. If anyone acted weird or looked suspicious, they would take note and have a word with the person out in the parking lot.

FJ, dressed in black slacks, long-sleeved white shirt, and a red bowtie, was in the family snack area nibbling on his third chicken leg, talking with Mike and Innocence's BFF, Ashley. With the amount of food brought in by friends of the family, most of it would go to waste. Luckily, the funeral home and the parents had worked it out with the *Salvation Army*, to come over after visitation tomorrow morning, after the body was taken to the church for the funeral mass, to take a small amount of food to Ray's house and the rest to their soup kitchen.

Betty and Tom were busy greeting the endless line of visitors. Father Riney was finishing the funeral arrangements with Margaret, Stephanie, and Charlotte. This was not their first time planning a funeral. All the readers and readings had been selected, as well as the hymns, the four Eucharistic minsters, and the six pallbearers.

At five o'clock, FJ dodged his way back into the viewing area. He found Betty sitting on a tall chair beside the casket.

"Hi sweetie," he said, sliding up to her. "Where's Tom?"

"He went to get us a bottle of water."

"How are you doing?"

"Hanging in there, Dad. You?"

"I'm tired."

"Why don't you go on home and get some rest? It's going to be a long day tomorrow."

"I know. I bet you're just as tired. (Betty nodded) If you can do this, so can I."

"She looks beautiful, doesn't she?" Betty commented, looking at her daughter.

FJ couldn't look at his granddaughter. He could only nod. Thinking of Innocence lying in the casket beside them made his eyes tear up. To distract himself, FJ allowed hate to dull his pain, and thoughts of what he was going to do to the man that murdered his granddaughter clouded his vision. Whether Ashley knew it or not, their conversation in the snack room had given him an idea of who the murderer might be. He should tell Ray, he knew he should, but that would eliminate his burning desire for revenge, and that was not going to happen today.

People kept coming and coming and coming, and FJ didn't know any of them. That's not true, but he didn't know most of them. His neck was getting tired from having to look up so much, but it wouldn't look right if he just stood there staring at their crotches. He looked along the line, trying to see if it was getting shorter. It wasn't. Suddenly, he froze. He couldn't move. He wanted to turn and flee, but his feet and legs wouldn't respond. He couldn't speak. The Lord knows he wanted too, and the words he wanted to scream would make Pluto, the circus strong-man, blush. Seconds passed. When he finally thawed, only two words came out of his mouth.

"Oh, shit."

It was at that moment; Betty exclaimed, "Mother?"

Zoe Payne had aged well. She was still slim. *She must be*

working out, FJ thought. She was always an exercise freak. To work the trapeze, you had to be. Her long, raven hair was now salt and pepper, mostly pepper. The sexiest thing about her, she still had. Her smile. That smile, the same smile Betty and Innocence inherited. It was embedded in their DNA. FJ felt something warm and sweet in the pit of his stomach. Then he remembered how Zoe had run out on them years ago, and the feeling in his stomach turned cold and sour. Back then she had a choice, stay or leave. She chose to leave, leaving him and Betty standing on a railway station platform. She left him and her daughter, as if she didn't care. *Did she ever care?*

"Dad, please don't make a scene," Betty whispered and begged. "Not here. Not now."

"I've got this," FJ whispered back. "But, I don't have to talk to her. When she passes, I'm going to ignore her. Betty, sweetheart, I do have two 'hell' questions for you. First off. Who in the hell found her? And, second. Who in the hell invited her?"

"Dad, can we talk about this later, when we're alone?"

"I don't know what we need to talk about."

"Dad!"

"Alright. Alright. But I'm not going to enjoy it."

The line kept getting shorter and shorter. Alright, the line wasn't getting shorter, but 'she' was getting closer. Only three people stood between Zoe and FJ. He wished there were a hundred. FJ prayed, and he never prayed, for the apocalyptic destruction of the world, as foretold in the *Book of Revelation,* to happen before she took one step closer. God must not have heard, for she took one step closer, and soon was standing over him.

"Hello, Frederick," she said, looking down.

"Hello, Zoe," he replied. *Oh shit, I said I wasn't going to talk to her.*

"You haven't changed much," she smiled — that smile.

"Nor you. What have you been–"?

"Hello, mother," Betty said, interrupting.

"Sweetheart," Zoe said, hugging Betty. "I'm so, so, sorry. I miss never having gotten to talk to her."

94

There you go again, FJ thought, getting angry. *It's all about you. It's always been about you.*

"She so beautiful," Zoe said, stepping up to the casket.

"FJ ... FJ ... Frederick!"

FJ looked up. "What Ray?"

"Let's get a coke," Ray suggested.

"Sounds good to me," FJ replied. "Maybe, we can add some whiskey."

"Later," Ray promised.

Chapter 19

It had been a long, tiring day for everyone. Tom had some papers to sign at the funeral home, after the last visitor left at nine-thirty. Now, everyone was at Mike and Stephanie's house for refreshments: sandwiches, chips, and drinks. Mainly drinks. Mainly alcoholic drinks. FJ was on the patio sipping on a gin and tonic.

"You know you can't avoid her all night," Ray said, taking a pull on his Jack and Coke.

"I don't know what you mean," FJ added, flatly.

"Bullshit," Ray exclaimed. "I've seen you staring at her."

"Ray, I don't have anything to say to her."

"Maybe you do."

***

Zoe and Betty were alone in the kitchen. Zoe was sipping on a Bud Lite.

"Mom, you can't avoid him all night," Betty said, taking a sip of her Margarita.

"I don't know what you mean," Zoe added, flatly.

"I've seen you staring at him."

"Betty, I don't have anything to say to him."

"Maybe you do."

***

"Ray, can you excuse us?" Betty asked as she and Zoe stepped out onto the patio.

97

"No problem," he replied. As he turned to leave, he looked over at FJ. "Maybe you do."

Zoe walked over and placed her drink on the patio table and turned to FJ.

"Frederick, it's been a long time. (Frederick nodded) Through the years, there hasn't been a day I haven't thought about you and Betty."

"I bet," Frederick spat back.

"Dad, that's not fair."

"It's okay, Betty," Zoe said. "He's earned the right to say that. No, Frederick. I think about you and Betty every day."

"Yeah, right."

"Damnit, Frederick. It's true. You two were the loves of my life."

"Then, why did you leave us?" Frederick asked. Finally, it was out. "You had a choice."

"Don't you think I haven't asked myself that same question? Frederick, I was scared."

"Scared?" he asked.

"Yes. Scared. I didn't know what to do. I've only known the circus."

"You could have trusted us," Frederick whispered.

"I know that now, but not back then. It broke my heart, leaving you that day, watching you from the train windows."

"Mom, what were you scared of?"

"Everything. If I left the circus, what would I do? Become a housewife. Sweetheart, I'm not and have never been housewife material. Get a job? Doing what? There are not many job openings out there for trapeze artists, and I'd be damned if I'd take a job as a waitress. At least, in the circus, I was a star."

"So, Miss Superstar, are you still swinging through the tent tops?" Frederick asked.

"No. Got too old for that, so I retired. But sitting around an apartment watching chrome rust was too boring. I never had a hobby, and I found out, you gotta have a hobby or something to do, if you want to retire. So, I asked for a job, any job, back in the circus. So now, I keep the books, sell tickets, hawk the arcade, and as *Miss Zoe, the All Knowing,* read palms. Traveling is in my blood. I'll never change. Honestly, I don't think I want to change. But I want both of you to know, I'm sorry for ever having hurt you. I hope someday you can forgive me."

"Mommy," Betty said, holding out her arms. They embraced. *One down,* Zoe thought.

FJ stood and went back into the house.

FJ found Ray in the kitchen, fixing another Jack and Coke.

"How'd it go?" he asked.

FJ shrugged.

"What does that mean?" Ray asked.

"Just," FJ shrugged again. FJ fixed himself another gin and tonic. "Ray, I wondered how Zoe found out about Innocence's death?"

There was a long pause.

"You can blame me for that," Ray finally confessed.

"You just took it upon yourself to find her and let her know? You did that without asking me first."

"Asking you first? Hell no. I did it because Betty asked me. (FJ frowned) FJ, you're my best friend, but I love Betty as I love my own daughter, and she wanted her mother here. How could I say, no?"

"You could have opened your mouth and said, 'NO!'"

There was another long pause.

"So, how did you find her?" FJ asked.

"Do you remember Special Agent Lisa Clark with the FBI? (FJ nodded) During our last meeting with her, she said, she knew about Zoe, and was about to tell us where she was until you stopped her."

"I remember that. So?"

"So, I called Lisa and told her about Innocence's death, and how I needed to get in touch with her grandmother. Lisa was happy to give me her address and phone number."

"I bet she was ... Well, you should have asked me."

"And what would you have said?"

99

"Probably, no."
"That's why I didn't ask."

Chapter 20

Students at Innocence's school had been excused for the funeral and committal, and three busloads of kids and teachers showed up at St. Mary's. There were so many people in attendance at the funeral; they had to set up a big screen in the parish hall for the spillover crowd. The church's parking lot was overflowing, so much so, Ray had to park at the *Piggly Wiggly* across the street from the church.

The weather forecast said nothing about a thunderstorm, but there was thunder and lightning and buckets of rain during the funeral and the graveside committal. With every lightning strike, everyone jumped. The little kids thought it was funny. Thankfully, the funeral home furnished lightning rods, a.k.a. umbrellas, for the family. Everyone else was on their own. Plywood sheets had been placed around the open grave to cut down on the mud. The problem with plywood, it gets slippery when wet. Once, an older person had been saved from slipping into the open grave, something which Margaret would never live down.

It had been hard on Tom and Betty, picking out a burial plot for their daughter. To them, it probably was one of the worst things a parent ever had to do. They bought three plots, one for Innocence, and for when the time came, one for each of them. That way, the family would be buried together. The Greenlawn & Shadyrest Cemetery opened in the late 1800's, and had grown to forty acres, with approximately 16,500 occupied graves. That was almost twice the number of people in the city of Franklin. Everyone was tired and soaked by the time the funeral was over. No one would ever say it, but everyone was glad it was over.

The family and extended family migrated to Ray and

Margaret's home to relax. It turns out, the Harris's home was located right beside the cemetery. And, because Ashley was the best friend and taking it so hard, she had been given the day off from school. Margaret asked Ashley's mother if Ashley could come over to their house and hang out. They would bring her home later.

Margaret, Stephanie, and Charlotte made sandwiches from the funeral home leftovers, and everyone ate a late lunch. It was quiet in the house, with everyone lost in their thoughts. But that was okay. It was the being together, that would jumpstart the healing process. Late in the afternoon the rain finally stopped, the sun came out, and the humidity took over.

Margaret, Stephanie, and Charlotte were busy cleaning up in the kitchen, whispering about how good Father's homily was, and how great the music was, and on the number of people who attended. Tom and Betty sat on the deck, staring across the road at the cemetery. Zoe joined them, with her cigarettes. Tom's parents had gone home right after lunch, saying they would see Tom and Betty tomorrow. Ashley was in the backyard playing with Ray's dog Roy, earbuds in place, listening to *iTunes*. Ray sat in his easy chair, thinking about how the case was going, or not going. Right now, he needed a break, anything that could get him one step closer to solving the murder. If things continued as they were, this was going to end up being a cold case. Dave was busy tap-dancing in his head to the tune of *Amazing Grace*. Ray needed an aspirin.

FJ stood at the sliding doors, watching Ashley playing in the backyard with the dog. His thoughts were on his conversation with Ashley at the funeral home. Not knowing what brought it up, Ashley had mentioned Innocence's date with Randy Bennett, and how bad it went. According to Ashley, Innocence told her Randy thought himself a stud, and she, Innocence, was his next conquest. During their one date, Randy was pushy, grabby, wanting Ashley to give him oral sex. He couldn't keep his hands off her, trying to grab her boobs and her butt. He kept trying to put his hand between her legs. She warned him if he didn't stop, she was going to tell her Uncle Ray. Ashley thought that was the end of that, but then she saw Randy and Innocence together the day she died.

God only knows why, but it looked like they were getting back together. FJ had asked her why she hadn't gone to the Sheriff with this information. She replied, "It would be his word against mine. And if Randy found out, I told the authorities he would hurt me. (FJ had frowned at her) No, he really would. Nobody knows what kind of jerk he really is, not even his parents. You should hear how he brags to the other boys, about what Innocence lets him do to her, and what she's done for him. He says, she's nothing but a whore." FJ wanted to tell Ray, right then and there, but Ashley pleaded and begged him not too. She was almost in tears. Besides, who would believe her? Randy's rich dad would make sure of that. Randy would somehow hurt her. FJ finally gave in. On that day, FJ had felt his stomach turning over. On that day, his pain turned into hatred.

Today, at this moment, FJ's head was throbbing. He needed another drink.

Chapter 21

FJ was drunk. He couldn't argue the fact. He was somewhere between puking and passing out. He didn't know which would be better. He moaned through closed eyes. There came a knock on his door. Maybe. Could be. He wasn't sure. He opened his eyes. He lay there listening. Nothing. He closed his eyes and took a deep breath.

"Dad."

"Holy shit," FJ exclaimed, springing up. "You almost gave me a fricking heart attack."

"Sorry, Dad," Betty laughed.

"How'd you get in?"

"The door was unlocked."

"Note to self, 'Lock the damn door.' Betty, what brings you out my way?"

"You left Ray and Margaret's pretty drunk yesterday. I was worried about you."

"You could have called."

"I've been trying all morning."

"Oh. Betty, sweetheart, I'm good."

"Dad, you don't smell good."

FJ burped.

"Jesus, Dad."

"Sorry."

FJ farted.

"Holy crap," Betty exclaimed, standing up, waving her hand in front of her face. "What crawled up inside you and died?"

FJ smiled.

"I'm serious, Dad. Did you just shit your pants?"

FJ laughed.

"Dad!"

"Okay, Betty, I'm getting up. I just remembered; I've got something to do this afternoon."

"Are you in shape to do anything?"

"A shower will clear a lot of things up."

"Are you sure you can make it to the shower?"

"You're funny. You know that?"

"Mom is leaving in a couple of days."

"Good for her."

"That's all you have to say?"

"Yep," he said, stumbling toward the bathroom.

***

"Lunch time. Finally," Randy Bennett laughed, as he and his buddies made their way through a maze of students in the hallway.

"Are you eating in the cafeteria?" a friend yelled over his shoulder.

"Sure. I'll meet you guys there, after I have a smoke," Randy replied.

"Don't let Coach catch you. I heard him telling one of the teachers he smelled cigarette smoke on some of the player's breath."

"I'm parked out in the back-parking lot. No one's going to see me out there. Besides, I've got mints."

Randy looked around, making sure no one saw him as he was about to get in his car. What he failed to notice was a blue Audi parked one row over and three cars down.

"So, that's where you park," its driver whispered.

***

FJ felt like shit, if shit could be hung over. The shower hadn't helped. It was a quarter to five, the time Ashley told him the basketball players showed up for practice. FJ wasn't interested in

106

the whole team, but only one person, one person in particular. Randy Bennett. FJ knew what he looked like, because Ashley had pointed him out at the funeral. FJ also knew he shouldn't be here. All visitors were to check in at the office, but screw that. What would he have said? I'm here to see Randy Bennett. I'm going to beat the shit out of the little creep. *I don't think they would have let me in.*

FJ stood at the mouth of the hallway that led from the lockers to the gym. A couple of players came out, giving him the eye. Either they had never seen a dwarf, or they knew who he was. What would he say if one of the coaches approached him? *No clue.* He was here to talk with Randy. That wasn't true. He was here to kick his ass.

A couple more players passed. It was then; FJ noticed how tall these guys were. *Of course they're tall, they're basketball players for Christ sake.* It was easy to see, that most of them had been working out. It was also then; FJ began to doubt his ability to kick the shit out of anyone, let alone a beefed-up basketball player. It didn't matter now, for coming from the locker room was Randy Bennett. FJ felt his temperature rising.

"You got a minute?" FJ asked.

"Sorry, Mr. Johnston, but we're running late."

"How do you know my name?"

"I saw you at Innocence's funeral. You're her granddad."

"You and I need to talk in private," FJ demanded.

"I have nothing to say to you."

"Listen you little shit," FJ said to the guy standing two feet taller than he, "you'll talk with me, or you'll talk to the cops."

"What in the hell does that mean? I've already talked to the cops."

"Let's go someplace private, and I'll explain."

Two more players came out of the locker room.

"Having a problem with the midget?" one asked.

"No. Just a disagreement," Randy commented. "You guys go on. He's leaving."

"The hell I am," FJ spat, "not after everything you did to

Innocence."

"What I did to Innocence? You little creep, you're out of your fricking mind," Randy bellowed.

FJ jabbed Randy in the balls.

"Shit," Randy exclaimed, bending over. It was then FJ slapped him across the face, which sent Randy's head spinning. The two players who had been watching, shook their heads and realized something bad was going to happen, and this was not the place to be. They turned, one going back to the lockers, the other backing into the gym.

"You little bastard," Randy spat. "I don't care if you're little or not, you're still an adult, and you can't do that to a minor."

"You say," FJ whispered, as he stomped Randy's foot making him hop. Swinging his fist, FJ slammed the knee of the leg Randy was standing on. Randy fell to a sitting position. Stepping in, FJ kicked Randy in the side.

This is easier than I thought, he thought taking a step back.

"Hey, leave him alone, you old fart," someone said, as he was passing.

"Go screw yourself," FJ said, turning to the kid.

Randy, getting his wits, swung a left that caught the distracted FJ on the right cheek.

"You asked for it, you little turd," Randy said, gaining his feet.

A hard left and then a right bloodied FJ's face. A kick to the ribs backed FJ against the wall. Trying to protect himself, FJ brought his hands up across his face. The blows to FJ's face were followed by a kick to the middle section, which knocked the breath out of him. FJ bent over, grabbing his belly.

"You had enough?" Randy asked, through sobs.

FJ spat out a mouthful of blood and raised a stubby middle finger.

"Suit yourself."

No one knows how long Randy beat on FJ, nor who all watched, but when it was over, FJ was lying curled up in a fetal position, alone in the hallway.

Chapter 22

Ray stood before the door to ICU room 205. He received a call fifteen minutes ago from Margaret, that FJ was in Intensive Care. Taking a deep breath, he entered to find Betty standing on the left side of the bed, Charlotte standing on the right, Margaret and Stephanie at the foot, Mike and Zoe sitting on the visitor's couch whispering to each other.

Because of bandages, Ray could see very little of FJ's face, but what he could see reminded him of a purple prune. Tubes ran from his mouth and nose. He had a breathing tube sticking out of his throat. Monitors where flashing. Squiggly lines were being drawn on graphs. FJ laid there with his eyes swollen and closed. He seemed lifeless. It didn't look good.

"Mother of God, is he in a coma?" Ray exclaimed.

"Doctor induced," Charlotte replied. "He was hurting really bad, so they put him under. They said it was for the best. They're going to give him a couple of days to start healing, before bringing him out of it."

"The tube in his throat isn't as bad as it looks," Betty assured him. "They put it in to help him breath. Ray, somebody beat the shit out of him. He's got a light conclusion, a sprained wrist, three broken ribs, one of the ribs tore a small, very small, hole in his lung, and the Lord knows how many bruises."

"Do they know who did it?" Ray asked.

"No," Mike said from the couch. "Nobody's come forward saying they did it, or that they saw who did."

"I heard the call come over my radio, but it didn't say who it was, only that someone had been beaten up at the high school and was taken to the hospital. I thought a couple of boys might have

109

gotten in a fight, so I sent one of the deputies over to cover it."

"When the EMTs brought him in, the Emergency Department people thought he was a kid at first, so they put him in the pediatric section," Mike said, laughing. No one else thought it was funny.

"Did he say anything before they put him under?" Ray asked.

"No," Betty answered. "He was moaning and groaning so bad."

"Who found him at the high school?"

"The EMTs say one of the players was heading back to the lockers and found him lying in the hall. The player told a coach, who called it in."

A nurse stuck her head in, looked around, and quickly left. Five minutes later, a man, who said he was the Physician on Duty, came strolling in.

"I'm sorry, but the patients in ICU are allowed only two visitors per room, per visit. Most of you will have to leave for now. We have a nice waiting room down the hall."

"Doctor, do you know who I am," Ray asked.

"Yes, you're the Sheriff of Franklin. I voted for you, but that doesn't carry any weight in ICU. Two visitors per room, per visit. That's the rule. You decide, but most of you will have to leave."

"I'll go," Zoe said, rising from the couch.

"Me too," Betty said.

"No. You and Ray stay," Zoe said. "Maybe you two can make some sense out of all this. I know, I sure as hell can't."

Ray walked around to the right side of FJ's bed after everyone had left.

"Who would do this?" Betty asked.

Ray shrugged his shoulders.

"Knowing FJ," Ray said, "I bet he went to the high school looking for trouble. Has he been drinking?"

"He hasn't stopped since the funeral."

"Well, that could explain it. He's has a lot bottled up inside, and alcohol could have let it out."

"But why the high school?"

"Could be he thought one of the students killed Innocence.

He knows I interrogated several students there the other day, and so far, I haven't questioned a single adult. That's the conclusion I would come up with."

"You think one of the students did this to dad?"

Ray nodded.

"You are really telling me; you think one student did all this?"

"Betty, FJ is not a spring chicken. One student, a basketball player maybe, could have done this, or it could have been the whole damn team. But I doubt it. I think FJ went there thinking he knew who murdered Innocence, and he called him out."

"If he thinks he knows who murdered her, how does he know that, and you don't?"

"That's the first thing I'm going to ask him when he wakes up. I'm going to tell him; I'm glad he's okay. Then, I'm going to kick his ass."

Chapter 23

Ray parked his cruiser in the Franklin-Simpson High School visitor's parking lot, again. At seven o'clock that morning, he had called his favorite guidance counselor, Mrs. Harriet Taylor. He asked if she could have the basketball team, the cheerleading squad, and all the coaches assembled, so he could have a word with them about the incident yesterday.

After walking through security, again, Ray met Mrs. Harriet Taylor in the main office, and together they made their way to the gym.

"Sheriff Harris, we're so sorry about what happened to Mr. Johnston yesterday. If there's anything we can do to help, please, please, let us know."

That sounds like the same damn speech you gave the last time I was here. Do you have it memorized? Is it fill in the blank, as in, we're sorry what happened to 'fill in the blank'?

That's what he wanted to say, but what came out was, "Thank you, Mrs. Taylor. I'm sure the family would appreciate that. Has everyone been assembled?"

"Yes, Sheriff, per your request. This won't take long, will it? I mean, the children are missing class and all."

"No, Mrs. Taylor, this won't take long. I'm just trying to find out who beat the shit out of a dwarf in your school."

"Sheriff, I didn't mean it that way. You ... You take as long as you need."

"Thank you, Mrs. Taylor. I knew you would want to cooperate."

The school must have done some remodeling lately, because

113

the gym was laid out like most new school gyms today: a small stage on one long side of the basketball court, folding bleachers on the opposite side, and several basketball goals mounted around the perimeter. One section of the folding bleachers was pulled out, and everyone was present. The coaches sat on the first few rows, followed by the cheerleaders, with Ashley, Mary, and Janice among them, and then the basketball players. Ray could see Randy and Danny. Randy didn't seem very happy. The school principle, Oscar Owen, met Ray at the free throw line. Speaking through a cordless mic, Principle Owen said, "We'd like to welcome Sheriff Harris to our school. Yesterday, something horrible happened here, and like the Sheriff, we want to get to the bottom of it. So, please give our Sheriff your undivided attention. Sheriff, the students and facility are all yours."

"Thank you, Principle Owen," Ray said, taking the mic. "I'm sure all the buzz around here today, is about what happened to Mr. Johnston yesterday afternoon. It's my opinion, Frederick came here, on his own, to talk to one or more of you, about the death of his granddaughter, Innocence Hall. While here, it appears, a fight broke out with Frederick and an unknown student, or students. Today, Frederick is at the hospital in ICU in a coma. *(There's no reason to tell them it was induced)* We're not sure when he will wake up *(True)* or if he will ever wake up. And we don't know what or who started the fight. That's why I'm here with you today. If you've saw anything or heard anything, please come forward now. The family of Mr. Johnston desperately need your help. *(That should move them)*"

No one moved. There were whispers and glances toward Randy Bennett, but no one came forward.

Come on, people. The person who did this is sitting among you, and you know who he is.

"Okay, maybe you feel uncomfortable about coming forward right now. I can understand that," Ray assured them. "If you think of anything, please contact your guidance counselor, Mrs. Taylor, or your principle, Mr. Owen, and they will call me. Maybe, you're afraid you'll be in trouble. Don't worry. *(Unless you're the shit that*

114

did this) I'm only here wanting answers."

Still, no one moved.

"Thank you, Principle Owen," Ray said, handing the mic back. "If anyone comes forward, give me a call." *It's not going to happen.*

"As soon as it happens," Principle Owen promised.

"Principle Owen, I'd like to see where Frederick was beaten."

The principle led Ray to the opposite end of the gym, where a hallway made its way past the bleachers to the locker room. Ray stood at the point they found FJ. There were only three ways the attacker could have left here. He could have walked back into the locker room, or into the gym. If the bleachers were pulled out that day, he could have gone under the bleachers and exited on the other side. Ray's phone dinged. It was a message from Betty:

```
"The doctor says, he's planning to start
waking Dad up sometime this morning.  He
doesn't know how long it will take.  But,
seeing Dad's not under very deep, it probably
won't take more than an hour or so."
```

Ray texted back:

```
"K"
```

Ray found George and Special Agent Jenny sitting in the bar at the Brickyard Café. They were sipping coffee.

"Ray, we ordered you a cup," George said.

"Thanks. I need it."

"Busy morning?" Jenny asked.

"I met with the students at the high school."

"I bet that went over well," Jenny said, as their server placed a cup before Ray.

"You know it did," Ray laughed, taking a sip. "A lot of somebodies know what happened, but nobody's coming forward."

"Maybe they're afraid. Afraid of getting into trouble, or afraid of the boy or boys that did this."

Ray nodded.

"I don't see it going any further," Ray confessed.

Jenny nodded.

"How's Fred?" George asked.

Ray glanced at his watch. "The doctor should be waking him up about now."

"I'm surprised you're not there."

"They said, it'll probably take a couple of hours. So, I've got plenty of time. I wanted to see if you guys have anything new."

"Sorry, Ray," Jenny confessed. "Everything's turning into dead ends. So, moving on. I'm the stranger in town. Did either of you notice anything during the funeral, either during the visitation or the funeral mass?"

"It was a beautiful service," George commented.

"I think Jenny meant; did we notice anything out of the ordinary with those attending?"

"Oh, sorry," George said. "No. There were a lot of people there, but no one seemed any different from anyone else."

"I agree with George," Ray added. "I noticed Danny Harper came to visitation, but I didn't see him at the funeral."

"I noticed that too," George stated. "Randy Bennett was at both, as was Janice Carson and Mary Austin. The girls seem genuinely upset."

"So, where do we go from here?" Jenny asked.

"I don't know about you," Ray said, "but I'm off to the hospital."

Chapter 24

Zoe was standing in the hallway outside ICU room 205, when Ray walked up.

"Why are you standing out here? Everything alright?"

"I just got back from having a smoke. The doctor's been in there for over an hour. He's bringing Frederick out of the coma. So he ran everyone off, except Betty. Mike and Stephanie went to the gift shop. Charlotte went home to check on Reggie, her cat. Margaret went home to check on Roy. So, I guess, I'll head back out and smoke another cig."

Ray wished he could go out and have a smoke. Ten years now and smoke free, but still he remembered the taste, the smell.

"How did it go at the high school?" Zoe asked.

"As well as I thought it would. Those little bastards know what happened, but they're not talking. I don't know about kids today. When you and I were their age, if a police officer talked to us, we'd be scared shitless. But, not the kids today. There's no fear. There's no respect. That sounds like Rodney Dangerfield, doesn't it?"

Zoe laughed.

I'm not sure, but I think that's the first time I've heard you laugh since you've been back.

"I think I'm going to stick my head in," Ray said, reaching for the doorknob.

"Beware. It's the same doctor that ran us out yesterday."

"That's great."

Every light in the room was on, and the room shone bright, like the middle of the day. Betty stood at the end of the bed, and when she saw Ray, she motioned him over. He joined her, putting his arm around her waist.

"How's FJ?" he asked, whispering in her ear.

"Look for yourself," she replied.

The doctor stood on the left side of the bed, with his arm across FJ's face, fiddling with a tube. "You'll feel better with this out," he said. When the doctor pulled his arm back, Ray could see both tubes were now removed from FJ's nose, but the tube in his throat was still in place.

FJ lay there with most of his face bandaged, but what Ray could see was still red, purple, and puffy. His eyes were swollen, almost shut.

"You look like shit," Ray laughed.

FJ gave him a thumbs up.

"He can talk, sort of," Ray exclaimed.

"We'll remove the trach shortly," the doctor said, patting FJ on the shoulder.

"I didn't think it would be this soon," Ray commented.

"We didn't either, but all his vitals greatly improved since yesterday. We've found patients heal quicker when they feel more comfortable, and having tubes stuck up your nose and a trach stuck in your throat, is not comfortable — been there and done that. Also, tubes and a trach make it harder to talk, and patients can't eat solid foods, with a trach blocking the esophagus. Trust me, Frederick; you will feel a lot better when all of this is out. And I can't stress this enough, you should not attempt to talk, until we remove the trach. You could damage your larynx. If you keep improving as you are now, you should be going home sometime tomorrow."

FJ gave the doctor a thumbs up.

There was a knock on the door, and before anyone could say anything, Special Agent Jenny Broxon walked in followed by George.

"How's the patient?" she asked.

"Much better," Betty replied.

"Mr. Johnston, glad to finally meet you."

FJ gave her a small wave.

"Excuse me, but two visitors per room, per visit," the doctor stated.

"What?" Jenny asked.

"Two visitors per room, per visit."

"Excuse me, but do you know who I am?" Jenny asked.

"I do not."

"I'm Special Agent Jenny Broxon from Frankfort."

"Well, Special Agent Jenny Broxon from Frankfort, two visitors per room, per visit. My hospital. My rules. If you have a problem, I suggest you take it up with the Medical Director. Oh, that's right. That would be me. Right now, two of you, and I don't care who, must leave."

"So, you're the Physician on Duty and the Medical Director?" Ray asked.

"We're a small hospital. There's no room in the budget for two people."

"He doesn't look critical," Ray commented. "I don't see why it—"

"Have you not been listening? Two visitors per room, per visit," the Doctor said, interrupting. "My hospital. My rules."

"I need to get something to eat," Betty said, patting her dad on his foot. He gave her a thumbs up.

"I'll go with you," George said, holding the door open. "Good seeing you, Fred."

Another thumbs up.

"I'll need some help getting the trach out," the doctor said, as he walked toward the door. "I'll be back in a minute. Don't run off."

FJ gave him a thumbs up.

"Any idea who did this?" Jenny asked Ray, when the door closed.

"I have an idea, but I need FJ to tell me. Then I'll arrest the little bastard."

"Give him a name. If he gives a thumbs up, then you have your man, as they say. Or the little bastard, as you put it."

"I should have thought of that," Ray confessed. "FJ, did Randy Bennett do this?"

Thumbs down. Ray frowned.

"Come on, FJ. Did Randy Bennett beat the shit out of you?"

FJ gave him two thumbs down.

"You're lying."

FJ pumped three thumbs down.

"Why are you protecting him?"

FJ shrugged his shoulders.

"You know, there is a way to find out, even if Frederick doesn't want to help," Jenny said.

"How's that."

"Give Randy Bennett a lie-detector test."

"That's a great idea, but our little police department doesn't have a machine."

"What kind of Special Agent would I be if I couldn't help out a fellow officer? If you want, I can call and have one here later this afternoon."

"Works for me," Ray stated.

FJ was pumping thumbs down, but the other two weren't paying attention to him. The doctor and two nurses came back with a cart.

"You two will have to step out," the doctor said, pointing toward the door. "You don't want to see this."

"Is it nasty?" Ray asked.

"A little bloody," The doctor replied to Ray. "And a little painful. But it's quick. I'll ask Mr. Johnston to cough, and I'll give it a big jerk, and it pops out. Well, most of the time it pops out. Sometimes, there's clotting around the tube, and it sticks a little. But it will come out. I promise."

FJ was pumping thumbs down.

Ray stood against the wall opposite FJ's room, while Jenny walked down the hall, with her cell stuck to her ear. She nodded as she passed Betty and George.

"What's Jenny up to?" George asked, nodding in her direction.

"She's getting us set up with a lie-detector."

"That's awesome," George said.

"You going to use that on Dad?" Betty asked.

"No. On the person, I think beat up your dad."

"It's a shame," Betty laughed. "I have a couple of questions I'd like to ask Dad."

"Me too," George admitted.

"As would I," Ray remarked, laughing. "But not this time."

Jenny returned, pocketing her cell phone.

"It'll be at your office around five today."

"You know, we may have jumped the gun on getting the lie-detector."

"How's that?"

"The kid (He didn't want to mention his name around Betty) is a minor, I would have to get his parent's permission first."

"You could be right," Jenny agreed. "Maybe, you should get a court order."

"That's a great idea, but when you meet Judge Chu, don't stare."

Chapter 25

Judge Sarah Chu met Ray and Jenny in the hallway, between her chambers and the courtroom. The judge stood four-foot-three, and because she was of equal proportions she was, what one would call, a "short person," and not a dwarf.

"I'm running late, but what can I do for you today, Sheriff?" she asked.

"I have a court order I'd like for you to sign, Judge."

Judge Chu stopped and held out her hand. "Let me see it." Scanning both pages, she handed the papers back to Ray.

"I have a couple of questions for you Sheriff, which I don't have the time to ask right now. And, I'm sure the boy's father and his lawyer–yes, I know the father and his lawyer– I'm sure they will have a few questions as well. With a lie-detector, you're close to invading the privacy of the minor. It's one o'clock now. I'll have someone serve papers on Mr. Bennett and his lawyer, and I'll see everyone in my chambers, at, say, two o'clock tomorrow afternoon. Will that work for you?"

"Yes, your honor. We'll see you at two tomorrow."

The Judge opened the door to the courtroom, and Ray heard the bailiff bellow, "All rise for the honorable Judge Sarah Chu." Then the door closed.

"That went well," Jenny said, turning to leave.

"I hope it goes as well, tomorrow," Ray said, joining her.

"She was short, wasn't she?" Jenny said, leading the way.

123

Chapter 26

"I wonder where Jim Bennett and his lawyer are?" Ray asked, looking at his watch.

"Right behind you," Harold King, of *King, King, and King* replied. "Sheriff, after reviewing your court order, I feel, not only are you wasting our time today, but also the judge's."

"We'll see," Jenny commended.

The door to the Judge's office opened. "Come in," Chu said, turning away. Jenny still wasn't used to the judge's height and was staring; staring until Ray poked her in the ribs.

Chu's office was spacious. A sitting area with a couch, two chairs, and a coffee table, were nestled next to a gas fireplace. Next to the fireplace was a liquor cabinet. Judicial books filled several bookcases on the opposite side of the room. A mahogany conference table, big enough for ten to twelve people, T-boned the Judge's mahogany desk. All four walls matched the judge's mahogany desk. On the floor was a large oriental rug, covering most of the hardwood.

"Have a seat," Judge Chu said, indicating the conference table. Chu walked around her desk to her chair. Once she was seated, Ray noticed it looked like she was looking down at them. Leaning back in his chair, Ray stole a glance around the corner of her desk and noticed the judge's chair resting on a raised platform. Ray, Jenny, and George took one side of the conference table, while Jim Bennett and Harold King took the other. It had the appearance of a tag-team wrestling match.

"Your honor," Harold began, "I feel this meeting will be a waste of ours and your valuable time. Randy Bennett is a minor

125

and as a–"

"Hold on Counselor," Chu said, raising her hand. "I think I know where you're going with this. Randy Bennett is a minor, but his father is present, and so, it appears, is the boy's lawyer. (Harold nodded) Be that as it may, I guess my question to you Sheriff, is– what hard evidence do you have that Randy Bennett was involved in the death of Innocence Hall?"

Everyone turned to Ray.

"None your honor, but that's not the reason we're here. Nor is it the reason I requested a lie-detector test."

"It says here; you are investigating the death of Innocence Hall."

"Yes, your honor; everything points back to the death of Innocence. That's the reason, I feel, Frederick Johnston went to the high school. He thinks he knows who killed Innocence. It's the reason, Frederick was beaten. I'm trying to figure out who gave Frederick an ass-kicking. Pardon my French. And, Randy Bennett refuses to answer my questions."

"And you think Randy Bennett was responsible for the ass-kicking? (Ray nodded) Do you have evidence that proves that, or even points to that?"

"No, your honor."

"Were there any witnesses?"

"I'm sure there was your honor, but no one's come forward."

"Why is that?"

"I think it's because of Randy's father and his influence in the community."

Springing from his seat, Harold King protested, "Your Honor, I object to that statement."

Judge Chu raised her hand. "I'm sure you do Mr. King. But, please save your dramatics for the court room. This is not a trial. Sheriff, I warn you to be careful what you say."

"Sorry, Your Honor."

Judge Chu continued. "Has Mr. Johnston told you, or anyone else, who beat him?"

"No, your honor, he hasn't."

"And why is that?"

"I wish I knew."

"You have no evidence, no witnesses, and a victim who's not talking. (Ray nodded) You don't have probable cause. Hell, you have nothing else to go on. (Ray nodded) If I were to sign the court order, what's to keep you from wanting to test every student at the high school?"

Ray was about to answer, but Judge Chu stopped him, with a raised hand.

"Sheriff, the only thing you're going on, is a feeling in your gut. Is that it?"

"You just about summed it up, your honor."

"Have you thought, maybe you have indigestion. It could be–how did Ebenezer Scrooge put it– an undigested bit of beef, a blot of mustard, a crumb of cheese, a fragment of underdone potato. No Sheriff, I can't sign this paper. (Jim Bennett and Harold King stood up shaking hands) Gentlemen, please sit down. I'm not done. Sheriff, I can't sign your court order, not today anyway. But, if you come up with any shred of evidence, a smoking gun if you will, even if it's a cap-pistol, come back and see me. Then I'll sign your court order." She said the last part staring at Jim Bennett and his lawyer.

Out in the hallway, after Jim Bennett and his lawyer had turned a corner, at the end of the hallway, Jenny turned to Ray. "I was hoping the judge would sign the damn order."

"Me too," Ray confessed.

"Where do we go from here?"

"I don't know. I need to keep bugging Frederick. Whether he knows it or not, he has the answer that could solve Innocence's murder. Hopefully, he'll be getting out of the hospital in the next couple of days. Then I'll increase pressure on him. Right now, I'm only spinning my wheels."

"I know how you feel," Jenny confessed. "I'm in the same boat. The report came back on the fingerprints and the DNA evidence. (Ray frowned) The condoms. (Ray nodded) There were too many. Too many fingerprints and too much DNA. With the abandoned house being party central, there's no way to tell how old the samples are. I'm afraid unless someone comes forward, this will turn into a cold case."

"That's what I fear. So, what's your plan?" Ray asked.

"I'm heading back to Frankfort. When I have it written, I'll send you a copy of my report. It won't say much more, than what you already know. Sheriff ... Ray, if you come up with anything new, please send it to me. I want to help. I want answers for her parents, her extended family, and for Innocence."

"Thank you, Jenny," Ray said, hugging her.

"Ray, what are you going to do now?"

"While I'm waiting for Frederick to get out of the hospital, I'm going to interview the basketball players, one on one, away from prying ears. I plan on taking them away from their peers; then they may say something."

"That sounds like a plan and something you don't need me here for. Ray nice meeting you," she said, shaking his hand. "And you," she said to George, shaking his hand.

"So. What now, Sheriff?" George asked, watching Jenny's rear-end as she walked away.

"I guess, you need to get back to doing, whatever County Mounties do. I'm going to the hospital. If you think of anything, call me. If I think of anything, I'll call you."

George gave him a thumbs up.

Chapter 27

Ray walked up to ICU room 205 and found the door wide open and no one in the room, not even the patient. A closer inspection showed the bed was made with fresh linen, and the whiteboard, which normally had FJ's name, his nurses, and a funny quote for the day, had been erased. Backing out into the hallway, Ray checked the room number again. Room 205. *Right room.* Making his way to the nearest nurse's station, Ray asked, "Has Frederick Johnston been released?"

"No, Sir," a nurse, who looked too young to be nurse, replied. "He's been moved to Transitional Care, room 7."

"Thanks," Ray said, heading for the elevators.

Ray found the whole gang plus Zoe, crowded in FJ's room.

"How'd it go?" Mike asked from the window seat.

"Her honor said no," Ray replied, looking straight at FJ. It appeared to Ray; FJ let out a big sigh. "I'm running out of leads ... How are you feeling, FJ?"

"My throat's a little scratchy," FJ whispered.

"At least, you can talk now. (FJ nodded) Then, who in the hell beat you up?"

FJ just laid there.

"Charlotte's cat got your tongue?"

FJ just laid there.

"Maybe, he'd couldn't tell," Mike said. "Have you thought of that? Maybe all he could see were crotches."

No one laughed.

"Ray, I'd rather not say," FJ whispered.

"Why in the hell not?"

FJ just laid there.

"You know, I know you know. So, I ask myself, why aren't you coming forth with a name? Could be, you started the fight, and Randy's a minor. You see, I'm guessing its Randy that beat you up. So, Randy's a minor, and you know it would be you, who'd be in trouble. Randy hasn't come forward and pressed charges. The only reason I can come up with that you're not telling is, because you're not through with him. You want revenge. FJ, if that's true, it's not the way you should handle this. If you hurt him, you'll be in deep shit. And at your height, it doesn't have to be too deep. Give me a name. Who beat you up?"

"Okay, Ray," FJ replied. "I'll tell you."

Everyone leaned in.

"It was the whole basketball team. (Ray rolled his eyes–Betty snickered) They came at me all at once. I could have taken them one on one, but not the whole damn team. You should have been there. I put up a pretty good fight, and I'm sure some of them are in the hospital. If not here, maybe in Nashville. You should check out Vanderbilt. I bet someone videotaped it, and it's on Facebook, even as we talk."

Ray stood there, staring at FJ, and FJ could see steam coming out of Ray's eyes. Suddenly, Ray smiled.

"I'll be back later," he said, as he headed for the door.

"I wonder, where's he's going?" Mike asked.

"He's probably calling Vanderbilt," FJ replied.

Oscar Owen, the principle of the high school, met Ray as he went through security.

"Thank you for seeing me this late on a Friday," Ray said, shaking hands.

"Anything to help. What can we do?"

"I'd like to see the gym again, if I could."

"I don't see why not. They should be finishing up practice for today and getting ready for school to let out, but we shouldn't be in their way. What do you think you missed?"

"I don't know until I have a look."

The gym was busy. At one end of the gym, basketball players

were running half-court laps. Some were shooting baskets, while others were practicing bounce passes. The other half of the gym found cheerleaders going through their routines. Ray saw Ashley waving, and he waved back.

Standing at the spot where FJ got his ass kicked; Ray slowly looked around the ceiling.

"Is there something in particular you're looking for, Sheriff?" Principle Owen asked.

"Yes, as a matter of fact, there is, and I think I've found it."

Principle Owen followed Rays' pointing finger.

"Oh, the camera," Owen said.

"I assume it works?" Ray asked, indicating the camera.

"Yes, of course. I'm not sure how much it will pick up on the hallway, but we can take a look."

"How often is the tape erased?"

"Once a month the tape is overwritten," Principle Owen replied.

"So, yesterday should be on there?"

"Of course."

Principle Owen led Ray back to the office, and together they queued up Thursday. The camera lens was wide angle, but not wide angle enough to catch the entire hallway, only enough to catch the first two rows of bleachers and part of the hallway.

"I don't see how much this will help," Principle Owen confessed. "You can't see the spot where Mr. Johnston was attacked."

"Could you fast forward to where the boys were coming out of the locker room for practice?" Ray asked. Owen pressed a key, and the video speeded up. Suddenly, a boy appeared.

"Stop it there," Ray said, pointing. "Okay, now play it forward at normal speed."

The boy walked out onto the gym. He was followed by two more boys. A few minutes went by before another boy appeared. This time the boy was backing out onto the floor.

"Stop it there," Ray said, pointing. "I'd like to talk to him. You know who he is?"

"I do, but I'm not sure school policy allows me to give out

that info."

"It will take me some time," Ray sighed, "but, I can get a court order. We're talking about a murder, and–"

"I thought this was about the attack on Mr. Johnston."

"That's what I meant. So, give me a name and an address, or Damnit, I will be back."

"Sheriff, I've seen these kinds of tactics before, on *Law and Order*. Wait here a minute while I call the school's lawyer." Principle Owen disappeared into his office. When he returned a few minutes later, he said, "So, our lawyer said, I should play your game. Go ahead and get your court order. Give me a call when you have it, and he'll be here to take a look at it. If he says okay, I will give you both a name and an address."

By the time Ray returned with the court order, the school was letting out. He had called Principle Owen when he left the judge's chambers, and the principle said he and his lawyer would be waiting.

"Good to see you again, Sheriff Harris," Harold King, of *King, King, and King*, said offering his hand.

"You're the school's lawyer?" Ray asked. Harold smiled.

"I assume you have something you want me to look at?" Harold asked, holding out his hand. Ray handed over the court order. Harold skimmed over the pages and repeated the process, this time much slower.

"Owen, it looks like everything is in order. As the school's attorney, I direct you to give the good Sheriff the name and the address of the boy on the video."

Principle Owen reached into his jackets inter-pocket, pulled out an envelope, and handed it over to Ray.

"Mr. King, when you talked with Principle Owen earlier, you knew the judge would sign it, didn't you?" Ray asked.

"Yes," Harold King answered.

"Then, why make me go through all the hassle?"

"Sheriff, I don't much like you," Harold King replied with a smirk.

"Fair enough, Counselor," Ray said, as he turned to leave.

Then he stopped and turned back to Mr. King. "I should warn you. I'm thinking about cracking down on speeders. Two miles over the speed limit will get you a ticket. People who run stoplights, people who coast through four-way stops, jaywalkers, hell, people who spit on sidewalks will get tickets. People, especially lawyers, should keep that in mind."

"Are you threatening me?"

"Hell, yes. I'm the Sheriff."

As the Sheriff was threatening Harold King, Randy Bennett was hurriedly making his way to his car. His hair was still wet from the shower he took after practice. He was in a hurry because he desperately needed a smoke. Approaching the driver's side door, he noticed a folded piece of paper stuck under the wiper. He looked around, checking to see if anyone was watching. There wasn't. He unfolded the piece of paper. It was a typed note.

```
We need to talk.  If you don't want the
police to know what you did, you should go
to the old MacGregor house.  Be there no
later than five o'clock today.  Come alone.
```

Randy sat behind the steering wheel, wondering what he should do. Two rows over a blue Audi pulled out of a parking space and headed toward the exit. Randy didn't notice the car or the driver. It took two cigarettes, before his mind was made up. He pulled out of his parking space and turned in the direction of the MacGregor house.

Chapter 28

Ray knocked on the door, even though there was a doorbell. He turned and looked back down the street. The Henderson home stood at the end of a cul-de-sac. The houses in this part of town had been built in the mid-fifties, but you couldn't tell it by their appearances. They had been well maintained. The lawns were well manicured, the flower beds weed free, and busting with rainbow colors. *I wonder who mows your lawns.*

"Can I help you?" a voice said, bringing Ray back to the reason he was here.

Ray turned and smiled. Before him stood an attractive middle-aged woman. She was wearing cutoff jeans, sandals and a tie-dye t-shirt with no bra. *Wannabe hippie.* She was sporting round *Harry Potter* spectacles. *Looks like a wannabe wizard, as well.*

"Can I help you?" she asked again.

"Mrs. Henderson?" Ray asked.

"Yes, I'm Monica Henderson. Sheriff, how can I help you?"

"You have a son, Eugene?"

"Yes," she replied nervously.

You act like you just got caught smoking pot.

"Is your son home?"

"Is he in trouble?"

"No, ma'am. But, he may have seen something at school that–"

"Are you referring to that little person that got hurt at school yesterday?"

"Yes, ma'am. What do you know about that?"

"All I know–Eugene had nothing to do with it."

135

"Yes, I know, ma'am. But, he may have seen something. That's what I want to talk to him about. He's not in any trouble."

"Should I have my lawyer here?"

"Is his name, Harold King?"

"No. Does that make a difference?"

"No, ma'am. It doesn't. You can have your lawyer present if you wish. But I assure you, a lawyer is not required, and Eugene is not in any trouble. As I said, I just have a few questions I'd like to ask him. This will only take a few minutes, and I'll be out of your hair. I promise."

"I guess it'll be alright. But I will be in the room."

"I would not have it any other way."

Monica led Ray into the family room. *The Grateful Dead* was playing somewhere in the background.

"Have a seat, and I'll get Eugene. He should be finishing his homework."

When Eugene and his mom walked in, Ray could see Eugene was the boy in the video, and he was very nervous, but not as nervous as his mom.

"Eugene?" Ray asked.

"Yes, Sir."

"You look nervous."

"I am, Sir."

"I'll tell you, as I told your mom, you're not in any trouble. I can't say this enough. You are not in any trouble. Relax. Take a deep breath. It will help."

Eugene took a deep breath and exhaled slowly.

"Did it help?"

"What, Sir?"

"The deep breath."

"Yes, Sir. Thank you, Sir."

Is this kid real with all the 'sirs' or just nervous? Nervous.

"Eugene stop calling me sir. It's starting to bug me."

"Yes, Sir. I mean, Okay."

"I know you were in the gym yesterday when Mr. Johnston was attacked."

Eugene shook his head.

"I don't know what you mean," Eugene said.

"Really? Eugene, we have a video of you backing out of the hallway, at the time of the attack."

"Eugene, did you have anything to do with it?" his mom asked, sternly.

"No, mom. I didn't."

"I know you didn't have anything to do with the beating," Ray assured him. "I've already said that. But I know you saw the beating. Surely, you can't deny that. Eugene, son, we have you on tape."

Eugene looked up at his mom.

"She can't help you," Ray said, forcefully. "If you don't help me with this, I could arrest you for obstruction. But I don't want to do that. I really don't. I just need answers."

"Sheriff, he's a good kid," Monica pleaded.

"Mom, I saw what happen," Eugene blurted out.

"Finally. Eugene, it's okay," Ray assured him.

"It was Mr. Johnston who started it."

"I can believe that."

"He smelled like he'd been drinking."

"I can believe that as well. Go on."

"He threw the first punch."

"I can see him doing that. Eugene, who did he punch?"

"Randy Bennett."

***

Randy Bennett stood in the darkened room wishing he had bought a flashlight or something. His heart was pounding. The late afternoon sunlight fought its way through the cracks of the boarded-up windows, throwing alternating streaks of light and dark across the floor and walls. Dust particles floated in the light streaks and disappeared into the dark streaks. The mood was surreal. Standing in the dining room, he could just make out what appeared to be a pool of what he knew was dried blood, and he knew this is where it happened. A cold chill ran down his back, and he wished he hadn't come.

After all, this was still a crime scene. *Hell, didn't I have to duck under the yellow police tape blocking the front door?* If he got caught, he would be in a shitload of trouble. But the note he found under his windshield wiper earlier said, if he didn't want the police to know what he had done, he should come here, alone, and be here no later than five o'clock. Randy had no idea what the note meant, nor who left it.

Didn't want the police to know what? Did the person know it was me who beat up the dwarf? Did the jerk-off who wrote the note see me? What kind of evidence does he have? Hell, everybody carries a cellphone. He could have recorded it. Maybe he knows dad's rich. Does he want money? Would he settle for money? Maybe, it's something else. Jesus!

Did the bastard know me, and Innocence are, were, a couple? That we had been seeing each other without our parents knowing? That we had been having sex? It's always about the sex. How would the asshole know that? Good God, had he been watching us? Randy began to sweat. He knew Innocence's age, and he knew it would be considered rape. He didn't want to go to prison. Innocence didn't want him to go to prison. That's why they had been keeping it a secret, and why they were going to keep it a secret, until they were of age. They loved each other. Adults wouldn't understand. Was that what the dickwad was going to tell the police, that he and Innocence were having sex? *Get ahold of yourself, Randy.*

It was ten minutes after five. He stood there, wondering whether he should leave or stay a few more minutes. "What kind of sick joke is this?" Randy whispered. It was then he thought he heard a noise. Slowly turning his head, he tried to determine the direction of the sound, or if he could make out anyone standing in the room, but the streaks and deepening shadows made that almost impossible. Maybe, it was only his nerves playing tricks on his mind. *That's it — tricks of the mind. Hell, it happens to everyone.* Then he heard the noise again, coming from his left. Someone just stepped on a loose floorboard.

"Who's there?" Randy shouted. Silence answered back. "Damnit, I heard you." Again, silence. It was then, that the warm afternoon became frigid.

Enough of this shit.

Turning toward the exit, he slowly took a step, and then another. Soon he found himself standing in the doorway leading into the family room. His palms were sweating. The outside door was on the other side of this room. Merely twelve feet away, but to him, it could have been across town. He tried to force his eyes to adjust to the darkness, but it was useless. The room was full of shadows; shadows deep enough to hide a herd of elephants, or something worse. Twelve feet away. That's all it was. Twelve feet. If he dashed, he could surely do that in two seconds, max.

Taking a deep breath, Randy lunged forward. Halfway across the room, he fell. Something tripped him up; something he was sure wasn't in the middle of the room, when he came in. While rising to his knees, the back of Randy's brain exploded in pain, and the darkness became even darker.

***

"So, you're telling me, you saw Mr. Johnston punch Randy Bennett."

"Yes, sir. He punched Randy in the nuts."

"Randy!" Monica shrieked.

"That's what he did, mom. Hit him square in the balls. Randy bent over. And he, Mr. Johnston, hit Randy in the face."

"You're sure of that?" Ray asked.

"Yes, sir. Mr. Johnston hit Randy in the face."

"Then, what happened?"

"I really, don't know. (Ray frowned) No, really, Sheriff."

"Then, what did you do?"

"I said, 'Oh, shit.'"

"Randy," his mom exclaimed.

"No, Mom, I did. I said, 'Oh, shit.' Cause I knew something bad was about to come down, so I got the hell out of there."

"Did you see Randy hit Mr. Johnston?"

"I heard Randy cursing, and I saw him take a swing at Mr. Johnston, but as I said, I got the hell out of there."

"Was there anyone else with Randy when the fight broke out?"

"No, Sir."

"Stop calling me Sir."

"Yes, Sir."

Chapter 29

Ray burst into FJ's room.

"FJ, we need to talk right now."

FJ held up a hand for silence and pointed toward the corner of the room, where Charlotte sat with her head buried in her hands. Ray walked over and took a seat on the couch beside her.

"What's wrong, Charlotte?"

"It's Reggie."

"Reggie?"

"Yes, my white Persian cat. Oh, Ray, I ran over him."

"I'm sorry Charlotte. When did this happen?"

"This morning when I was heading to daily mass. I was backing out of the drive, when I felt a bump."

"Are you sure you ran over him?"

"There was a black tire track going across his head. (Ray fought back a smile) Ray, don't you dare laugh. There was blood coming out of his nose and mouth. His eyes were crossed. (A snicker came from FJ's bed) Go to hell, FJ."

"Charlotte, losing a pet is the same as losing a child," Ray assured her. "I cried and cried when we put Cleo down. I know what you're going though. Do you want me to go over and bury him?"

"Why?"

"That's what you do when a pet dies. You bury them."

"Who said Reggie died?"

"You just said you ran over his head."

"I did, but that didn't kill him. Ray, I put him in a cardboard box, and I ran him by the Crocker Animal Hospital. The way he

141

was acting, I knew he was going to die, so I wanted the vet to put him down. I hated doing it, but I didn't want him to suffer. It turns out; all Reggie has is a broken jaw, which cut his tongue. That's where all the blood came from. The vet said he'll be back to normal in a month or two. But, I'll have to feed him soft foods during that time, which is okay. He loves soft food. His eyes were crossed because he was in shock and pain. He's calmed down now, and his eyes aren't crossed anymore. I'm giving him little drops of kitten morphine for the pain."A laugh exploded from FJ's bed.

"FJ, I know who you got into the fight with," Ray said, approaching FJ's bed.

"So?" FJ came back.

"So, I don't know who's in more trouble. You for hitting a minor, or the minor kicking your ass, with you being a little person and all."

"Does it matter?"

"Not to me. Randy Bennett hasn't come forward and pressed charges. He's probably waiting to see what you're going to do. What are you going to do, by the way? You think he had something to do with Innocence's death?"

"Yes. I believe he did. You think that as well," FJ stated flatly.

"Yes, but I didn't get my ass kicked. Do you know why I haven't arrested him? (FJ shrugged his shoulders) It's because I don't have any evidence. FJ, it's all about the evidence. What evidence do you have, that would make you want to hurt him? Tell me, and I'll go right now and arrest the little bastard."

FJ laid there, staring at the muted TV hanging on the opposite wall.

"Come on," Ray continued. "You must have had some reason."

"My reasons are my reasons."

"Damnit, FJ, that's not helping. Tell me what you know so that I can put the creep away."

"Put him away? Hell, he's a minor. He won't do time. And if he does, he'll be in some kiddy prison with pool side service, ice cream, and video games. His daddy's money will see to that. No,

Ray, I have nothing to say to you."

"Then, without your help," Ray sighed, "this case may never be solved."

"It'll be solved someday," FJ promised.

"What in the hell does that mean?"

FJ unmuted the TV.

Chapter 30

Ray popped three aspirins and had just washed them down with a big gulp of Bud Lite, when his phone rang. He never liked receiving phone calls late in the day, but this one was from George.

"George, when you call this late, someone has died."

"Ding, ding, ding. Winner, winner, chicken dinner."

"Really? Who died?"

"You're not going to believe this; number one suspect, Randy Bennett."

"You're right. I don't believe it," Ray exclaimed. "He can't be dead."

"Well, no one told him that. Cause, I'm looking at him right now, and he looks dead to me."

"Don't tell me, Billy Hayden found him at the MacGregor place?"

"Are you psychic, or what?"

"George, have you been drinking?"

"How did you know? Oh, that's right. You're psychic."

"What time did Billy find Randy?"

"Billy was on his way home from work. With the baby on the way, he's been working doubles. He drove by the old house and saw a car parked in the lane, up close to the house. It turns out; vehicle registration says the car belongs to Randy Bennett. Anyway, Billy Hayden knows the place is still a crime scene, so he calls me. That was about, let's see, thirty minutes ago. Do you want to guess how he died? Go ahead. Guess."

"Blunt force trauma to the back of the head?"

"Quick, give me five numbers and a number for the Powerball."

"Have you called Nicole?"

"She just arrived."

"I'm on the way."

"Are you kidding me?" Margaret asked, as Ray buttoned up his shirt. "Someone else died in that old house. (Ray nodded) Somebody should tear it down."

"I agree, Margaret. I'd better get going. I told George I'd meet him out there."

"Be careful, Ray."

Once in the patrol car, Ray stared at his phone. *Should I, or shouldn't I?*

"Would you connect me to Transitional Care, room 7, please?" Ray asked the hospital answering service.

"Just a minute."

Thirty seconds went by.

Damnit FJ, you better be there.

Ten more seconds went by.

"Hello," a sleepy FJ said.

Thank you, Jesus.

"FJ, its Ray."

"Why are you calling this late in the evening? Has something happened?"

"Nah, nothing's happened. I just wanted to make sure you're okay."

"That couldn't wait till the morning?"

"No. I had to be sure, or I wouldn't be able to get to sleep."

"Ray, have you been drinking?"

"A couple of beers, but I just wanted to make sure you're feeling better."

"That's sweet, Ray. But Ray, tell me again, has something happened?"

"What do you mean, has something happened? Can't a friend call his old buddy?"

"I'm fine buddy, old pal."

"That's great, FJ. I'll see you sometime tomorrow."

"Okay, Ray. Goodnight."

"Goodnight, old buddy."
Ray heard the word 'asshole' as FJ disconnected.

Chapter 31

Can you say, Déjà vu?

The same two firetrucks, ambulance, Nicole's M.E. van, and George's patrol car, were throwing multi-colored lights across the abandoned house. Here was something new. A small, expensive sports car had joined the party.

Has to be Randy's.

As before, George was standing on the front porch.

"Evening, Ray."

"George."

"I thought about not calling you, but I thought you'd want to be here."

"Thanks. Did he die in the dining room?"

"You missed that one. He died in the family room."

"The same shape and size of wound like Innocence's?"

"Now, you're on a roll."

"Any other wounds?"

"Nope. I feel like giving you a 'Clue' accusation. Colonel Mustard did it with the candlestick in the Billiard Room, but that would be tacky."

"In this situation, tacky is not the word I'd use. But, if it makes you feel better, that's something Frederick would say."

Police tape from the first murder still hung across the entrance, and new tape had been added. Ducking beneath the tape, Ray entered the living room. Portable lights tore through the darkness. Techs were busy collecting evidence. Looking around, Ray made the sign-of-the-cross. Nicole was bent over the body.

"Don't get up, Nicole," Ray said, as he walked up.

"I hadn't planned on it. How are you doing, Ray?"

"I'm okay. You know, we're going to have to stop meeting like this. People are starting to talk."

"Like you're my type."

"What kind of type, is your type?"

"Are you going to stand there flirting with me, or are we going to get down to business?"

"So, as our Medical Examiner and not the object of my flirtation, what can you tell me?"

"Right now, it looks like the young man died from blunt force trauma."

"A blow to the back of his head?"

"There, but that's not the only one. There are several blows to his shoulders, back, and arms. The wound to the back of his head looks like a glancing blow, but without further examination, I can't say it was enough to kill him. He'll tell us more when we get him on the table. The other blows could have been overkill. From his core temperature, I'd say he died around four or five hours ago. Ray, if I were to guess, it's the same person who killed Innocence."

"Why do you say that?"

"Same murder scene. The wounds appear to be the same size and shape as the wound Innocence received. I would guess the same weapon was used in both cases. Both victims went to the same school, were in the same class, and both were sexually attracted to each other, and not in a bad way. That's too much of a coincidence."

"Has anyone found the murder weapon?" George asked the techs. All shook their heads.

"Nicole, how do you know the last part?" Ray asked. "The part about Randy and Innocence being sexually attracted. Are you one-hundred percent sure?"

"I'm not sure about anything," Nicole confessed. "It's a gut thing. Do you ever have gut feelings?"

"Too many. I've been told it's probably indigestion. Most of the time, my guts wrong and gets me in a shitload of trouble."

"But sometimes your gut's right. So, what's your gut telling you now?"

"As much as I hate admitting this," Ray confessed. "I think Randy did have sex with Innocence, but I won't go as far as to say it was mutual. I don't see how any of this helps now, that he's dead. He was my number one suspect. Hell, my only suspect. I'm afraid; we're back to square one. George, when are you planning on going over to the Bennett's?"

"I'm heading over there now. You want to ride along?"

"Truthfully, no. But I probably should. I've been riding them hard about Randy."

"You want me to follow you back to your house, so you can drop off your car? We can take the county's car over to their house."

"Works for me ... See you, Nicole."

"See you, Ray."

Once they had dropped Ray's car off at his house and were backing out of Ray's drive, Ray's phone rang. It was dispatch.

"Hello ... Okay ... No. Tell him I'm coming over right now ... Okay. Thanks."

"What's up?" George asked.

"Jim Bennett just called dispatch. He wants to report his son missing. They haven't seen him since he left for school this morning. They don't know where he is, and he hasn't answered his cell."

Chapter 32

George parked out on the street, because the Bennett driveway was full of cars, four to be precise. "Who's going to tell them about Randy?" George asked, before getting out.

"It should be you," Ray stated flatly. "He was found in your jurisdiction."

"But they live in yours," George came back.

"No, seriously," Ray said, shaking his head.

"But they don't like you already," George assured him.

They sat there, deadlocked.

"Odd or even," Ray suggested, holding up a fist.

"Ray, you call it."

"Even. One. Two. Three."

Ray had one finger. George had two.

"Odds," George exclaimed. "You have to tell them."

"Crap," Ray whispered, opening the car door.

I wonder if they have raw eggs.

One of the city's new LED streetlights was casting a bright white glow across the yard.

I wonder who does your lawn, Ray thought, as they walked up the sidewalk to the front entrance.

Jim Bennett opened the door before they were on the porch.

He must have been watching for us.

The egg sucking moment was rapidly approaching.

"Come on in," Jim said, holding the door for them. "Sheriff, I called your office about Randy. Why is George Watson with you?"

"We both need to talk with you."

Jim led them to the back of the house, to the real family room.

This is where you could take off your shoes and put your feet on the coffee table, like normal people. A bigscreen hung on a decorative brick wall. It was turned off. Old black and white family photos covered the walls, which were of Lebanon Cedar. The walls, not the photos. The floors were expensive inlaid Italian tile. Harold King was standing at the bar, fixing a drink. Three people were sitting on the couch; an older version of Jim Bennett, a white-haired lady that had to be the older version's wife, and a woman who had to be Jim the younger's wife.

"Can I get you a drink?" Jim the younger asked, indicating the fully stocked bar across the room.

"Nothing for me," Ray replied.

"Or me," George added.

"Excuse me," Jim the younger stated, "where're my manners. Let me introduce you to everyone. You know Harold King, of course. (Harold nodded) These are my parents, Jim Senior and Julie, and my wife, Heather." Ray nodded. Ray wondered where the possessed Cindy Lou was. Then it dawned on him, this late in the evening, she should be in bed. Visions of *The Exorcist* floated through Ray's mind. Instead of Linda Blair being tied to the bed, it was little Cindy Lou. He could see Cindy's sweet, innocent face one second, and her puking green vomit the next.

"Sheriff Harris," Harold King said, interrupting Ray's nightmare. "I know we've had our differences, but I hope we can conduct this in a civilized matter. We are here for the same reason, after all."

Play nice Ray, Ray thought.

"Yes, we are here for the same reason," Ray assured him.

"Sheriff, what is it you have to tell me about Randy?" Jim Jr. asked, but staring at his wife. "We haven't seen him all day. He won't answer his phone, and that's not like him. His mom and I are worried."

Egg sucking time, Ray thought, *but not for me.*

"Jim, I'm here only for support. It's George who has something to tell you. Go ahead, George."

"Well ... Mr. Bennett ... I ... We have some bad news for you,

154

and there's never a good way to say this. Late this afternoon, your son, Randy, was found dead at the old MacGregor place."

Heather slumped back on the couch and burst into tears. Julie reached over and pulled her daughter-in-law to her. Jim Bennett Jr. went and sat down beside his wife, placing his hand on her knee. Jim Sr. joined Harold King at the bar and poured himself something strong.

"What happened?" Jim Jr. asked, fighting back the tears.

You're not the hard-ass I thought you were, Ray thought. *Shame on me.*

"We're not sure, right this moment," George said, softy. "The M.E. has taken his body to the morgue. As soon as we know something, we'll be in contact with you. I'm sorry Mr. Bennett ... Mrs. Bennett."

"Was he murdered?" Jim Sr. asked.

"Right this second, it looks that way, but we'll have to wait for the Coroner's report."

Looks that way. You're a good liar George, Ray thought.

"I'd like to see my baby," Heather sobbed.

"That will be arranged," George assured her. "Let me get with Nicole, the County's Coroner, and set up a time tomorrow. I'll need your phone number, Mr. Bennett."

"Did he die like Innocence Hall?" Harold King asked.

"I can't say right now," George replied.

"Why would anyone want to kill my son?" Heather asked, looking at Ray.

Mrs. Bennett–"

"Please, call me, Heather."

"Alright ... Heather, we don't know. I know that's not the answer you want, or need to hear right now, but it's the truth."

"You think he was killed for the same reason, as the young woman?"

She wasn't a woman. She was just a child, Ray almost said out loud.

"Again, it's too early to jump to conclusions," George assured her.

"What if we were to offer a reward for any information?" Jim Sr. asked.

"It might work, but I doubt it," Ray confessed. "As much as we've dug into all of this, no one, and I mean no one, has come forth. If you do go public and offer a reward, you will have all the crazies coming out of the woodwork."

"So, what now?" Jim Jr. asked.

"We'll start asking around," George said, "while we're waiting on the autopsy report. I'm sure Sheriff Harris will assist us during our investigation. (Ray nodded) I will call a Special Agent friend in Frankfort and see if she can lend support as well. I promise we'll do everything we can to find the person, or persons responsible for this."

Back in George's cruiser, Ray and George sat there in silence, wondering if they had said the right things. You never know in these situations.

"You did well Grasshopper," Ray said, hoping George would catch the reference to the television series *Kung FU.* "You made it sound like we had something to do, things to investigate, instead of being up shit creek without a paddle."

George laughed, "Thank you, Master ... So, Ray, what are we going to do now?"

"I don't know, George. I'm at my wit's end. The best thing we can do right now, is to walk away from both murders for a day or two. (George had a puzzled look on his face) There's so much to decipher, it's starting to muddy the water. I think I'm taking the weekend off. Lord knows I need it. My head's been throbbing for eight days, and aspirins ain't cutting it.""Monday morning, I'll go in to work like any other day and do some Sheriff stuff. In a couple of days, I'll holler at you. Maybe we can get together at the Cracker Barrel and see if there's an angle we haven't tried."

George nodded.

"And what if Frederick or the Hall's or the Bennett's call, asking you where we stand on things?" George asked.

"Then, I'll have to do the worst thing I've ever done."

"What's that?"

"I'll have to lie to them."

156

Chapter 33

Ray watched George drive off, after dropping him at his house. Like *Motel 6,* Margaret had left the light on. He stood on the front porch deciding if he was going in or not. It was almost midnight, but he wasn't sleepy. Tired, but not sleepy. Margaret would be crashed. Roy would be curled up on the foot of their bed sound asleep. There was too much running through Ray's mind, and he knew it would be hours before sleep found him, if then. His head was pounding. Besides, Dave wasn't through with *Don't cry for me Argentina.*

The drive to the MacGregor house was quiet and lonely at this hour. There were no headlights in the rearview mirror, nor were there any approaching. Ray felt like the last man on earth. He had no idea why he was out here, but here he was. His headlights shone on the old house's vine covered façade, causing Ray to smile. It wasn't as alien looking as it was with the rescue vehicle's multicolored lights dancing all over it. It just looked spooky. Crickets that had been chirping earlier in the evening had gone to bed for the night, and it was deathly quiet and still, like the moments before a storm. Ray wondered if there was a storm brewing. Grabbing his flashlight, Ray turned off the headlights. Now, it was beyond spooky. He thought about starting the engine up, putting the car in gear and heading back home.

The flashlight's beam jumped around the living room. From its intensity, everything within the beam appeared almost black and white. The darkness outside the beam was darker than India ink. *God, this is creepy.* Nothing had changed since he was last here. Well, the flood lamps were gone, as well as Nicole and George.

The forensic techs were also gone, other than that, nothing had changed. Ray could hear the pitter-patter of raindrops beginning to fall on the tin roof. When he was little, Ray's home had a tin roof, and Ray loved falling to sleep to the pitter-patter.

The flashlight zeroed in on the chalk lines where Randy's body was found. Yes, they still use chalk lines. Looking closer, there seemed to be very little blood. Of course, it was blunt force trauma, and with BFT, it doesn't always have to be messy. Ray rubbed his head, trying to rub away the throbbing.

"Knock it off, Dave. Give it a rest, please."

Dave wasn't listening.

Why am I here? The techs have combed through everything, and they're better at that than I'll ever be. A moan floated through the room, causing Ray to jump. *What the ...* There it was again. *Now what?* The melancholy sound reminded him of his own spirits. It came from the next room. Innocence's room.

Tiptoeing through the doorway, Ray paused to listen. If something grabbed him right now, he knew he would shit his pants. His flashlight dodged here and there searching for the source of the sound. When it came again, it was from the fireplace on the far exterior wall. Walking over, Ray placed his head close to the black opening. Close, but not too close. He didn't know what was going to spring out on him. He thought about pulling his gun. *That's silly,* he thought as he unsnapped the gun's tie-down. The moan came again, this time from inside the chimney. Ray smiled because he knew what it was. At least, that's what he told himself. With the rain, had come the wind, and it was blowing down the chimney, causing something to vibrate in the flue pipe, which in turn caused the moaning. *Knew it all the time,* he thought as he snapped the gun's tie-down.

Crossing back to the table, Ray shone the light on Innocence's chalk lines. If nothing came along to disturb them, how long would they remain? A month? Six months? A year? Two years? *Would they still be here when I'm dead and gone? Would Innocence's death be unsolved when I'm dead and gone?* Ray knew now; it was the idea of Innocence's death, becoming a cold case that nagged at him. It had been a little over a week, and he was no closer to solving her murder than the day it happened. Ray had cable and was a fan of *The First 48,* and he knew what happens when you go past forty-eight hours, and he was well past forty-eight. His number one suspect, his only suspect, had been murdered, murdered in the next room. With Randy, there was motive, no matter how small. He and she were having sex. Mutual or forced, Ray didn't know. It didn't matter now. If only he had Innocence's diary. She probably would have written something about it. Maybe, Randy was worried Innocence would spill the beans. Perhaps, he thought she was pregnant, and he wasn't ready to start a family. Randy knew she was Catholic, and an abortion to her would have been murder. That was the only thread, the only connection Ray had. But now, it was broken. There was someone else in the equation, someone unaccounted for. But who? He had to solve these murders, or it would drive him crazy, crazier.

When Ray got home, it was pouring.

Chapter 34

It was close to noon, before Ray rolled out of bed. From the sound outside, it was still raining. His dreams that night had been full of moans, groans, and small black hairy things with wings, red eyes, and fangs, pouring out of the fireplace in droves. In his dream, bullets did not affect them.

"I was getting ready to come in to check if you were still alive," Margaret said. "Rough night?"

"You don't know the half of it."

"Why don't we take some time and go somewhere. We could fly down to Tybee Island and get away from everything and everybody. I bet the sun is shining down there."

"And who's going to work the case. I mean, cases."

"Ray, you're not the only police officer in town. Besides, the cases are outside your jurisdiction. Ray, you need to remember, you're not a spring chicken anymore. You're liable to have a heart attack. Let George handle it."

"I can't, Margaret."

"Why not? You don't think George can handle it?"

"No. He's as thorough as they get."

"You think everyone will call you a quitter? Ray, they know you better than that."

"Margaret, I just can't."

"Ray, you look worn out."

It was the phone that ended the argument Margaret was winning.

"Hello, Nicole," Ray said, pointing at his phone.

"Ray, I know it's Saturday, but I found something interesting, and I want you to see it before I send it off."

"What is it?"

"I'd rather you see it. Could you come down to the office?"

"Right now?"

"Yes."

"I'm on the way."

"Nicole wants you to come to her office?" Margaret asked. "I caught that part. I take it; she found something that can't wait till Monday?"

"I guess it can't," Ray replied. "She said she wanted to show it to me before she sent it off."

"Sent what, where?"

"I don't know the answer to either of those questions."

"You haven't had anything to eat, and you know how sick-to-your-stomach you get when you haven't eaten anything."

"I'll grab something after I've seen Nicole."

"Make sure you do. I've noticed you haven't had much of an appetite lately."

"Yes, ma'am."

Nicole was waiting at the rear entrance to the building when Ray pulled up.

"Come in out of the rain, Ray," Nicole laughed, holding the door open for him. "Wait till you see what I found."

Walking into the autopsy room, Ray noticed a covered body, and he knew it had to be Randy.

"So, what is it you were in such a hurry to show me that it couldn't wait till Monday?"

"This," Nicole said, holding a small plastic bag in front of Ray's face.

"I can't make it out," he confessed. "But it looks like a hair."

"It is a hair."

"And this is why you called me out in the rain? For a hair? Nicole, I've seen hair before."

"Oh, Ray. Follow along. What color is the hair?"

"White, or blond."

"Very good. What color was Innocence's hair?"

"Blond."

"What color was Randy's hair?"

"Black, I think."

"Do you want to make sure? He's lying over there," Nicole said, indicating the covered body.

"Black. I'm sure it was black."

"You're right. So tell me, why did I find this blond hair in the wound on the back of Randy's head?"

"I would guess it got there from the weapon the killer used."

"The same weapon that killed Innocence," Nicole finished. "The hair was transferred from Innocence's head to Randy's head via the murder weapon."

"Are you sure it's hers?"

"Not one hundred percent. The only way to get DNA from a hair sample is if the hair follicle is present, which it is in this case. We also have Innocence's DNA on file. That's why I'm sending both samples to Special Agent Jennifer Broxon. I called Jenny earlier today, and she said to send her the samples, and she'd put a rush on it. I'd bet your paycheck it's Innocence's. Ray, you know what this means?"

"Yes. The weapon that killed Innocence is the same weapon that killed Randy. That's all it proves. It doesn't tell us if it was only one person."

"Damnit, Ray. What's the odds it wasn't the same person?"

"I would say pretty close to zero percent. Good job, Nicole. Good job. But I think we need to keep this among you and me, and George of course."

"Of course," Nicole agreed. "Now comes the hard part."

"What's that?"

"The waiting."

Even in the pouring rain, Ray was upbeat on the way home. So much so, he stopped in at Hardee's and ordered two quarter-pound Angus Bacon Cheddar Melts, a large fry, and an apple turnover.

"You're wolfing it down," Margaret laughed, as she watched Ray consume the meal. "Somebody must have been hungry."

"You don't know how much."

"So, what did Nicole show you that made your appetite return?"

Ray chewing with his mouth full, just stared at her. Margaret waited. Ray took another bite.

"It's the public thing again. Isn't it?"

Ray smiled. His phone rang. Caller-ID said it was FJ.

"You think you can take me home?" FJ asked, before Ray had a chance to say hello.

"Sure. When?"

"As quick as you can get here. They will have the release papers ready for me to sign as soon as you're here, to prove I have someone to take me home."

"Are you sure you need to go home right now?" Ray asked.

"I'm not going home right now. Betty made a big fuss, so I'm spending some time with her and Tom."

"That's a good idea. Let me take a pee, and I'll be right over."

FJ was dressed, sitting on the bed with everything packed on a cart to be taken down to the car.

"About time you got here," FJ exclaimed.

"What's got your panties in a wad?"

"Her."

"Sheriff Harris, we're asking Mr. Johnston to leave," the head nurse, holding the clipboard with the release papers, said.

"What does that mean?" Ray asked.

"It means, they're kicking me out."

"I wouldn't say it that way," the nurse stated, "but, yes, we are kicking him out. Sheriff, he's so demanding. Get me this. Fetch me that. This is too hot. That's too cold. Can I have a Gin and Tonic with my supper? Can I get a body massage? I think it's time for my bath. Are there any pornographic channels on the TV? Sheriff, there's not a woman in the hospital he hasn't hit on. He's like a little Banty Rooster that wants to screw every hen in the chicken coop. So, yes, we're sending him home. There's nothing wrong with him, except, maybe, his testosterone level is way too high, which at his age should have significantly dropped."

"If you got it, flaunt it," FJ said with a smile. "That's what my momma always said."

"You were abandoned at birth," Ray said. "You don't know who your momma was."

"Maybe, it was one of the foster moms who said it."

The drive from the hospital to Betty's and Tom's was short.

"Ray, have you come any closer in figuring out who killed her?"

"No. I'm sorry. George and I are hard at it."

"Was it the same person who killed that Randy kid?"

"I can't say."

"I read in the paper where he was killed. It was about the time you called and woke me up. You don't think I had anything to do with that, do you?"

"I think you're a lot of things, but a killer isn't one of them."

"I won't lie to you, Ray. I wanted him dead. I wanted revenge for Innocence's death."

"I know you did."

It was all silence until they pulled into Tom's lane.

"FJ, why did you go to the school that day? Surely, you knew you'd get hurt."

"No. I didn't know I'd get hurt. Do you think I went out there hoping someone would beat the shit out of me? No, I honestly thought I could take him, but I didn't take into account how big basketball players are."

"You still haven't answered the question 'why?'"

"Let me think on it, Ray. I'm not ready. Not yet anyway. I need to talk to someone. Then maybe I'll be ready."

"I have no idea what that means, but I'll give you a little time. Not a lot, mind you, a little."

"Good enough," FJ said.

Betty, Tom, Ashley, and Zoe were waiting for them with umbrellas, as they came to a stop.

Chapter 35

"Come in here, Ray," Margaret yelled from the living room as soon as Ray had entered the house.

"What is it?" Ray asked, coming into the living room.

"Look on the TV. It just came on. I swear."

"There's no need to swear."

There on the television was Jim Bennett with Heather at his side, the Mayor and George Watson. They were standing in front of the Sheriff's Station. Looking over Jim and Heather's shoulder was Harold King, all decked out in his thousand-dollar suit and all smiles. Beside Harold was Jim Sr. and Jim Sr.'s wife. Ray couldn't remember her name. All were covered under a canopy of umbrellas. They were surrounded by a sea of reporters. Most of which were also under umbrellas. George didn't look so happy.

"Thank you for coming out in the pouring rain," Jim Jr. began. "I wanted to have a press release today. As you know, I lost my son yesterday about this time. The police are working as hard as they can, but my wife and I feel a little incentive could help. That's why today, we're offering a $100,000 reward for anyone who has information leading to the arrest and conviction of our son's killer. Please take one of these sheets of paper. On it, you will see an 800-number. Please call if you have any information."

"Mr. Bennett, I'm sorry for your loss," one of the reporters said. "But what can you tell us about your son's death?"

Jim looked at George, who stepped up to the mics.

"No one will be taking questions today. Thank you."

George turned to walk away.

"Why not?" another reporter asked. "The public is entitled

to know."

George turned back to the mics.

"And they will. When the time is right, I'll call a meeting. But now is not the time. And, when I do call a meeting, I promise you, it won't be in the pouring rain. Now, go home, back to work, or anywhere else. I don't give a crap where you go, but you can't stay here. Thank you and have a nice day."

George turned and walked back into the station, out of the rain.

"Way to go, George," Ray yelled, knowing full well George couldn't hear him.

Chapter 36

Today was a "non" event day, for which Ray would be eternally grateful. At least, it was supposed to be. The morning began with early mass at St. Mary's followed by breakfast at the Cracker Barrel with the crew. FJ had skipped mass, as usual, but met them for breakfast. The manager seated them himself. Mike brought it up that he had seen Randy Bennett's OB in the paper that morning. He was a good-looking kid. There were rumors floating around town that Randy had committed suicide after killing Innocence, and the Police were covering it up with their own story that Randy was murdered. In his heated response to the rumors, Ray had almost used the word "bullshit" in his statement to the press.

Randy's visitation would be tomorrow afternoon from two to seven, and his funeral Tuesday morning at ten o'clock. Both visitation and funeral would be at the Calvary Baptist Church. Everyone planned on attending; everyone except FJ. Ray would be there looking for suspects. The rest of the crew would be there because Franklin was a small town, and in a small town, everyone knows everyone.

After breakfast, Margaret had run off to Charlotte or Stephanie's house. Ray didn't know which. FJ and he had settled in for an afternoon of beer and a western classic: *The Good, the Bad and the Ugly*. Ray had watched this movie over a dozen times, knew every line by heart, and it still hadn't gotten old.

FJ was sitting on pins and needles. Today he was going to tell Ray why he went to the school that day, and why he picked a fight with Randy. The reason he hadn't told Ray so far, was that someone, someone close to them would be in trouble, nothing serious, but

169

still in trouble, and he didn't want that. He wondered how much of the things the person told him were lies. Besides, Randy was murdered. There was no need throwing dirt on a dead kid. But still, Ray needed to know. Maybe after the movie. Maybe.

It was near the end of the movie and Tuco, the bandit, is running through the spiraling ring of graves looking for the grave marker of Arch Stanton. Tuco is in focus, while all the markers are whizzing around him out of focus. Ray loved this part, especially Ennio Morricone's musical score, and Sergio Leone's choreography. Suddenly, the camera freezes on Arch Stanton's wooden marker with his named hastily painted on it. Ray's phone rings. Special Agent, Jenny Broxon's name appeared on the Caller-ID.

"Sorry, FJ. I need to take this."

"No problem," FJ said, popping open another beer.

Ray pressed the TV's pause button. Sometimes, he wished there were a pause button for his phone, but not this time.

"Hello, Jenny. I haven't heard from you in a while."

"I know, Ray. Sorry. I've finished up my report on Innocence Hall, and I'll be sending it to George tomorrow. A special courier just now delivered samples from your coroner. I'll put a rush on them tomorrow."

"Why not today?"

"It's Sunday, Ray. Most people, normal people, take Sundays off."

"Priests, don't."

"Okay, priests don't. Tomorrow–"

"Doctors, EMTs, firefighters."

"Okay."

"Cops, nurses, thieves."

"Enough! Tomorrow will be fine. I *will* put a rush on it. What normally takes us a couple of weeks, I'm hoping will take a couple of days."

"That sounds great, Jenny. Thank you, but you didn't have to call for that."

"Ray, that's not the reason I'm calling you."

"Okay."

"Friday, we had a case dropped in our lap, because the local authorities weren't making headway. It reminded me of your situation."

"What? The not making headway part?"

"No, nothing like that. There was a homicide in Park City."

"Jenny, people are being murdered every day somewhere in America. I read somewhere there were over 18,000 people murdered in the U.S. last year. Nothing against Park City, but why should they be left out?"

"Ray, listen to this. Here's the crime scene scenario that appears in their report: abandoned house, dead body, female, and cause of death: blunt force trauma to the back of the head."

"Jesus," Ray exclaimed. "When did this happen?"

FJ perked up. *What happened?*

"Three months ago," Jenny continued. "Ray, that's not all. As you know, Park City and Franklin are along the I-65 corridor. So, I set up a query in our database, searching for murders with the same scenario as ours, I mean George's crime scene, all along I-65."

"Tell me you got hits."

FJ leaned in, wondering what in the hell "hits" meant. He wished he could hear what was being said on the other end.

"Ray, I got hits. Do you believe that? Four fricking hits. Six months ago, a similar murder happened in Munfordville. Three months later, it was Park City. One month ago, Bowling Green. And now Franklin. Ray, all these towns are along the I-65."

"Jenny, are you telling me, we have a serial killer operating along I-65?"

A serial killer? FJ thought.

"God, I hope not," Jenny sighed, "but Ray, it looks that way."

"That's horrible, but it's more than I've got right now. Jenny, if you were here, I'd kiss you."

FJ rolled his eyes.

"Let's not go there," Jenny laughed. "Ray, you're old enough to be my grandfather."

"That hurt, Jenny."

Hurt? What hurts, FJ thought.

171

"The truth sometimes hurts," Jenny laughed, again.

"Jenny, please tell me you have a lead."

Jesus. An I-65 Serial killer? A lead? FJ thought, trying to eavesdrop.

"I have a lead. There was a reliable witness in the Park City murder. The suspect is between five-ten to six-foot in height. Thin. Around one-twenty to one-fifty. Caucasian. Probably mid-twenties. Dark hair. Walks with a limp. The witness says, from his clothing and his lack of grooming, he has to be homeless. That would account for the abandoned houses."

"How reliable is this witness?"

Witness? FJ could barely contain himself.

"She saw the suspect running from the house the day the body was found."

"You know, that doesn't mean he did it."

"No. Even if he didn't, he still may know something that could help us. Ray, he's worth finding. He could breathe new life into something that's slowly dying."

"Agreed. Where do we start?"

"I already have. I've got a BOLO out on him, along with a sketch made by the witness. I'll email both to you shortly. Because no one has seen him, I would guess this guy isn't standing on a street corner begging for handouts. He's more of a dumpster-diver."

"I know the Chief of Police in Munfordville. I'll call him tomorrow," Ray said, wanting to get back to the movie.

"Why not call now?" Jenny asked. "I'm sure he's working. Probably chasing all those thieves, that are breaking into houses today."

"You think you're funny, don't you?"

"I don't think ... I know."

"I don't think you know, either."

"Now who's the comedian? Ray, don't give up your day job."

"Okay. Okay. I'll give Munfordville a call and see where it takes us. Thanks, Jenny. I'll get back with you."

"What's going on? What do you mean, a serial killer? There's a witness?" FJ asked as soon as Ray put his cell phone away. Ray sat there staring at FJ, wondering if he should tell him. *What harm could there be?* It'll be coming out sooner than later. Maybe it should come out sooner. And, there's nothing that says this man is a suspect. He might be another witness himself. It would make all those involved feel like the police were actually accomplishing something. So, for the next few minutes, Ray repeated his phone conversation with Jenny, stressing the man could only be a witness, and not necessarily the suspect.

"Holy shit. A witness," FJ whispered. "So, call Munfordville already."

Chapter 37

Ray googled the Munfordville Police Department, went to their website and got their phone number.

"This is crazy," Ray said to himself. "Gary won't be in today. It's Sunday, after all."

The phone picked up on the first ring.

"Munfordville Police Station. Chief Reynolds here. What can I do for you?"

"Gary, it's Ray Harris."

"Ray? So, what can the Chief of Police of Munfordville, do for the Sheriff of Franklin?"

"First off, why in the world is the Chief of Police of Munfordville working on Sunday? You guys do away with your dispatch?"

"Our dispatch is on paternity leave, or at least, one third is. We're shorthanded around here, so I'm filling in today. So, Ray, why are you calling me?"

"To the point. Gary, I heard you had a murder six months ago."

"We did. Do you have something for us? Lord knows we need something, anything."

"Sorry. Nothing for you, but maybe you can help me."

"Ray, I heard you had two murders in the last couple of weeks, but I don't see how we can help."

"Your murder took place in an abandoned house. So did ours. Your victim died from blunt force trauma to the back of the head. Same for our two."

"You're telling me, both of your vics died the same way?"

"Both."

"In the same house?"

"The same house."

"The same day?"

"About a week apart."

"Jesus. Ray, I'm not sure we can help. We don't have much to go on. No prints. No DNA. No witnesses."

"Park City has a witness."

"Park City has a witness to my murder?"

"No, Park City had a murder of their own. Same scenario: abandoned house, cause of death–blunt force trauma to the back of the head."

"That's too weird."

"You don't know the half of it. Six months ago, you had a murder. Three months later, it was Park City, and they have a witness. One month ago, Bowling Green, and now Franklin. Gary, all these towns are along I-65."

"That's smart, Ray."

"I wish I could take credit, but it was an agent in Frankfort who came up with it."

"I'd like to shake his hand," Gary said.

"He's a she."

"Then I'd like to give her a big old sloppy kiss."

"Gary, you're old enough to be her grandfather."

"If you say so, but I'm not her grandfather ... am I?"

Ray laughed. "Probably not. Gary, what can you send me? Better yet, can I come up your way and you can show me around. I'd especially like to see the crime scene."

"Sure, come on up. I need to stay on dispatch the rest of today, but I can free up some time in the morning. Say around ten."

"I'll be in your office at ten. Thanks."

"No, thank you. I need to solve this for her parents," Gary confessed.

"Her parents? How old was she?"

"*She* is Phyllis Steele. Caucasian. Thirty-five. Single. Pretty girl. Five-four. A hundred and twenty pounds. She worked as a waitress at Murray's Restaurant on Main Street. How old were your vics?"

"Both were sixteen. One girl. One boy."

"Were they raped?"

"No."

"Ours was. Post-mortem."

"Jesus."

"I know. Ray, I need to go. There's a call coming in. Probably, some kid's screwing with Mrs. Calhoun's chickens again. I mean messing with her chickens. Every Sunday about this time, she calls in saying somebody's messing with her chickens. So, like always, I'll send somebody out there, and all the chickens will be present and accounted for. I should start charging her."

"Gary, I wouldn't want someone screwing my chickens," Ray laughed. "I'll see you tomorrow at ten."

"Who's screwing chickens?" FJ whispered, before Ray could disconnect.

Ray frowned and shook his head.

Ray put his cell phone back in his pocket and un-paused the TV. A few minutes went by. Blondie, Angel Eyes, and Tuco are standing in the cemetery's stone circle court, staring holes into each other, their hands closing in on their pistols. It's dying time.

"No, you can't go," Ray whispered, not taking his eyes off the screen.

"Shit," FJ whispered back.

After the phone conversation and what it could pertain to, FJ's confession to Ray on the reason why he went to the school that morning, had been put on hold.

Chapter 38

It was a pleasant one hour drive up to Munfordville. Ray felt like country music that morning. Not that modern country crap, but classic country. Johnny Cash, Hank Williams, Merle Haggard, Patsy Cline, and the Carter Family flowed from station WGGC, filling the airways and the inside of Ray's vehicle. If someone had passed, they would have seen Ray jamming to the music. If they were lucky, their windows would be rolled up, because Ray couldn't carry a tune in a bucket.

Ray had hopped on I-65 heading northeast, taking the 31W exit southeast straight into Munfordville. The Munfordville Police Station was located at the intersection of 31W and South Street. Easy-peasy. Ray thought about using his siren and flashing lights on the way up, but he wasn't in a hurry. Not today. Besides, he was in the mood for country. For some reason, Dave was sleeping in. Maybe, it was because the case was finally moving again. Depending on his mood and just for fun, it would be sirens and flashing lights on the way home.

In a large Manilla envelope, on the passenger-side seat was the Park City murder report and the witness's sketch. Ray wasn't impressed with the sketch. The suspect looked like a cross between an alien and a Sasquatch–maybe their love child.

Gary was standing outside the station, smoking a cigarette when Ray pulled up. In the old days, Ray and Gary would have taken a smoke together in Gary's office over a cup of coffee. With the no-smoking-in-public-buildings laws, those days were long gone, but not Ray's urge for a cig. Gary waved as Ray got out of his cruiser.

"Right on time," Gary said, looking at his watch.

Gary was African American, about ten years younger than Ray, heavier, and with the aid of a razor, completely bald. He was wearing black-rimmed glasses. Ray wasn't sure he was wearing glasses the last time they were together. *When you get older, your eyesight is the second thing to go.* The first time they had worked together was fifteen years ago on a hit-and-run that happened on the Munfordville's south-bound on-ramp to I-65, Gary's jurisdiction. The suspect had hightailed it back home to Franklin, Ray's jurisdiction. During the investigation, both men had become friends, not close friends mind you, but friends. They normally saw each other at the yearly state police convention held in Louisville. During the three-day event, they would hang out together. Ray knew enough about Gary to know he was a widower, had three grown children, two grandchildren, liked to fish, was Methodist, and was an all-around good guy.

"You're car or mine?" Ray asked.

"Mine. It'll be easier with me driving. Besides, if I remember correctly, you can't drive worth a crap."

Ray settled in the passenger's seat, but he didn't have long to get comfortable. The ride took only five minutes. During those five minutes, they went from small town America, to a rural setting of pastures, clusters of trees, and fields of corn and soybeans. Gary pulled onto a narrow asphalt lane off Coren Mill Road.

"This section used to be the old Coren Mill Road, before the Interstate went through and cut it off," Gary commented. "They had to build a new road into town. This stretch dead ends at the Interstate."

A quarter of a mile later, Gary pulled into a densely wooded area and stopped beside a rundown single-story shack.

"We're here," he said, turning off the engine. Ray could hear traffic on the I-65. He could also see the Interstate, through a line of trees that ran alongside the highway.

Ray climbed out of the car, stretched and turned to look at the house. It wasn't much of a building. From what he could see, it did have four walls of faded, white-washed boards and what was left of a rusted tin roof. There was an opening for a door and an opening for a window. Vines covered most of the walls and roof. The vines were probably the only thing keeping the building from falling down.

"Is it safe to go in?" Ray asked.

"Sure. I wouldn't touch anything unless you're up-to-date with your tetanus shots."

Together, they waded through weeds and sticker-bushes toward the front door.

I wonder, who does your lawn? Ray thought with a smile. There used to be a front stoop, but it had rotted away. Do-not-enter police tape, making a big "X," still covered the dark opening. Gary pulled out two flashlights, handing one to Ray.

"You first," he said, motioning the way.

Turning on his light, Ray ducked under the tape and went inside.

It smelled like the old MacGregor place. *Why is that?* Ray thought. *Is there a law that says old rundown buildings must smell the same? And who makes sure they do?* Cobwebs grew in the corners, and Ray hated spiders with a passion. He prayed he didn't walk into a spider-web. He didn't want Gary to freak out when he saw him panicking and throwing a hissy fit. Trying to forget about nasty, blood-sucking, plate-sized spiders, Ray looked around at the walls. They were covered in brightly painted graffiti of cuss words and drawings of aroused body parts and gigantic breasts. A chalk line of a human body could barely be seen on the floor.

"This is where she was found," Gary said, pointing.

"We're way off the beaten path," Ray commented. "Who found her?"

"The farmer who owns the land. He came up here one morning, getting ready to burn the shack. He plans on increasing his corn acreage. He found a car setting in the trees and her body here. The VIN number said it's her car."

"How long had she been dead?"

"Her autopsy said two or three days."

"Any evidence?"

"None."

"Was she dressed?"

"Nude."

"And she was raped?"

Gary nodded.

"Did you find the murder weapon?"

"No. Nothing."

"Were there any other wounds on the body?"

"None. But there were wood filings in the head wound."

"Why this house?" Ray whispered, mostly to himself.

Gary thought Ray must have been talking to him. "The only thing we came up with, is the killer either knew this place, or he saw it from the Interstate."

"Do you think you could see this house through those trees going sixty-five miles-per-hour?"

"No, not really. But you could if you were hitchhiking. Yes, it's illegal to hitchhike on an Interstate, but you know as well as I, people do it every day. He probably saw the house from the shoulder of the road, climbed over the right-of-way fence and settled in for the night. It kept him out of the rain, mostly. If you walk along the right-of-way fence, it's only half-a-mile to a Wendy's on North West Street. He probably begged for money or food there. I figured, he liked it here so much, he decided to stay for a while."

"What can you tell me about her?"

Gary opened the report he had been carrying under his arm. "Like I said over the phone yesterday. Her name is Phyllis Steele. Caucasian. Thirty-five. Single. Pretty girl. Five-four. A hundred and twenty pounds. Worked as a waitress at Murray's Restaurant on Main Street."

"How did the murderer get Phyllis to drive him out here?"

"That we don't know. We do know; she clocked out at midnight. What happened after that is anybody's guess."

"Where'd she work again?"

"Murray's Restaurant."

"Did she have problems with anyone at work?"

"None that anyone admits. Still looking into that angle."

"Yesterday, you said over the phone she had parents. Did she live with them?"

"No, she had her own apartment. Her boss at the restaurant thought she was taking a few days off. So, that's why no one reported her missing."

"Her own apartment. It sounds like you're telling me she wasn't married."

"Never been married. Before I forget, here's a copy of the crime scene photos. I warn you, the ones of the vic are pretty graphic."

"Thanks. I'll look at them later ... What was the condition of her apartment? Anything missing or disturbed?"

"Nope. Her bed was made, like she had never gone to bed."

"And you don't have any witnesses?"

"Nope. Ray, what do you think?"

"I think you're screwed, just like Mrs. Calhoun's chickens."

Chapter 39

It was a twenty-minute drive down I-65 from Munfordville to Park City. The drive had been in silence, no siren, no flashing lights, no country music. Ray wasn't in the mood. What he saw in Munfordville hadn't help. He didn't know what he expected to find, but whatever it was, he didn't find it. He doubted if he'd get anything at Park City, but they did have a witness. That was something at least. Ray rubbed his forehead. Dave was back in all his glory.

Park City is so small they can't budget their own police department. So, they rely on coverage from the Cave City police department. Before he left Munfordville, Ray had called Cave City and talked with Chief Marty Aud, who said he'd meet Ray at the Shell Station on the Mammoth Cave Parkway, just off the Interstate. Ray was to take a left from the off-ramp onto the Mammoth Cave Parkway. As soon as he went under the Interstate, he would pass a Dollar General Store on the right. The Shell Station was on the same side of the street and right beside the Dollar General. He couldn't miss it, and the Chief was right.

Already, there was a Cave City police car parked in the parking lot of the Shell Station. A young man, dressed in a brown uniform and wearing a brown Smokey the Bear hat, stood leaning on the hood of his car with his arms crossed. Ray pulled in beside him. The man looked to be in his late twenties; too young to be a Chief.

I bet I have underwear older than you.

Ray climbed out of his car. "Chief Aud?"

"No, I'm Deputy Gideon Raley. Chief Aud sends his apology that he couldn't meet you, but he's tied up back in Cave City. We've

185

got a bear problem that needs immediate attention."

"You have a lot of bear problems?"

"No. Bears don't normally come out of the park, but for some reason, this one got a hankering for shaved ice with cherry syrup. Half an hour ago, the bear broke into the one of the shaved ice stands at the Kentucky Action zip-line and go-cart park. Luckily, everyone saw him coming and got out of his way. A dozen tourists started yelling and waving their arms at the bear, scaring the crap out of him, literally. The bear took off at a gallop across the horse farm in the valley, where tourist do trail rides.

"The Chief said, the manager of the zip-line said, it looked like a scene out of the black and white movie, *Frankenstein,* where the villagers are chasing the Monster with torches and pitchforks. I wouldn't know. I haven't seen the movie. The Chief is currently with the park rangers. They're tracking the bear, and when they find him, they plan on tranquilizing him and releasing him deep inside the park. His shaved ice days are over."

"Do you know why I'm here?" Ray asked.

"No, Sir. I do not. The chief didn't fill me in."

"I heard you had a murder here about three months ago."

"That's true. I worked the case."

"I'd like to see the murder scene."

Nonchalantly, the deputy pointed across the street. Looking, Ray noticed an empty house.

"It happened over there?" Ray asked.

"Yes, Sir."

"I mean, it's right on the street; in plain sight of everyone."

"That's where she was found."

"Could I have a closer look?"

"Yes, Sir. Let me drive."

Leaving the parking lot, the Deputy took a right, back out onto Mammoth Cave Parkway. At the stoplight, he took a left onto Louisville Road, and shortly after that, a left onto Mammoth Cave Avenue. The Mammoth Cave Avenue looped around on itself and dead-ended back at the Mammoth Cave Parkway. From where he sat, Ray could see his car, across the parkway at the Shell station.

As Ray got out of the car, he noticed the front yard looked like it had been mowed, but only to knock down the weeds. It was easy to see; an edger or trimmer hadn't touched a blade of grass in months.

I wonder who does your lawn.

The house wasn't as old as it looked, from a distance. As a matter of fact, with paint and a little TLC, this wouldn't be a bad looking house.

"Can we go in?" Ray asked.

"I'll have to get one of the owners to come and unlock the door. Since the murder, the owners put in deadbolts."

"I don't blame them, but I really need to have a look inside."

"Not a problem."

It took thirty-five minutes, before one of the owners was located and arrived, to unlock the front door. He didn't want to go into the house and said he'd wait in his car, until they were through. Then he would lock up. Ray thanked him for any inconvenience. After three months, police tape still covered the front door.

Once inside, Ray knew this wasn't an abandoned house. He knew because of the smell. It didn't smell like an abandoned house should smell. Also, there wasn't a lot of rot or trash. And thank God, no spider-webs. *With a little paint and some elbow grease, this place could be fixed up.* Ray guessed, because the house was empty and in need of some repair, it was classified as abandoned. On the floor was another chalk line.

"Your report said it was a young woman."

"It was. Elizabeth "Lizzy" Fulkerson was twenty-nine when she was murdered. She was a nice-looking lady. African American. About five-nine. One hundred and forty pounds. Very fit. She liked jogging. Why anyone would like jogging is beyond me."

"Who found her?"

"I did. Dispatch got a call from Joyce Boarman. She works at the Shell Station across the street. Joyce was out having a smoke when she saw the suspect running from the house. While I was waiting for you, I got a Sunkist, and it was Joyce I paid. So, if you want to talk with her, she's over there now."

187

"I most definitely will, but first a few questions for you. Was Elizabeth married?"

"Divorced. No children. Her Ex is currently living in L.A. We did some checking, and the day the coroner says Lizzy died, her husband was giving an all-day lecture at UCLA. I think the subject was on Global Warming and why it ain't happening. Can you say boring? Anyway, with over a hundred alibis, there's no way he could have done it."

"Did she have a boyfriend?"

"Girlfriend would be more like it. That's the reason for the divorce. But, no, nothing serious. We checked the few ladies she's been seen with lately, and they all have air-tight alibis. Before you ask, Lizzy was a model citizen. She wasn't into drugs or alcohol, that we're aware of. She's never been arrested. Hell, she's never gotten a speeding ticket."

"Where did she work?"

"She worked at the South Central Bank over on Louisville Street. We passed it coming here."

"Did anyone there have a problem with her being a lesbian?"

"None. Everybody liked Lizzy. Sheriff, we're a small town, smaller than Franklin, and everybody knows everything about everybody, but we look the other way on most issues. Lizzy's sexual orientation was one of those issues. She was my friend. She was everybody's friend. I used to joke with her that if she went out with me, I could change her sexual orientation. She thought I was crazy, but she said, she could look over that shortcoming.

"The day of her funeral, the whole town showed up. You see, there's this hate group somewhere up north that tries to crash funerals claiming, "God hates faggots." And we heard rumors they were coming here. That's why the whole town came to her funeral. A motorcycle gang, that looked a lot like Hell's Angels, came to the funeral. They hate that hate group. Most of the law-abiding citizens of Park City brought baseball bats and sawed-off two-by-twos. Some brought shotguns, but Chief Aud said if he saw a single gun the whole lot would be arrested. I tell you, Sheriff, if those bastards had shown up, they would have gotten an ass-kicking they would never have forgotten, and the police officers would have looked the other way. Lucky for them, they didn't show."

"Good for you, Deputy Raley," Ray said. "Good for you ... You said you found her. (Raley nodded) Was she dressed or naked?"

"It's in the report."

"I know, but I like to hear it from the horse's mouth."

"Let's see. She had on a pair of shorts and a tank-top."

"Bra? (Raley shook his head) Panties? (Raley nodded) Was she wearing shoes?"

"Flip-flops."

"And, she was not raped?"

"That is correct."

"I can still see some traces of blood here. Was she murdered here?"

"The coroner says no, but she was dumped here."

"Have you found the place she was murdered?"

"Not yet."

"Were there any other wounds?"

Raley was about to say, "It's in the report," but being the horse's mouth, he replied, "No. Not a mark. Sheriff, there were no apparent defensive wounds or anything under her fingernails. She didn't put up a fight. The only wound was a pipe or something, to the back of the head. I believe she knew her killer."

"Would she have known a homeless man?"

"Good point, Sheriff. I would guess not, but that doesn't mean he didn't approach her. Hell, he could have asked for a handout, and she refused. If he'd been on drugs at the time; that could have set him off. He could have killed her and dumped her here."

"Good point, Deputy. I'll keep that in mind ... I think it's time we have a word with the witness. What's her name again?"

"Joyce Boarman."

"Let's have a word with Joyce Boarman."

On the way back to the Shell Station, Deputy Raley pointed out the bank where Lizzy worked. He also promised Ray, that afternoon as soon as he got back to the station, he'd fax copies of the crime scene report. Once back at his car, Ray noticed the Shell

189

Station was more than just a gas station. It was a combination gas station and convenience store. Ray and Deputy Raley were greeted by an electric door chime as they walk in. Bebe Rexha and the Florida Georgia Line's song *Meant to Be* filled the room. At the far end of the store was a tiny pizza parlor. Next to it was a display case with an assortment of cookies, donuts, chips, and those kinds of things. Next to that was a case containing sandwiches and hot wings. There were several isles of assorted overpriced household items: soaps, toilet paper, dishwashing stuff, etc. etc. etc.

A young, slightly overweight woman, probably in her late teens, stood behind the counter. Her wide smile displayed a mouth full of stainless steel and wire. Her hair was strawberry red, and her face covered in freckles. Ray would have bet, this was Joyce Boarman. Why? He didn't know.

"Miss Boarman?" Ray asked. Joyce nodded. "I'm Sheriff Harris from Franklin. Could I ask you a few questions about–"?

"The woman who died over there," Joyce said, finishing Ray's sentence for him.

"Exactly. You saw–"

"A man running from the house. Yes, I did. He looked homeless. Our manager said someone had been going through our dumpster."

"*Why would he … I am giving you a chance to second guess what I'm about to say, oh well, times up …* Why would he be going through your trash?"

"We throw away tons of food every day: left over pizza, cooked chicken wings too old to sell, breakfast sandwiches, you know, those kinds of things. Jerry Gates, he's the owner, said he didn't care if the man raided our dumpster, as long as he didn't leave a mess."

"When you first saw him, where was he?"

"He was coming out of the house, in a big hurry. That's why I watched him. He seemed scared. That's why I called 9-1-1."

"Scared of–"

"Seeing the dead woman."

"Seeing the dead woman. *(Jesus)* So, maybe she was already dead when he found her, and that's why he was scared and running.

Maybe, he didn't want people drawing their own conclusions."

"I don't know. Could be. I haven't thought of it that way."

Ray handed her the sketch he had been sent. "This is the sketch you came up with?"

"That's him, alright."

So, Sasquatch is our suspect? Ray wanted to ask.

"Have you ever seen this man before?" he asked instead.

"No, sir."

"Okay. Now think. When was the first time you ever saw him?"

"Oh, I saw him a couple of days before they found the girl."

"So, you have seen him before."

"I guess I have."

"Only that one time?"

"Yes. I think so."

"You think so?"

"Yes. That one time and the day I saw him running from the house."

"Was he limping the first time you saw him?"

"I don't think so. Maybe. Sheriff, I don't remember."

"That's okay. Probably not important anyway. Have you seen him since?"

"No, sir."

"You're sure of that?"

"Yes, sir. I'm sure."

"When you saw him running from the house, which way was he going?"

"Toward the Interstate."

"And that was the last time you saw him?"

"Yes, Sheriff. I think I answered that already."

"You have. But sometimes repeating the same question over and over again helps to bring out something new. I hope you understand. It has nothing to do with you. It's part of my job."

Joyce smiled.

"I think we're through here," Ray said, smiling. "But, if I think of something else, I hope I can come and see you again. (Joyce nodded) And, Miss Boarman, if you see this man again, here's my card. Call me immediately."

Joyce nodded.

Standing by his car, Ray looked at the house and let his eyes wander toward the Interstate.

"You asked Joyce if the man was limping the first time she saw him. You also told her it wasn't important. But that's not true, is it?"

"Maybe. Maybe not. If he developed the limp while he was here, how did he injure his leg? Did he interrupt the murderer, they fought, and that's when he injured his leg? If so, he's seen the murderer up close and personable. He would be able to recognize him. That's why we need to find this man.

"Now, if the homeless man already had a limp, then the point is mute. Still, he may know something, and we still need to find him. Deputy keep your eyes open. He may not have left the area."

"Sheriff, I'll pass this on to the Chief."

The deputy's phone suddenly started playing the *Battle Hymn of the Republic.*

"Text message," Deputy Raley laughed. "It was my dad's favorite song ... It looks like the bear is on his way back home."

"As am I, Deputy. As am I."

It was too late in the day to stop in Bowling Green, and Ray needed to hurry and get back in time for Randy's visitation at the Calvary Baptist Church. Even though Ray's dark mood had deepened, and Dave was pounding on a base-drum, the siren was blasting and the lights flashing.

Chapter 40

The first thing Ray noticed when he pulled into his driveway was the number of cars. Mike and Stephanie's car was parked up close to the garage, in his parking space for Christ's sake, making room for FJ's van. Betty and Tom's car was parked behind Margaret. The only car not there was Charlotte's. He and Dave didn't need this right now. Once inside the house, he was greeted with a Jack and Coke.

"Have a seat, Ray," Margaret said, pointing to his favorite recliner. "We can't wait to hear how your day went."

"Charlotte, where's your car?" Ray asked. "I didn't see it in the car lot outside."

"I rode over with Mike and Steph. They're giving me a ride to the funeral home. If it's as crowded as Innocence's, parking will be limited. Ashley's riding with us." Ray nodded to Ashley. Ashley, sitting beside FJ, nodded back. Ashley didn't have a car, that Ray was aware of. Zoe was here, seated between Betty and Tom. They silently sat there staring at Ray, waiting.

"Listen," Ray started. "I know what you want. You want me to tell you I know who the murderer is, but I can't do that. Right now, I don't know. I need time to process everything. Give me a day or two, and we'll get back together." Ray noticed everyone's mood suddenly changed, for the worst. He had to give them something. "One thing I can tell you. We have a person of interest. He's a white guy, mid-twenties, from his appearance, probably homeless, and he walks with a limp."

"Why is he a person of interest?" FJ asked.

"He was seen leaving the scene of one of the murders, on the day of the murder."

Everyone perked up.

"Tomorrow, after the funeral, I'm heading up to Bowling Green. For those of you who don't know, they had a murder up there."

"Was the homeless man seen up there?" Ashley asked.

"I haven't even been there yet," Ray laughed. "Let's not get ahead of ourselves."

The visitation that evening went off without a hitch. Nothing happened out of the ordinary: tons of people, bushels of food in the family snack area, flowers and gifts out the wazoo. Hell, even the governor had sent a flower arrangement.

Later that night, sitting in the dark on his patio, Ray raised his arm so he could read his watch, from the light streaming through the glass sliding doors of the family room. It was close to midnight. Everyone had gone home. Thank goodness. It wasn't that he didn't want their company, but it had been a long day and he just wanted to be alone. He had too much to think about, too much to process.

Margaret and Roy had gone to bed. Ray was dead tired, but too tired to fall asleep, even if he went to bed. He was afraid of the nightmares that were waiting for him in the dark. And then there was Dave, who was becoming his constant companion. Aspirins couldn't slow Dave down. Ray's third Jack and Coke this evening wasn't helping.

From what he saw and heard in Munfordville and Park City; he could have saved himself a trip by flipping a coin. Heads–go to Munfordville. Tails–go to Park City. The reason– the answers to his questions were the same in both places. The victims had no enemies. They were nice people. No one saw anything to speak of. The one and only witness's description of the suspect sucked, unless Sasquatch really did do it. So, in truth, it was like having no suspect at all. Hell, it could have been anyone down on their luck. It appears, the victims weren't killed in the places they were found. But that wasn't the case with Innocence and Randy. There was no murder weapon, no DNA, no fingerprints, and nothing whatsoever to go on. The worst thing, there was absolutely nothing to tie the murders together. The first murder was a woman, and she was raped. The second murder was a woman, but she wasn't raped. Ray's murders were a girl and a boy. Neither one molested. These murders were leaning toward being random. Still, there was always Bowling Green.

Chapter 41

The morning was overcast and threatening rain. In other words, it was gloomy, just like Ray's spirit. He had already been to one too many funerals in the last week, and he dreaded going to this one. His one and only suspect was being buried today. He should feel sorry for the kid, but knowing what Randy could have done to Innocence, he just couldn't. If this weren't an active case, he would have stayed home.

The church for the funeral service was packed, but not as crowded as Innocence's. Randy would be buried in a private family section of the Greenlawn & Shadyrest Cemetery. After the services, Ray noticed Ashley talking with Harold King and Mr. and Mrs. Bennett, Randy's dad and mom.

Probably paying her last respects. You're a good kid Ashley. I wished more kids were like you.

Ray noticed the lawyer and the parents staring at him now and then.

Probably wondering why I'm here. We never really got off on the right foot.

Ray nodded. They nodded back.

It was close to noon when the last car pulled out of the cemetery. Ray kept looking at his watch. He was hoping to run up to Bowling Green and be back before the rain set in. The Weather Channel said a thunderstorm was moving in, with lightening and damaging winds. According to the Weather Channel, the cold front was slow moving and wouldn't arrive till around seven tonight, but they have been known to be wrong. Stephanie had an app on her phone that predicted when a storm, within minutes, was going to hit. The funny thing was, most of the time, her app was right. Ray dreaded the thought of driving on wet pavement. Especially with little or no visibility. Ray's eyes weren't as young as they used to be, and he was also starting to have trouble seeing while driving after dark. Something he would never tell Margaret about.

The drive to Bowling Green was uneventful. Thankfully, the rain was holding off. Ray listened to Nashville FM Country 103.3 on the drive up. Chief Gary Reynolds, of the Bowling Green Police Department, told Ray to meet him at the Ace Storage facility on Sutherland Drive, just off Three Spring Road. To help him locate the storage facility, Ray had looked it up on *Google Maps* before he left. He noticed an interesting fact. The storage facility backed up to I-65.

"Chief," Ray said, as he got out of his car.

"Sheriff," Chief Reynolds replied. "You said earlier when you called, you wanted to see where our victim was found."

"If I could."

Chief Reynolds looked to be in his mid-forties and starting to get a beer-belly. He was Hispanic, but with no trace of an accent. Chief Reynolds reminded Ray of Stewart Granger, the classic Stewart Granger, with his jet-black hair and only a touch of white just above the ears. Some men would die for hair like his. Ray was one of them.

"Let me get someone to unlock the gate," Chief Reynolds said, pressing a call button. "Normally," Reynolds continued, "the gate is open from seven am to ten pm, every day. But, since the homicide, we're asking the owners to keep it locked. If someone wants to get into a locker, they have to have the manager come and unlock the gate."

"I bet they like having to do that."

"No, but until we can clear this thing up, it is what it is."

"Was the gate unlocked when the murder occurred?"

"I'm sure it was."

"So, the abandoned house is inside the storage facility?"

"It's not an abandoned house, but an abandoned trailer home. I know what the report says, but the report is wrong. Someone years ago, paid to store their trailer here, and it's been sitting on the back lot next to the Interstate right-of-way all these years. I think whoever owned the mobile home didn't want it and couldn't sell it, so they paid one month's rent, parked it, and never came back. The people who currently own the storage facility don't want to pay the expense of having it removed. So, it sits there rotting and rusting. It's an eyesore from the Interstate. It's a black eye for the city. I've been begging the town counsel to send the storage owners a warning saying, if they don't do something about the trailer, there will be a hefty fine. Now to make matters worse, with this murder, the trailer has to stay put until the case is solved, which could be never."

The storage facility lent Ray and the Chief a golf cart to run to the back of the lot, which Ray would be forever grateful. Ray had never told anyone, not even Margaret, that he was having problems with his left hip. It starts to hurt when he stands on it a long time, or if he walks more than a long city block.

Turning the corner of the last storage locker, the trailer home jumped into view. "Good Lord," Ray exclaimed. From a distance, it looked like a giant reddish-brown brick. At some point in its life, someone tried to burn it. All it did was melt the vinyl siding, revealing the steel sheet metal decking beneath, which through years and years of downpours, ice, and snow, was slowly turning into a red pile of rust.

"Surely, no one in their right mind would set foot in there?" Ray asked.

"They didn't. Because of the rot, I'm not sure the floor's support system would hold any more weight than itself. Whoever killed Jessy Clark tried to hide her body under the trailer's frame. Since no one comes back here normally, the coroner thinks she'd been lying there for three or four days."

"Was there a missing person report?"

"Her husband reported her missing a week before her body was found."

"If she'd only been lying there three or four days and missing for a week that means–"

"Yea. For several days, she could have been alive after being abducted."

"So, she was kidnapped. Was there a ransom note?"

"No. And it doesn't appear she was tortured."

"Was she sexually molested?"

"Can't tell. From all the rain and heat, and the worms and maggots, her body was in no shape to do a full autopsy. We know she was of average height. From the bloating, we couldn't tie down her weight. So, we're saying average weight. She was Caucasian. We can tell from the massive head wound how she died; blunt force trauma."

"Did her husband have an alibi?"

"Airtight. He's was delivering a baby in Boston."

"Boston?"

"His daughter's."

"He was in Boston delivering his daughter's baby, his own daughter's baby?"

"I know. That sounds so weird to me too. I wouldn't want to see my daughter's you-know-what. Anyway, he has an alibi, no matter how sick it is. That's all I cared about."

"Why wasn't his wife in Boston? It's her daughter too."

"Actually, it's her step-daughter. The real mom was there, and there's a hate-hate relationship between the two. According to the husband, it's better to keep them apart as much as they can, if you know what I mean. Besides, the daughter didn't need all the additional stress."

Ray nodded.

"Any boyfriends on the side?"

"We haven't found any. Still looking."

"How'd she get out here, behind a locked gate and all?"

"Remember, before the murder, the gate was always open. The lock on the gate now is new."

Ray couldn't see any blood. But being outside and in the elements, it easily could have washed away.

"Was there a lot of blood when they found her?" he asked.

"No. And from the blood that had soaked into the ground, the coroner says she was killed somewhere else, probably where she was being held hostage and dumped out here."

"Any leads or witnesses?"

"No, and no. The case is going cold."

"What was she wearing?"

"A cotton blouse. It's hard to tell the color, from all the oozing body fluids. I would guess white. Cut-off jeans. Nothing else. No shoes; no underwear."

"Did you hear about the murders in Munfordville and Park City?"

"I did, and I haven't seen a homeless man who limps. I've checked all the homeless shelters. Nothing. According to the staffers, there's been no limpers lately. That makes sense. During the summertime, most vagrants hang out under overpasses. Keeps them out of the rain. But, again, we haven't seen anyone who limps. That being said, that doesn't mean he hasn't already come and gone. May be down your way by now."

"You've heard about my deaths?"

Chief Reynolds nodded. "Sheriff, we've covered all the bases: her workplace, her church, the PTA, secret boyfriends, secret girlfriends, jealous wives, jealous husbands, neighbors, aunts, uncles, cousins, the woman who does her hair, her dog groomer. She didn't hang out in bars. She never used dope. She didn't smoke. She didn't cuss. She was squeaky clean. I have copies of the crime scene and all the photos for you. You can't sense what she looked like from the crime scene photos, so I put her wedding picture in the folder. It's the best photo they had of her. They're back at the car."

Ray shook his head. "I appreciate it. I take it the crime scene pic of the vic is pretty graphic."

Reynolds nodded. Ray hated graphic crime photos.

"You have to remember," Reynolds explained, "she'd been exposed to the elements for several days. It's been hot and rainy. She became a smorgasbord for the worms, bugs, and rats ... Sheriff, we'll keep our eyes out for your homeless guy, in case he shows. If we see him, we'll detain him for you. But the same holds true if you see him. I want to have a word with him as well."

Chapter 42

Ray stopped in at the office, after he grabbed a burger at the Waffle House. Susan was manning the front desk.

"Why are you out here and not at your desk?" Ray asked.

"Buddy called in sick. If you'd come to work in the mornings, you would know that."

"You knew I was going up to Bowling Green this morning."

"Did I?"

"Of course you did ... Didn't you?"

Susan stared at him. The truth is, he had told her yesterday, he was driving up to Bowling Green, but she liked pulling his chain.

"Okay, maybe you didn't," she said, "but you could have called."

"And interrupt your 'special' meeting with some redheaded floozy?"

Ray laughed.

"How do you know she's redheaded?"

"All floozies are redheaded."

"Margaret is redheaded. Are you calling her a floozy?"

"I didn't say all redheads were floozies. I said all floozies are redheaded. Don't go putting words in my mouth, Sheriff."

"Could you get me a cup of coffee?" Ray asked, heading toward his office.

"If you make it," Susan answered. "And, when you make it, you'll be standing there at the coffee machine, so you can save yourself some time and trouble and get your own cup. While you're at it, you can get me one as well. Black. Straight up."

"Any calls?" Ray asked, walking toward the coffee maker.

"That sweet little girl from Frankfort called. She wants you to call her back."

Ray made a pot of coffee, and while he waited, he wondered what Jenny had found out. Ray placed a streaming cup of black, straight up coffee on Susan's desk. "What time did Jenny call?"

Around nine. She's probably wondering what's taking you so long to return her call."

"You should have called me right after she called."

"I don't want to get on your floozy's bad side."

Back in his office, Ray dialed Jenny's number and got her answering machine.

"Hey, Jenny, Ray, here. I just got back in the office. I've been up in Bowling Green all morning. Give me a call when you get a minute."

Five minutes later, Susan hollered, "Miss Jenny's on line two."

"Hello Jenny," Ray said, picking up.

"You're welcome," Susan yelled from the front desk.

"Ray, we got the results of the samples Nicole sent," Jenny said. "We're ninety-nine-point-nine percent sure the hair found in the wound on Randy's head is Innocence's."

"Only ninety-nine-point-nine percent?" Ray laughed.

"We can't say one-hundred-percent in case we make a mistake."

"How could a sample that close to perfect, be a mistake?"

"It could have come from a twin."

"She didn't have a twin. So, it's Innocence's hair."

"Exactly. Which tells us," Jenny continued, "it was the same weapon that killed both Randy and Innocence. I would guess one person killed both, and before you say, 'I told you so,' Ray, we had to be sure. Now I think we are."

"That's all well and good, but that leaves me hanging."

"How did your visits up North go?"

"There are so many things that just don't add up. Yes, a person was killed at each location. Yes, it was blunt force trauma. It happened in an abandoned house next to I-65. But, Jenny, these people had nothing in common. They were different ages. They come from different walks of live. They have absolutely nothing in common with my two murders."

"You know what that means?"

"I'm afraid I do. I've got the worst kind of murderer–a serial killer who randomly picks his victims. He's smart and goes out of the way to make sure we can't come up with a clear motive, other than he likes to kill ... Have you heard anything on the homeless man?"

"No. But, it's still early. You don't believe he did it, do you?"

"Not really, but he could have seen something. That's why we need to find him."

"Ray, I've been thinking about a new twist."

There was silence.

"Ray?"

"I'm listening."

"Have you thought about Randy's dad?"

"His dad? Are you talking about Jim Bennett? I don't get it."

"Okay, follow along with me, and don't get your panties in a wad if I say something derogatory about Innocence. (Again silence) Let's say, Randy's dad, Jim, found out Randy and Innocence were a couple and were having sex. What if he thought Innocence was stringing Randy along, trying to get pregnant, so that she could get at his money."

"Okay, my panties are in a wad," Ray hissed slowly. "Innocence wasn't that kind of girl."

"I know that, but does Jim Bennett?"

"Doesn't make sense to me," Ray confessed. "Innocence doesn't need money. Her dad is loaded, and the kids were using condoms."

"Again, you and I know that. Ray, I've checked. Jim Bennett could buy Tom Hall five times over and still have money to burn. The man's embarrassingly rich. Yes, Randy and Innocence were using protection, but that doesn't mean dear old dad knew. Maybe, he's been following them, spying on them, and several times, they've ended up at the abandoned house. What if Jim asked Innocence to have a talk with him in private? So, Bennett takes Innocence out to the house to be alone, to the kid's secret hide-a-way, and he confronts her. In the beginning, all he wants are answers, nothing more. 'Have you ever been here?' he asks. 'No,' she replies. He knows she's lying. 'Are you pregnant?' She swears up and down she's not pregnant and has no desire to be. But he doesn't believe her. All he can think—she's trying to get my money. Ray, the guy's a fricking multi-millionaire. He probably still has the first dollar he ever earned.

"There are rumors floating around Frankfort, he's thinking about running for the U.S. Senate. How would it look if his underage son knocked up an underage girl? Do you think he'd be elected? What if he keeps pushing, and Innocence keeps saying no. Still he doesn't believe, and the more she says no, the more he believes she's lying. Suddenly, he loses control, and he kills her."

"Okay, that shit happens, and that would be one hell of a motive. What you're saying makes me want to go to his house right now and kick his ass. But, to kill his own son?"

"Could be, Randy found out somehow that his dad killed Innocence. So, he calls him out to the scene of the crime, and one thing led to another, and Jim kills his son. Ray, this would not be the first time a father has killed a son, to cover up another murder."

"Okay, let me ponder your idea, even though I think it's way out there."

"You have anything better?" Jenny asked.

"Jenny, I have nothing, except a homeless man I need to find, and a fricking never-ending headache. I will check out Jim Bennett, but I can't stress it enough, we can't forget about the homeless man."

"And we won't. If anything turns up, I'll call you immediately."

Dave was tap dancing on Ray's temples.

Ray would spend the rest of the day doing paperwork and thinking over Jenny's idea, of Jim Bennett being the killer. And the more he thought about it, the more it seemed reasonable.

Chapter 43

"And the vision that was planted in my brain
Still remains
Within the sound of silence"
- Simon & Garfunkel

Ray wandered through an endless expansion of darkness and the feeling of total emptiness and despair. Ahead, in the middle of it all–a speck of light, which, as Ray got closer, revealed itself to be a slowly rotating platform. Mounted on the platform, in rows of three, were posts. And mounted to each post were brightly painted wooden swans, horses, elephants, dragons, pigs, unicorns, spiders, and bears. Each post moved up and down on gears, simulating a galloping motion. Instead of carnival music, Simon & Garfunkel's *The Sound of Silence* floated softy from unseen speakers. This carousel had "seats" for hundreds of riders, but currently, Ray could only make out five ghostly figures. As the carousel rotated, each figure came closer and closer into focus.

The first to appear was Phyllis Steele. Ray knew she was Phyllis from her crime scene photo. She was completely nude, riding astride a giant black spider with dripping fangs and glowing red eyes. One of the spider's arms shot out, grabbing at Ray as if he were the brass ring, causing Ray to jump back, his mouth open to scream. But nothing came out. Ray stared as she rode by, and as she passed, he noticed the back of her head, or what was left of it. Hundreds of thousands of tiny spiders, with red glowing eyes, were crawling from the open wound. Ray couldn't tear his eyes from the laceration, until she was out of focus.

Next came Elizabeth Fulkerson astride a wooden black bear, whose mussel was covered in shaved ice and cherry syrup. Lizzy was licking what appeared to be blood from her fingers, but upon closer inspection, Ray could see it was only cherry syrup. As Lizzy rode by, she reached over to Ray with a cherry covered hand, as if he could rescue her. Before she disappeared, Ray noticed the back of her head and tank top were stained with a deeper shade of red, which Ray knew wasn't cherry syrup.

Jessy Clark, in her long flowing wedding dress, appeared riding a white wedding cake swan. The corner of her face was covered in cake and icing, where she and her husband had fed each other during the cake cutting ceremony. Perched on her shoulder, a giant rat was licking the icing off her face. As she rode by, she threw her bouquet at Ray. It passed way over his head, and as he watched, it slowly dissolved into shining particles, like fairy dust, to finally fade away into nothingness. When he turned his attention back to Jessy, the bouquet was once again in her hand. As the bride slowly disappeared around the turn, Ray noticed the long flowing wedding veil that covered her head was drenched in blood, worms, and maggots.

The next row to come into focus had two riders. One was riding a gray toy elephant and the other a pink pig with a blue collar. Innocence loved elephants. Ray remembered buying her one for her tenth birthday. He remembered seeing dozens on Innocence's bed. As Innocence passed, she threw Ray a kiss with her right hand, and Ray went through the motion of catching the invisible kiss and placing it on his heart. Innocence sadly smiled and placed her hand over her heart. Ray tried to reach out to her like she was the brass ring, but she passed within inches of his fingers.

Randy sat there upon his pig; his right hand holding Innocence's left. He turned his attention from Innocence and stared straight into Ray's eyes. Ray tried to break contact but couldn't. Randy mouthed, "I told you I didn't do it. But you wouldn't listen." Then Randy turned his attention back to Innocence. Before they disappeared, Ray notices they had identical stains, the shape of hearts, on the back of their clothing.

It was then, Ray saw movement at the rear of the platform. Just within sight, but out of reach, stood the shadow of a man. Ray couldn't make out any features, other than the shadow was the embodiment of darkness itself, and it radiated pure evil. The shadow man's hands rested on the controls of the carousel. He could start or stop, slow, or speed up the platform. It was by the shadow's hands that the five were doomed to their eternal ride, for Ray knew, the shadow man was their killer. Ray also knew the shadow man's most ungodly desire—to fill the hundreds of empty "seats" on the carousel. Ray walked around the carousel toward the shadow, but the shadow man would limp away, staying within sight, but just out of reach, his hand always upon the throttle.

Ray stopped and stood there in disbelief. Waiting. Waiting for what? Then he knew. For coming into focus again was Phyllis Steele completely nude, riding astride a giant black spider with dripping fangs and glowing red eyes. It was beginning again; this never-ending loop which would take Ray into eternity, and there was nothing Ray could do about it.

Chapter 44

Ray was saved from the never-ending loop, by Dave pounding on his temples to Tony Orlando and Dawn's tune, *Knock Three Times on My Temples If You Want Me.* And by the fact, Margaret was shaking the shit out of him.

"Ray! Ray! For God sake, wake up! You're scaring me!"

Ray sprang wild-eyed from the bed like a charging bull, almost knocking Margaret over.

"What's going on, Margaret?" he shrieked.

"That's what I want to know," she shrieked back.

Ray sat back down on the edge of the bed.

"It's just a nightmare," he confessed, rubbing his forehead. "I've been having a lot of them lately."

"Maybe you should see someone about them."

"Maybe, I will." He knew he wouldn't.

"Good. You need too." She knew he wouldn't. "What's on your plate for today?" she asked.

"I need to go into work before Deputy Glover heads out on patrol. Then, I'm going around to the shelters. We need to find this homeless man."

"Ray, be careful. He may have killed five people already, and I don't want you becoming number six."

"Me either," Ray laughed.

Ray walked into the station ten minutes before Norman Glover was scheduled to go out on patrol, and he found Norman talking with Susan. Glover was the newbie, fresh out of cadet school, and still wet behind the ears. Glover was good looking and well-built. He was clean shaven and sported a military style haircut.

His uniform was always clean and pressed. You could see your face in his shoes. He made the Franklin Police Department look good, and Ray would have hired him just to walk around in public wearing his uniform. He was the spitting image of his father, who was a police officer up in Owensboro. Not only did Norman look the part, but he had a policeman's mind. He knew what questions to ask, and he had the gift of seeing through lies. He knew what to look for. Norman had attended the Police Academy in Somerset and graduated in the top one-percent of his class. There was very little Franklin could offer this up-and-coming officer, and Ray was overjoyed when Norman decided to settle in Franklin. Ray knew the Owensboro Police Department wanted Norman. Ray guessed; Norman turned them down, because he didn't want to have to prove himself, in his father's shadow.

"Deputy, I want to talk with you before you head out."

"What?" Susan exclaimed. "No, good morning, Susan. Or, how are you doing this morning, Susan? You look different, Susan. Are you sporting a new hairstyle, Susan? Are you losing weight, Susan? By the way, Ray, you're not carrying a box from 'Best Donuts.' The bottom line, Ray, where are the donuts?"

"Good morning, Susan," Ray laughed. "How are you doing this morning, Susan?"

"I'd be better if I had a jelly donut."

"Wouldn't we all," Ray admitted. "Norman, while you're out on patrol, I want you to circle around to the local restaurants. I want you to go in and talk to each manager and learn if anyone's been going through their garbage in the last few days. Then, I want you to go out and check the dumpsters yourself. It's going to take a while, and you might not get done today, but if you do, I want you to drive along I-65 and check the over and under passes for vagrants."

"How big a radius, Sir."

"I don't know. All of Franklin for sure, and any restaurant within, say, a mile of I-65 from Bowling Green down to the state line."

"That's a lot of territory."

"I know. I'll be checking out the homeless shelters. I'll get done before you, so, I'll call you and see where you are. Maybe, I can help shorten the time."

"What am I looking for, Sheriff?"

"A homeless man with a limp."

"Not the one-armed man, Doctor Kimble?" Susan laughed.

"I don't get it," Deputy Glover said, with a puzzled look on his face.

"Don't worry about it, Norman," Ray said. "It was before your time."

"What if I see him, this homeless man with a limp?"

"You call me immediately. Don't approach him. Don't let him see you. He could be dangerous. Did you get that Norman? He could be dangerous."

"Yes, Sheriff. I got it. He could be dangerous."

"Okay, finish whatever you were doing here and head on out. And remember, if you see him, call me immediately. Don't confront him. You understand?"

Glover gave Ray a thumbs up.

"I think you scared him," Susan said, watching the young deputy leave. "You scared me, and I'm not afraid of anything. Hell, I may not go home tonight."

"Come on, Susan."

"I'll probably sleep in one of the empty cells."

"Jesus."

"Ray, is the homeless man, that dangerous?"

"I hope not."

"You know what would help me feel better?"

"What's that?"

"A jelly donut."

Ray laughed as he exited the building.

St. Benedict's, St. Ben's as the locals called it, is a haven for homeless men. Their mission is to provide a temporary safe environment where homeless men can find a warm place to sleep, shower, and eat. St. Ben's helps men face everyday challenges by becoming independent, and they do so without being judgmental.

Fr. Riney, from St. Mary's, does Bible study and spiritual counseling there during the evenings.

"Hi Sally," Ray said, walking into the main office.

"Hey, Sheriff. What are you bringing us today?" Sally Blackman inquired from behind the register's counter. Ray and Margaret normally donated grooming supplies–deodorant, hand soaps, body lotions, shaving cream, and safety razors–once a month.

"Nothing today," Ray replied. "Maybe, you can help me."

"How so?"

"How many men are staying here on a regular basis?"

"It averages between fifty to seventy men. Right now, we're sheltering sixty-five men."

"Any of them have a limp?"

"A limp? Let me think. Sheriff, I don't think so, but I don't pay much attention to those kinds of things. Maybe Homer would know."

Homer, who never gives a last name, was one of the shelters homeless men, that five years ago, found a permanent dwelling place here. Homer was an African American gentleman, that looked to be in his eighties. He had more wrinkles than anyone Ray had ever seen. And when he smiled, which was most of the time, his wrinkles seemed to double in number. Normally, the men rotate in and out of the facility, but Homer was equipped to give something back in return. First off, he had been homeless, and he knew how embarrassing and hopeless times like these were, for those who came through the front door. Second, from the years on the road and living under overpasses and Shantytowns, he spoke their lingo. Third, he was funny, laid back, and easy going. Fourth, he was a hell of a cook. He swore up and down, that he'd never had culinary training, but he was an expert in comfort foods, especially fried chicken, mashed potatoes, pinto beans, and cornbread, which were the staples around here. He never complained or found it daunting, having to throw together a meal for fifty to a hundred men, on the spur of the moment.

"Is Homer in?"

"I think he's back in the kitchen."

Homer was indeed in the kitchen. It was his domain, and he was its king. Today, the king was peeling potatoes, fifty pounds of spuds, lucky for him he had three other volunteers helping.

"Morning, Ray," Homer said, looking up. "You come to peel taters?"

"Not today, Homer. But, I do have a question for you."

"Let's go over there," Homer said, indicating the walk-in pantry. "So, what has one of our men done now?" Homer asked, when they were out of earshot.

"Nothing I hope," Ray answered. "Homer, has any of the men that's been through here, in the last week or so, had a limp?"

"A limp, you say?" Ray nodded. "No, Ray, I don't remember anyone having a limp. Why? Does this have anything to do with Innocence's and the Bennett kid's murder?"

"Why do you ask that?"

"Ray, everyone in town knows that's the only cases you're working on, and that you've pushed everything else off on the rest of your department. Ray, your department understands, the town understands, and everyone looks up to you for that. If I knew someone with a limp, I'd turn him in in a heartbeat.

"Ray, did you know Innocence used to come down here with her mom and volunteer during Christmas and Thanksgiving? Hell, they used to come down here on days that weren't holidays. I can see her now, standing over there dishing out taters."

For a moment, the two men stood there staring at the empty spot behind a stainless-steel table. In their minds, they could see the young girl laughing and cutting up with the men standing in line. Innocence was the kind of person who never looked down on anyone. Ray's eyes started tearing up, as did Homer's. Homer put a fist over his mouth and coughed. "A limp, you say? Sorry, Ray. Have you tried the Presbyterian Church?"

"That's where I'm heading next. Homer, if a man comes in." Ray couldn't finish his sentence, because of the lump still in his throat.

"With a limp. I'll call you, Ray." Homer said, with a quiver in his voice.

215

The two men hugged each other, for both men loved Innocence Hall.

Chapter 45

Franklin Presbyterian Church is located on North College Street, just off Main Street. Michael Frey was their current pastor; young, tall, average weight, local boy, married to Lucy Frey, father of twin baby girls. Ray found him in his office, preparing this coming weekend's sermon.

"What can I do for you, Ray?" Michael asked, rising from his desk.

"Reverend, I'm looking for someone–a homeless man with a limp. Maybe, he's come through your soup kitchen."

"It's possible."

"You mean, you've seen him?" Ray asked, getting excited.

"No. I'm sorry. What I meant, if he was looking for a warm meal, then he could have come through here. I've haven't seen anyone who limps, but I'm not the one you need to talk to. We have several members who work in the kitchen. Let me get with them, and I'll get back with you."

"Could you do that now?"

"Right this minute? (Ray nodded) Is it that important? (Ray nodded) Okay, I'll have to look up their numbers. It'll take a while. You might not want to wait. I promise I'll give them a call and get back with you as quick as I can. Will that work?"

"That would be perfect. Thank you, Michael," Ray said, shaking the pastor's hand.

"Ray, have you been over to St. Ben's?"

"Just left there."

"How about the Good Samaritan?"

"They don't cook meals."

"No, but they do supply the ingredients to the kitchens, that cook the meals. They have the best food pantry in Franklin, which all of us have used on occasion. Who knows, homeless people could be stopping in there asking for canned goods."

"I haven't thought of that. Thanks."

Good Samaritan's is located in a historic building on South Main. When you walked through the main doors, it instantly hit you, they were extremely frugal. Maybe, that isn't the word for it. The main office space was ten-foot by ten-foot. It had a single wooden work desk, upon which were piles and piles of paperwork, a telephone, a rolodex, and a laptop. *Do people still use rolodexes?* Behind the desk was a chair, and behind the chair, a single door, which at the moment was open. Ray could see beyond the door, into a large room packed with racks and racks of canned goods and household products: paper plates, cups, napkins, and toilet paper. Beside the desk, to the left, was another door, which at the moment was closed. It was from this door that Ray heard a toilet flush.

"Hello," Ray said, trying not to startle the person behind the bathroom door.

"Just a moment please," came an answer.

The door finally opened and out walked Jerry Krampe. He was a large man. Five-foot-ten. Three-hundred-fifty pounds. Puffy face. Puffy hands. Puffy body. He was sweating. He was constantly sweating. He could sweat in a blizzard.

"Hello, Ray," he said, wiping sweat from his forehead with a paper towel. "What brings you in?"

"A couple of questions."

"How can I help?"

"Do you get a lot of families, individual's maybe, coming in asking for canned goods, those kinds of things?"

"About two hundred a month."

"Really? That many? (Jerry nodded) You haven't seen a man lately, that looks like he's seen better times and walks with a limp?"

"No, but it's funny, you ask."

"Why's that?"

"Earlier this morning, I had two guys, one Caucasian and one

African-American, stop in and they asked the same question."

"State cops?"

"I don't think so. They weren't in uniform, and they didn't show their badges."

"How were they dressed?"

"Both were wearing identical black suits, white shirts, black ties. They also wore dark sunglasses. I tell you, they reminded me of those guys in the movie *Men in Black*. I thought they were going to pull out their Neuralyzer's, you know, the thingy that makes you forget. Ray, I tell you, they looked like somebody's bodyguards."

"Can you describe the two men, their appearances, I mean?"

"They both were over six-foot. I'd say, around six-three or four. Big men, but not fat. They looked strong. Their suit sleeves were stretched to the max. The white guy had a head full of thick white hair. I'm not talking gray. I mean, pure white. The black man was completely bald, but you could see a five o'clock shadow on the crown of his head. I bet he shaves his head."

"How old did they look?"

"I don't know, mid-thirties, maybe."

"And they asked about a man that limps?"

"They did."

"And you told them?"

"What I told you. I haven't seen anyone who limps."

"What did they do after you told them you hadn't seen him?"

"They thanked me and left."

"That's it?"

"That's it. They were very polite."

"When they left, did they get in a car?"

"No, they walked up the street out of view."

"Okay, Jerry. If you see a man that limps, or the men in black again, call the station."

"Will do, Ray."

Ray sat in his car, wondering who these men were. They weren't state cops, this he knew. Jenny would have told him if anyone from Frankfort was in town. Maybe, they were private dicks, working for the families of the deceased. That made sense, but how had they heard about the homeless limper? Was it in the BOLO Jenny had sent out? Do private dicks get BOLO's? Could be someone from Park City; they knew about the limper. Ray hadn't let it out to the general public, that he was looking for a homeless man with a limp. The only ones that knew were Mike, Stephanie, Charlotte, FJ, Zoe, and Margaret, and they sure as shit wouldn't have hired private dicks. In Ray's mind, things were starting to stack up like large Manilla folders on a desk, each with its own label: Innocence's murder, Randy's murder, the Munfordville murder, the Park City murder, the Bowling Green murder, the man who limped, and now, the men in black. Ray rubbed his temples. "Hello, Dave."

Chapter 46

Wade McBride was enjoying a late lunch, or maybe it was an early supper at the Red Roof Inn just off the I-65 interchange. It was free; free as in lying in their dumpster, out of sight, and going through the scraps they'd thrown away earlier in the day. As he feasted on this wonderful cornucopia of half-eaten biscuits, burnt bacon, rubbery scrambled eggs, blackened bananas, leftover hamburgers, soggy fries, the little bits remaining on chicken bones, and the "I hate to waste it, but I'm full" food items, he thought about how he ended up here.

Two years ago, Wade came home from his first and only tour of duty in Afghanistan, code name Operation Freedom's Sentinel. He brought home with him a mind and body, that was twisted and scarred. He had gone into the service because, according to his father, he was a loser with no future. Wade hoped the service would teach him a trade, or perhaps, the military would turn out to be a permanent career move. No such luck. He came out, twenty-five years old, with no apparent skillset other than killing people. His expertise: the ability to silently sneak up behind a person in the dark, before cutting his or her throat. He came home with a fear of people and crowds. He also came home with PTSD.

There wasn't a night that went by he didn't relive the sudden deafening sound of the IED explosion, the ungodly sight of flying body parts, the smell of burning flesh, the sight and smell of blood, the screams of his fallen brothers-in-arms, and the intense pain in both his legs. Most nights, he would wake up in a cold sweat, filled with dread and anxiety. He had problems adjusting and coping, with life beyond that day in Afghanistan. He couldn't keep a job more than a couple of months, and after a while, finally gave up trying. His parents didn't understand PTSD. Most people didn't. His mother wondered if he needed help. His father said Wade's only problem was—weakness. And, Wade needed to grow a set. One night, after a horrible argument with his dad, Wade up and disappeared. His mom cried and cried, but prayed in the end, it would all work out. She truly believed Wade would straighten up someday and come back home. His dad's final words on the subject were goodbye and good riddance.

From then on, Wade found himself living out of trashcans and dumpsters, sleeping in cardboard boxes, or under overpasses. He slept with one eye open, in case someone tried to steal his two prized possessions— his weatherproof army overcoat and his military boots. He spoke very little. He had no friends. He wanted no friends.

When he returned home from overseas, it took months for his body to heal physically. His legs were covered in shrapnel scars, reminders of what happened on that eventful day in Afghanistan. His left leg was so scarred, twisted and damaged, that he would walk with a limp for the rest of his life.

***

Dave was doing the boogaloo on Ray's temples, which wasn't good, because Dave didn't have rhythm. Ray thought about doing something he normally wouldn't do. He thought about going to Convenient Care. No sooner had he put the car in drive, when his phone rang.

"Hello," he said, rubbing his temples.

"Sheriff, something weird is going on."

"What's that, Norman?"

"I just came out of Casey's General Store on 31W," Deputy Glover said.

"Okay. And?"

"I was talking to Freda, the manager, you see. And I'm asking her if someone's been diving in her dumpster. She says, not that she's aware of."

"What's weird about that?"

"Sheriff, that's not the weird part. What's weird, she said two guys came in earlier today asking the same questions. She also said these guys were looking for a man that had a limp. Sheriff, I hadn't mentioned the limp part."

"Let me guess," Ray said. "Two men that were both wearing black suits, dark sunglasses, and both looking like poster boys for a bodybuilding gym."

"You nailed it, Sheriff. Now that's weird. What do you want me to do?"

"Continue doing what you've been doing. Our number one concern is the limper."

"Okay, Sheriff."

"Norman, another question."

"Shoot."

"Freda didn't happen to see what the men were driving, did she?"

"She did. She saw them filling up."

Ray perked up.

"God bless her ... Did they pay with a card?"

"No. Cash. I asked. That would have been sweet."

"Did she know what kind of car they were driving?"

"It was a newer Lincoln Town Car."

"Norman, while you're looking for the limper, keep your eyes out for the men, or their car."

"And, if I see them?"

"Call me. Get their license number if you can, but don't put yourself in harm's way. Understood?"

"Perfectly."

"Good job, Norman. Be careful. I don't know who these guys are, or what they're up to."

Ray looked at his watch. It was 3:45 pm.

***

Special Agent Jenny Broxen looked at her watch. It was 3:45 pm, and she was bored stiff. She had spent the last two days doing paperwork, and it was slowly killing her. She much preferred being in the field, doing real police work; getting her hands dirty. Her phone rang.

"Broxon," she said.

"Special Agent Jennifer Broxon, this is the Sheriff of Franklin, Kentucky, Raymond Harris."

"Hello, Ray," Jenny laughed. "It's good hearing your voice. Tell me you're going to give me some fantastic news, about solving some murders?"

"I wish I had fantastic news, but sadly, I don't. The water's gotten muddier."

"How so?"

"I've got a couple of guys down here looking for our homeless man, and my gut tells me, they're not law enforcement. But my gut has been known to be wrong."

"Sorry, Ray. Our department hasn't sent anyone your way, or I would have known ... So, who are these guys?"

"That's why I called you."

"Sorry. I was thinking out loud."

"Can you think of anyone, besides us, who'd be looking for the homeless man?"

"Everyone's looking for the man. I put the BOLO out on him. Remember? I also read about the reward the dad posted. These guys could be bounty hunters. They could also be private dicks, but private dicks don't come cheap. The woman who got murdered in Bowling Green, if I remember correctly, her husband was a doctor. He could afford private detectives. Your own Jim Bennett could easily afford private detectives."

"I didn't think about that. Maybe, I should talk with Mr. Jim Bennett. I'll also give Chief Reynolds a call up in Bowling Green and have him check out Jessy Clark's husband."

"That's where I'd start," Jenny said, disappointed.

"You sound down in the dumps," Ray said.

"Just bored. The best fun I've had in a long time was when I was with you guys in Franklin. Just between you and me, I'm planning on asking for a lower level position. One that gets me out in the field more often."

"Well, I hope you get it. I need to get off of here and call some people. Come see us, Jenny. I think George would like to see you."

"Will do, Ray. I'd like to see George."

Ray called Chief Reynolds before he headed home and told him about the men in black. Reynolds thanked Ray and said he'd keep an eye out for them. Ray also told him what Jenny had suggested; that Jessy Clark's husband, the doctor, could be behind the men in black. Reynolds promised he'd have a word with the husband and get back with Ray.

Chapter 47

Ray swung his legs out of bed and sat there a moment, pinching the bridge of his nose.

"Good morning, Dave," he whispered. It had been two weeks since Innocence was murdered, and Ray was no closer to solving her case, nor was he any closer to solving Randy Bennett's case. The images of their lifeless bodies hung like cobwebs, in the corner of his mind. A strong cup of coffee was in order. Nothing clears cobwebs like a strong cup of coffee. Afterwards he'd give Jim Bennett a call and set up a meeting.

Margaret, the saint, was waiting for him in the kitchen with a hot streaming cup of Java.

"Ray, what do you want for breakfast?"

"Coffee's fine."

"Ray, you need to get something on your stomach. I noticed the aspirin bottle is half empty, and I know I just bought that bottle a couple of days ago. Ray, you need to cut down on the pills, or you're going to hurt yourself. Joe Bob's mom took too many pills for a migraine, and after a time, the aspirins ate a hole in her stomach."

"That's called an ulcer."

"Whatever. It still ate a hole in her stomach. You need to go in and see Doctor Carrico and have him check you out."

"I'll do that, Margaret."

"I know you will. I set you up with an appointment. The earliest I could get you in was nine o'clock tomorrow morning."

"Margaret, you shouldn't have. I've got too much going on right now."

227

"And if you don't see him, you could have a massive stroke or heart attack. Then where would you be?"

Duh. Dead, Ray thought.

"You're right, Margaret. I'll see him tomorrow."

"Promise?" Margaret asked, from the kitchen sink.

"I promise," Ray said, with his fingers crossed behind his back.

"Uncross your fingers, Ray," Margaret said, without looking around.

***

FJ sat on Betty's patio, under a patio awning, sipping a Bud Lite. The day was going to be a scorcher. He heard the sliding door open behind him, and a moment later, Zoe strolled up. Taking a chair under the awning, she lite a cig, took a long draw, and slowly exhaled.

"You know, that's another nail in your coffin," FJ said, taking a swig.

"So, how's your liver, Mr. 'Let's Have a Beer for Breakfast?' Just to let you know, it's nowhere near five o'clock."

"It's five o'clock somewhere in the world," he laughed.

"How are you feeling today, Frederick?"

"A lot better. Thanks. I'm breathing easier. According to Doctor Carrico, the hole in my lung should be healed by now. Everything else seems to be getting back to normal. I'll probably be heading home tomorrow. The way I look at it, I'm just in the way around here."

"It's good that you're feeling better," Zoe nodded. There was an uncomfortable pause. A small white butterfly floated across the patio and landed on a potted plant of posies beside Zoe. Frederick took a drink. Zoe took a draw.

"Frederick, you had Betty worried. Seeing you in the hospital and all."

"I know," Frederick confessed. "I had everyone worried. Hell, I was worried."

Another uncomfortable pause. The butterfly took off, flew in front of Zoe and landed on a potted plant beside Frederick.

"Zoe, thank you for being here. I know Betty appreciates it."

"Just Betty?" she asked, staring.

"I think I'm going in," Frederick said, standing. "Like my beer, I'm getting hot."

Startling the butterfly, it took off over the pool.

"Frederick, I need to tell you something."

"Can it wait?"

"No. It can't."

"Okay. Let's hear it," Frederick said, turning toward her. A naked robin flew past, snatching the butterfly out of the air.

"I'm leaving tomorrow," Zoe said, taking a drag off her cig.

"Tomorrow?"

Zoe nodded. "You're better, and Betty doesn't need me around here any longer. I'm just taking up space."

"Are you sure? I mean, about Betty not needing you?"

"Pretty sure. I got a call from Eddie Jessop. He bought the circus from old Mr. Campbell back in the nineties, and he's wondering when I'm coming back."

"You and he?" Frederick asked, tilting his head left and right.

"Heavens no," Zoe laughed. "He's half my age, and he has a boyfriend. The circus is heading to California for the Pacific Summer tour. The tour starts in San Diego next week. That's where Eddie wants me to join them. I'm the logistics manager for the circus. After that, it heads north along the coast. If all goes well, we'll finish up in Seattle sometime in October, just in time to turn around and head down to the Southern states, for the winter tour. Eddie told me a secret, he's going to ask Sam, Sam Vessels, to be his husband, and he wants me to be their maid of honor. You can do that in California now."

"What? Be a maid of honor?"

Zoe laughed. "No, silly. I mean two men getting married. Oh, you're being funny."

"Sounds like you have everything planned," Frederick said, walking away.

As Zoe watched him walk away, a tear formed in her eye.

"I could always change my plans," Zoe whispered.

Frederick didn't hear. He was already in the house. Zoe stood, dropped the cigarette butt on the tile floor, and crushed it under her shoe.

Ray pulled up in front of the Bennett's well-manicured yard. He sat there a moment marveling on how every blade of grass looked like it had been measured and clipped by hand. *I bet you don't mow your own yard,* Ray thought as he got out of his car.

Ray had called Jim from home and set up an appointment for ten o'clock. Looking at his watch, Ray saw he was five minutes early. Approaching the front door, Ray noticed a black Lincoln Town car sitting in the driveway. *There you are. Why am I not surprised? Note to self. Call Jenny and Chief Reynolds, and tell them I found Agent K and Agent J.*

Jim Bennett had asked to meet at his house because of all the crank calls he'd been getting at work, and the real reason, since Randy's death he couldn't concentrate at work. For years, Ray wanted to ask Jim how he made all his money. But that would be tacky. Anyway, as Sheriff, he could always check the tax records. Of course, it would have nothing to do with the case. Ray was just nosey. Harold King answered the front door and shook Ray's hand. "Come on in Sheriff. Everyone's waiting for you in the family room."

Jim Bennett was leaning on the fireplace mantel, holding a coffee mug. Randy's mom, Heather, was sitting on the couch sipping on a Bloody Mary. She nodded. Ray nodded back. Jim Bennett Sr. was having coffee, at the bar with the men in black. Harold King joined the three at the bar.

And there you are, Ray thought.

The two did look like Agent K and Agent J, sort of, if you squinted your eyes, and only if Tommy Lee Jones and Will Smith were younger, six inches taller, and on steroids. Each man wore a black suit, a thin black tie, and even in the house, dark glasses.

Together, the men approached Ray, each offering his hand. "Nice meeting you, Sheriff," Agent K, a.k.a. Tommy Lee Jones, said, shaking Ray's hand. "We'd planned on coming over today to have a word with you. This will save us some time."

"Yah," Agent J, a.k.a. Will Smith added. "We wanted to let you know why we're here, in your friendly little town."

"And why are you here, in my friendly little town?" Ray asked, shaking Agent J's hand. "And who are you, anyway?"

"Sorry, we should have introduced ourselves. I'm Ethan Monroe," Agent K said, "and this is Phillip Conrad. We own a small private investigation agency in Nashville."

"Conrad and Monroe Investigations," Agent J, a.k.a. Will Smith, now known as Phillip Conrad, added, smiling. "You can call me, Phil."

"So, Ethan and Phil, why are you here in my small town?" Ray asked again.

"We received a BOLO, on a person of interest in several murders, from Munfordville down to Franklin. We did some checking, and we've learned the person in question, is homeless and has a limp. We decided to check things out."

"Who told you the man had a limp?"

"A young woman who works at the Shell Station in Park City. I think her name is Boarman."

"And, being the nice guys that you are, you're offering your help pro bono," Ray inquired.

Both men looked at each other and smiled.

"We also heard about the reward Mr. Bennett was offering," Ethan said. "So, we thought we'd stop in and introduce ourselves."

"I bet you did," Ray stated.

"Sheriff, I want to thank you for coming to the house for our meeting," Jim Jr. said, taking the edge off the conversation, between the bounty hunters and Ray.

"Not a problem, Mr. Bennett."

"I've asked you before. Please, call me Jim."

"Okay, Jim."

"Sheriff Ray, would you like something to drink?" Heather asked, refilling her Bloody Mary at the bar.

"No, thank you, ma'am," Ray replied. "But, I would like to have a word with your husband, privately, if I could."

231

Jim Jr. motioned toward a sliding door. "We can talk out by the pool."

Jim's pool was twice as big as Tom's pool, almost Olympic size. *Why would anyone have a pool this big? Does size matter with pools?*

"Let's talk in the pool house," Jim suggested. "It's air conditioned."

The pool house was more of a sports bar, with a changing room.

"So, what do you want to talk about? Is it about Randy? Do you have something?"

"Jim, I need to ask you some questions, and you're going to be pissed when I ask them. I know I would, but they should have been asked weeks ago."

"I don't think I like where this is going," Jim commented.

"Understood. Jim, where were you the day Innocence died?"

"What are you insinuating?"

"Nothing, if you have an alibi."

"Sheriff, I think you need to be leaving."

"Really? All ready?"

"You need to leave."

"Jim, I told you, you weren't going to like the questions."

"I think you should go back to calling me, Mr. Bennett. Sheriff, if you have any more questions, they should probably go through Harold."

Ray nodded.

"Tell Mr. King I'll give him a call this afternoon."

"He's in the house. Why not talk to him now?"

"Because you and he need to get together and get your ducks in a row. I'll want to know where you were the day and time Innocence was murdered. I'll also need to know the same thing, concerning the time and day, of Randy's death."

"You really believe I had something to do with my own son's death? That's just sick."

"Mr. Bennett, here's what I think. You found out the two kids where having sex and–"

"You don't know that," Mr. Bennett interrupted.

"Know what? That they were having sex? (Mr. Bennett nodded) I hate admitting it, but I'm afraid I do. And so do you. They're both minors. You know that as well. At some point, you found out about the sex. (Bennett, staring at the floor, sadly shook his head) Not wanting your son accused of rape, or thinking Innocence was going to blackmail you, you killed her to keep her quiet."

"That's absurd."

"Randy found out, and he confronted you. Something he said, or something he did, set you off, and in a fit of uncontrollable rage, you–"

"Killed my own son?"

Tears were flowing from Jim's eyes.

"Is that a confession?" Ray asked softly.

"That's bullshit. That's what that is," Jim spat, wiping the tears away, "and you know it."

"It's not the first time a father has killed his son, to cover his sorry ass."

"Sheriff, you need to leave before I do something, we'll both regret."

Ray saw himself out.

Back in his car, Ray dialed up Jenny– punched up Jenny. You can't dial a cell phone.

"I thought I'd let you know; I just finished questioning Jim Bennett."

"How'd that go?" Jenny asked.

"Pretty good. I think."

"Really?"

"Shit, no. He's royally pissed. But, that's not the reason I called."

"What is?"

"I met the men in black."

"At the Bennett's?"

"Yes."

"Did he hire them?"

"Not according to them, but I wouldn't be surprised. Their

233

names are Ethan Monroe and Phillip Conrad. They run a detective company out of Nashville. Maybe you could run them through the system."

"I'm typing as we talk. When I collect their info, I'll send it down the pike."

"I appreciate it."

"What are you going to do now?"

"First, I'm going to call Chief Reynolds and give him the heads up on Monroe and Conrad. Then, I'm going to try and find the homeless man. Again, my gut tells me he didn't have anything to do with the murders, but he may know something critical to the investigation."

Chapter 48

"That good-looking man, Harold King, just pulled up in the visitor's parking space out front," Susan McCormick said, sticking her head into Ray's office. "If you're going to ask him if he wants coffee, you better make a new pot. Make it a full pot. I may want some later."

Ray smiled but didn't get out of his chair.

"When he comes in, bring him on back," Ray said, leaning back in his chair.

"Will do," Susan said. "You're not making coffee then?"

"Are you?"

"No."

"Neither am I."

"You're a hard man, Sheriff Ray. A hard man."

When Harold King walked in Ray's office, Ray stood and shook hands. Susan stood in the doorway, giving Harold King the once over.

"Thank you, Susan."

"No problem, Sheriff."

Susan didn't move.

"Susan, is that your phone ringing?" Ray asked.

"I don't hear nothing," Susan said, giving Harold King another once over.

"Thank you, Susan," Ray said, this time a little more forceful.

This time Susan got it and returned to her desk. Ray thought about closing the door, but Susan would have a hard time eavesdropping.

"Have a seat, Mr. King," Ray said, pointing to the two empty chairs in front of his desk. "I didn't expect you to show up here. I figured we'd talk over the phone."

"I like doing face to face," Harold smiled. "When I ask questions, I like to see the expressions on a person's face. I gain a lot of information that way."

"I'm the same way," Ray said, sitting back down. "So, I suspect you talked with Mr. Bennett."

"Oh, we talked alright, and he wasn't happy. I'm sure you can understand why."

"I wouldn't be happy either," Ray confessed. "But, you have to understand, I have to ask these kinds of questions, no matter how stupid, no matter how disrespectful, no matter how painful. Hell, I should have asked them the day the kids died. Mr. King, in my business, everyone's a suspect."

"You mean guilty until proven innocent."

"Exactly. But, you didn't hear me say that, and I'd swear in court, I didn't say it. Truthfully, I don't believe Mr. Bennett killed anyone. But I had to ask."

"If you didn't believe it, why ask in the first place?"

"Because I'm the sheriff, and it's my job to ask the hard questions. That's why I get paid the big bucks."

"Do you have any evidence that could incriminate my client in either murder?"

"I do not."

"I didn't think so, because my client is innocent."

"For his sake, I hope he is."

"I think we're done here," Harold said, rising and extending his hand.

Ray kept his seat and didn't offer his hand.

"I have something else," Ray said, pointing back to Harold's seat.

Harold looked at Ray, then the chair and back at Ray, then he sat down.

"I hope this doesn't take long," Harold said, looking at his watch.

"That's up to you," Ray replied. "Did you or Mr. Bennett hire

Monroe and Conrad?"

"If he did or I did, I fail to see any crime being committed."

"No. It's not criminal to hire detectives. People do it all the time. But most people own up to it. So, let me ask you again. Did you or Mr. Bennett hire Monroe and Conrad?"

"Mr. Bennett did ask me to inquire into a detective agency."

"And, you found Monroe and Conrad."

"Yes, they came highly recommended. Are we finished now?" Ray smiled.

"I guess not," Harold sighed.

"And if they find the homeless man before me?"

"What are you trying to get at?"

"It's simple. If they find the man, I'm sure they will do their civic duty and turn him in to the authorities."

"Of course. Why wouldn't they?"

"Why wouldn't they indeed?"

There was a moment of silence.

"Well?" Harold asked.

"I think we're done now. Thank you for coming in," Ray said, standing up and offering his hand.

Ray stood there a moment watching Harold make his way to the front exit. Susan stepped into Ray's office, watching Harold leave as well.

"I heard everything you said," she said.

"Of course you did."

"What does that mean?"

"Nothing. So, what do you think about Harold's answers?"

"He sounded sincere to me, but what do I know? All I do is answer the phone around here, keep everyone up-to-date on birthdays, and make coffee."

"While you're at it, get me a cup," Ray said, pushing Susan from his office, so he could shut the door.

"You're a hard man, Sheriff Ray. A hard man."

As Susan was making coffee, Wade McBride was enjoying a couple of appetizers, from the Brickyard Café. The first course, discarded cold Crispy Calamari, hand breaded and fried. Wade remembered his drill sergeant once telling him home cooking wasn't real home cooking, unless it was deep fried. The Calamari was more rubbery than crispy, but it had a good favor. Second on the menu was what was left of someone's order of Steamed Mussels cooked in a sauce of white wine, garlic, tomato, and basil. Yes, the eating was good at the Brickyard Café. The only patrons today, like every day, were the rats sharing the dumpster, but they were polite and friendly. Most kept to themselves, eating things even Wade refused to put into his mouth. Wade did have scruples. Wade's only regret—no one ever threw away a half empty bottle of Chianti.

With his belly mostly full, Wade climbed out of the green dumpster and ducked between it and the café. This was the second most dangerous part of dining out—escaping without getting caught. The first—not getting caught climbing in the dumpster, in the first place.

With no one in sight, Wade slid along the alley between the Brickyard Café and Donald's Car Service Center and stole a peek around the corner out into Franklin's downtown shopping square. One of Franklin's charms was its shopping square. From McDonald's to the north, to Puckett's Grocery & Restaurant to the south, visitors could stroll among the restored houses and buildings of the nineteenth century, tasting the southern comfort dishes of 55 South, along with its specialty drinks, or sitting under sidewalk umbrellas at the Frothy Monkey Coffeehouse. Of course, there was always the Brickyard Café. Which Wade highly recommended. If food and drink weren't on the bill, visitors could wander among the artsy galleries of fine prints and antiques. Wade wasn't in the mood for fine art. He couldn't afford a masterpiece, and besides, where would he hang it? This afternoon the square was sparse, which was a worry for Wade. It was easier getting lost in a crowd.

Down the street, Wade noticed a patrol car slowly coming to a stop, across the street from the United Methodist Church, the church where Johnny Cash and June Carter were married back in 1968. Getting out his car, the officer approached a park bench occupied by two old gentlemen. Could the officer have seen him, Wade wondered. Wade did a three-sixty, searching for an avenue of escape. The only escape was back down the alley, toward the dumpster. Even from this distance, Wade could tell the cop was a nice looking young man. He looked spiffy in his uniform. He must have known the old men, for he joined them on the bench.

A man, wife, and three kids strolled by, giving Wade "the" pity look. When they were several yards away, Wade dropped in behind them, making sure not to get too close. For the homeless, trying not to be seen was a challenge. The family went into *Cedars Flowers and Gifts,* leaving Wade alone and exposed, with his anxiety mounting. At the next corner, beside the *Best Donuts* shop, Wade turned south. He had been this way several times, since his arrival in Franklin. He knew the street's hiding places: the shrubs, the clump of trees, the recessed doorways, alleys that didn't dead-end.

It wasn't far to his abandoned warehouse on South College Street. This was Wade's second "home", since coming to Franklin two weeks ago. The first abandoned house, out by the interstate, had been too far away from most of the restaurants this fine community had to offer. Away from the crowd and prying eyes, Wade's confidence was up. He'd just finished a fantastic meal. He had picked up a few cigarette butts off the sidewalk earlier. Luck was with him, for he had found a half-used pack of matches. Mostly, no one had paid him much attention. Life was good.

A black Lincoln Town car crept through the intersection Wade had turned down. The two occupants watched as the man with the limp made his way out of the town square, toward the warehouse district.

Chapter 49

The drive to the Nashville Airport took a couple of hours, but at four o'clock in the morning little to no traffic was out. Betty and Zoe led the way in Zoe's rental. Mike, Stephanie, Charlotte, and Margaret followed Zoe's rental in Mike's van. Ray and Tom followed Mike's van in Tom's BMW. The mini convoy started running into morning traffic at Goodlettsville.

With boarding pass in hand and standing at the entrance to the TSA check-in line, Zoe said her goodbyes.

"What time will you get into San Diego?" Mike asked.

"Let's see," Zoe said, looking at her boarding passes. "The Southwest flight from Nashville to San Diego leaves Nashville at 7:55 am. That's an hour from now. So, I've got plenty of time. It arrives in San Diego at 1:20 pm, their time. I've got a layover in Chicago."

"We'll miss you," Stephanie said, hugging her.

"I'm glad you finally came back, but not for the reason you did," Ray said, kissing her on the cheek.

"You have our numbers. Call us," Margaret said, wiping a tear.

Charlotte hugged Zoe, whispering something in Zoe's ear. Zoe nodded and smiled.

"Please don't be a stranger," Tom said, giving his mother-in-law a long hug.

"I will miss you all," Zoe said, teary eyed. "Betty, could we talk in private?"

"Sure mom," Betty replied, taking Zoe's hand. Together they walked back past the check-in counters.

241

"Betty, sweetheart," Zoe began. "I'm sorry for all the years I wasn't here for you."

"Mom, it's–"

"No, Betty. I did you and your father wrong. I know now, I should have trusted you, both of you, but baby, I was afraid. For the life of me, that's the only excuse I can come up with. Because of that, I never got to meet my granddaughter. I've missed her first steps, her birthdays, her Christmas's, her boo-boos. Hell, I missed changing her poopy diapers. For sixteen years, I haven't been here for her. That's unforgiveable for a grandmother. But, from what I've learned, she was a beautiful, caring person, thanks to you and your friends, and no thanks to me."

"Mom, don't be so hard on yourself. You know, we've already forgiven you."

"We? I don't see your dad here. He hasn't forgiven me. Betty, I'm not sure he ever will."

"He has," Betty assured her. "He just has a weird way of showing it."

Zoe laughed.

"I wish he were here," she said. "There're some things I need to get off my chest; things he needs to hear. Betty, there's things I've done."

Zoe seemed to be in a world of her own. Another time. Another place, perhaps. Betty noticed but was afraid to inquire. She was afraid of the answers. So, she said, "Maybe next time, mom."

"And, there will be a next time," Zoe said, returning to the present. "I promise. It won't be as long as the last time."

"It better not be," Betty said, acting stern with her hands on her hip.

"I have your phone number, and I know how to use a cell phone," Zoe said, smiling. "I will call."

"I'm sorry to interrupt," Mike said, walking up. "But you need to get in the TSA line. It's starting to back up. There's a lot of people heading out for the weekend."

Zoe nodded. "Thanks, Mike." Leaning over, she gave Betty a

final hug. "I love you, my daughter," she whispered.

"I love you, mom."

Back in Franklin, FJ took a pull off a longneck. Maybe Zoe was right. Drinking beer at seven in the morning could be a disaster waiting to happen.

Screw it.

He took another pull. Looking down, he noticed there were already five dead soldiers lying on the floor at his feet. He also noticed, there was another person sitting on the other end of the couch.

"Who are you?" he asked. After a few seconds of squinting, he concluded, "Oh, it's only me." FJ raised the bottle to himself. "You're wondering why I didn't go to Nashville with the others, aren't you?" FJ asked his other-self.

"Why didn't you go?" his other-self replied.

FJ took a pull, emptying the bottle. Tossing the empty on the floor, he opened another. Now there were six dead soldiers lying at his feet.

"Why ain't you as drunk as me?" he asked his other-self.

"Because I'm not drinking, stupid. Again, why didn't you go to Nashville with the others?"

FJ shrugged his shoulders.

"I know why," his other-self said.

"No, you don't."

"Sure, I do."

"Bullshit."

"You would have been reliving the day Zoe left, all those years ago, and you're not sure you could have handled it this time."

FJ pitched his other-self a finger. "You don't know what you're talking about."

"Oh, really? I am you; you know. I know everything about you–I mean me–I mean us."

"Then screw you–Screw me–Screw us."

"Good come back, Frederick. Admit it. You've always loved her. Even after she deserted you and Betty. Hell, you love her now. That's why you're drinking so much."

"No fricking way."

"Yes, way."

"So, Bigshot, what if I do love her? She's already gone. It's too late."

"Call her. Beg her not to go. It's never too late."

"If she truly loved me, she wouldn't have left."

"That's what you thought the first time. You can't use that excuse again."

"The hell I can't."

"Just call her already."

FJ reached for his phone but was interrupted by a knock at his door.

"Are we being joined by another me?" he asked his other-self, but his other-self was gone.

FJ opened the door and squinted, from the bright sunlight bursting into the room.

"What?" he asked, shielding his eyes with his hand.

"Mr. Johnston, it's a pleasure meeting you," a large silhouette said.

"Who are you?"

"I'm Ethan Monroe, and this is Phillip Conrad. We own a small private investigation agency in Nashville."

"There's two of you?"

"Yes, sir," Conrad said from the side. "Could we come in, please?"

"Because you said the magic word, I guess," FJ replied, turning away. "Close the door behind you."

Monroe and Conrad entered the trailer and immediately took up all the unoccupied air space, and the trailer seemed to moan under their combined weight. Conrad closed the door behind him, making it easier for FJ to see both men. FJ raised an eyebrow.

"I know who you are," he said. "Which one of you is Agent K?"

"I guess that would be me," Monroe replied, smiling at Conrad.

"Then I'll have to be Agent J," Conrad laughed. "Believe it or not, we get this all the time."

"I bet you do," FJ said. "So, why are you guys here?"

"We're private investigators from Nashville," Conrad answered.

"You said something to that effect, at the door. And you're here investigating?"

"Randy Bennett's death."

"Not Innocence's?"

"We were hired to look into the Bennett kid's death, but we do believe both crimes were committed by the same person."

"So, what kind of questions do you have for me?" FJ asked.

"Mr. Johnston, we're not here wanting answers to questions. We're here to ask you if you'd like to meet the man, who murdered your granddaughter."

Chapter 50

FJ sat in the back of the Town Car with Conrad, while Monroe drove. They drove through the McDonald's at the Town Square, before heading toward the interstate. They ordered FJ a large black coffee, hoping the strong coffee would help sober him up a bit. Just outside Franklin, Monroe took the onramp south for Nashville. FJ had only sat in a Lincoln Town Car one other time. It was when he and his friends had been picked up by the FBI on Tybee Island. It had reminded him of an episode of the *X-Files*. This car was spacious as the one before, and the ride just as sweet.

"We going to Nashville?" FJ asked, carefully taking a sip of the scalding coffee. Conrad nodded.

"Our client has a warehouse in Nashville."

"And that's where you found the killer?"

"That's where we stashed the killer, after we apprehended him."

"So, why haven't you handed him over to the police?"

"We will, but our client wants some time with him before we do. Our client thought you might like some time as well."

"Who is your client?"

Conrad looked at Monroe in the rearview.

"Go ahead and tell him. He'll found out sooner than later."

"We were hired by Mr. Harold King," Conrad said, "on behalf of Mr. Jim Bennett."

"So, what you're telling me is that Jim Bennett hired you."

"Yes, Mr. Johnston, I guess you could put it that way."

"And, you have the killer, but you haven't turned him over to the cops. (Conrad nodded) Isn't that the same as kidnapping?"

247

"Technically," Monroe answered from the front seat. "But we will turn him over and collect the reward money. We're just taking our time. Today or tomorrow, what's the hurry?"

"Taking your time," FJ laughed.

"If we had turned him over, as soon as we caught him, you wouldn't be having this opportunity to 'question' him, and you want to 'question' him, don't you?"

"I want to do more than question him," FJ confessed.

"That's what Mr. Bennett said as well," Conrad said. "Mr. Johnston, we don't care how much you 'question' him, as long as you don't kill him. If you do happen to kill him, while you're questioning him, that would be considered Voluntary Manslaughter, and you ... Us... we would go to jail."

"And what if he turns up at a police station beat up and bloody?"

"It happens sometimes. The bad guy tries to escape, and we have to use extreme force," Conrad commented.

"Yes, it happens all the time," Monroe added.

"Then I would like to 'question' the murderer," FJ said, smiling out the window. "Does he have a name?"

"McBride, Wade McBride."

"And he admits killing both kids?"

"Of course not, but he will before we're through with him. But you shouldn't worry about all that. You just need to ask your 'questions.'"

Revenge for Innocence will be sweet, FJ thought, staring out the side window.

"There's something I'd like to ask you, Mr. Johnston," Conrad said a few minutes later.

"What's that," FJ said.

"You look like that actor–"

"I know who you're going to say," FJ interrupted. "I look like Peter Dinklage, the actor in *Game of Thrones.* I get that a lot."

"I've never watched *Game of Thrones.* No, that's not it. I'm talking about the movie where a P.I. steals a machine that can record and play back memories of other people. He uses the machine to

248

solve the death of the man who invented it. I don't remember the name of the movie, but you look just like the actor."

"Rememory," Monroe said, from the front seat.

"What," Conrad asked.

"The name of the movie is *Rememory*, and it stars Peter Dinklage; the same Peter Dinklage who plays Tyrion Lannister on HBO's *Game of Thrones*. I haven't missed an episode. I thought you looked like him myself."

"I get that a lot," FJ said, smiling.

Somewhere just north of Nashville, the Town Car passed Mike's Van heading north toward Franklin.

Mike pulled up in his driveway and turned the engine off. Everyone sat there a few moments before slowly piling out.

"My back and legs are screaming," Ray said, bending over trying to grab his knees. "I'm getting too old for long car rides."

"Hell, all our backs and legs are screaming," Mike stated. "You guys want to come in for a drink?" All shook their heads. They weren't in the mood. They had just said goodbye to a friend, and they didn't know when they would see her again, if they would see her again.

"Maybe another time," Tom said, taking Betty by the arm. "I think we need to head on home."

"Yes," Betty added. "We should be going. There's something I need to talk with Tom about." Tom raised an eyebrow.

Now's the time to talk about moving, Betty thought.

"After I take Margaret home, I'm going over to talk with FJ," Ray said, as he and Margaret got in their car. "He still hasn't told me why he tried to kick Randy Bennett's ass. It's time he did. You all know, what he tried to do is not like FJ. (All nodded) I think it's time he and I had a heart to heart."

"Be nice," Betty begged.

"I'm always nice," Ray said. Mike rolled his eyes.

FJ didn't answer the door after Ray pounded on it for five minutes. *Something's not right.* FJ's van was in the yard, so where was FJ? He couldn't drive any other vehicle, but it sure looked like he wasn't home. FJ was not the type to take walks. Ray pounded on the door a few more times. Still no FJ. Ray tried FJ's cell again. It went straight to voice mail.

I bet the lucky little shit hooked up with the WKU girls' volleyball team again.

"We want to thank you for not answering your cell phone, Mr. Johnston," Conrad said. "It would be embarrassing having to explain where we're going."

"Not a problem," FJ said. "It's only Ray, anyway. He probably wants to tell me how the trip to the airport went. That can wait till later."

Downtown Nashville on a Friday afternoon was a living organism of sights and sounds. The "in" crowd was already out in their cowboy hats, western shirts, tank tops, faded jeans, cut-offs, mini-skirts, and cowboy boots. Drunks and country music, classic and modern, spilled from the honky-tonks up and down Broadway. A billboard said *Jenny Lewis with The Cactus Blossoms* were playing at the Ryman Auditorium that night. On weekends, which includes Fridays, the Johnny Cash Museum and the Country Music Hall of Fame and Museum would stay open late, to accommodate the late-night restaurant goers. All this FJ noticed as they drove through downtown, toward the docks on the Cumberland River.

Stopping in front of a rundown, about to cave in (from the looks of it), three-story brick warehouse, Monroe turned the engine off.

"Lucy, I'm home," he said in his best Desi Arnaz accent.

"You're kidding. Right?" FJ asked, from the backseat.

"No. We're really here."

"I was talking about your Desi Arnaz accent."

Both men laughed.

"This place is an accident waiting to happen," FJ surmised. "It looks like it's going to collapse any second."

"Don't let the looks fool you, my little friend," Monroe said. "Back in the day, the warehouses along this part of the river used to make parts for trains. Carbon, Silicon, and Iron would be brought down the river on barges. The forges would belch black smoke, as they blended the three elements into cast iron, which was then poured into molds making parts for trains. The problem was – the parts were for the old-fashioned steam engines. The owners made millions, until steam driven trains went the way of the Dodo. For years, the buildings lay vacant, decaying and rotting, that is, until someone came up with the brilliant idea of turning these dilapidated old buildings into condos for the rich. Can you imagine the cost of an apartment overlooking the Cumberland River and only a few steps from downtown Nashville?"

"I guess Jim Bennett is one of those with the brilliant idea," FJ said.

"I don't know if he came up with the idea, but his family was the original owners of these buildings."

"So, that's how he made his fortune," FJ said climbing out of the backseat.

"One of his ancestors made the money. Jim only grew it, into what it is today. What do they say? It takes money to make money — something like that. Today, Jim Bennett is the sole owner of the three adjacent buildings you see before you. He will undoubtable make multimillions on this venture. Now Mr. Johnston, shall we go inside?"

"By all means. But–"

"But?" Monroe interrupted. "Are you chickening out? Do you wish for us to return you to your trailer? We will if you want. Just say the word."

"Hell, no. But, before we go in, I'd like to know how you caught the monster."

"It would be my honor," Monroe said. "Unlike the cops, who spend most of their time chasing speeders, or monitoring stop signs and jaywalkers, or delivering summons, ticketing people for spitting on the sidewalk, or tracking down litterbugs; we had only one thing on our mind, one mission if you will, that of locating the suspect. From the BOLO, we knew the suspect was homeless, and probably living out of trashcans and dumpsters. It was the latter that did Mr. McBride in. Everyone has to eat. We planned on spending a few days in Franklin, and if nothing panned out, we would move to the next town along I-65.

"For a few hours, we staked out the restaurants around I-65. From I-65, we slowly made our way into town, stopping now and then at restaurants, Convenient Stores and Quick-Picks, anything with trashcans or dumpsters. At the Town Square, we had a good view of several downtown restaurants. After that, it was just a matter of playing cat and mouse.

"Luck is a fickle lady, but yesterday she smiled on us. Around four pm, we saw Mr. McBride coming out of the alley, beside the Brickyard Café. He acted and looked like the man in the BOLO. He appeared homeless and walked with a limp. So we followed him, and he led us to a deserted warehouse, on the southern part of the city. We watched as he crawled through a missing section of a chain-link fence and climbed through a broken window. After parking our car, Mr. Conrad and I walked around the building looking for any other signs of egress, other than the broken window. We found none, but that doesn't mean there wasn't any.

"We flipped a coin to determine who was going to stay outside and guard the window, and who was going to enter the building, in search of the suspect. I lost. While Mr. McBride made it look easy crawling through the window, I have to tell you; it was all I could do, getting through the window, without getting stuck. It was all Mr. Conrad could do, to keep from laughing and giving away our presence.

"It turned out, the warehouse the suspect set up home in, is a massive structure of rusting beams and columns, flaking grey and yellow paint, cracked concrete, trash, and puddles of rainwater. The building is laid out in an open pattern; the entire length of the one-hundred-yard structure. On each end of the warehouse, large sagging metal doors marked the only access in and out. We have no idea what the structure was used for, but by the looks of things, it's been years since it was last occupied. From dozens of broken windows running down both sides of the building, dust and pigeon poop could be seen covering most everything.

"In the dust on the floor, a much traveled trail of footprints led away from the window, toward a small metal shed at one end of the building. I would guess, the shed was probably used as an office sometime in the past. As quiet as I could, I made my way toward the shed with my sidearm drawn. (FJ raised an eyebrow) Mr. Johnston, there's no way I could determine if the suspect were armed or not. As I got near the shed, I noticed piles of fresh trash scattered about. To me, it looked like the suspect had been there several days.

"Standing by the only entrance into the tiny shed, I could hear murmurings coming from inside. It was like someone was carrying on a conversation. I heard things like– Hang in there ... We're almost home free ... I'll die before letting them take us again ... We shouldn't venture out during daylight hours ... What do you mean? No, I don't know where HQ is ... If you think you can do better, then you take over ... You get us food and water ... You watch out for the Taliban.

"If Mr. McBride wasn't talking, then he was moaning or crying. The man was hurting, and I don't mean physically. I felt sorry for him, and I had to keep reminding myself this monster raped and killed several people.

"Backing away from the shed a couple of yards, I yelled, 'Come out with your hands raised.' With a roar, Mr. McBride charged out of the shed, with what looked like a baseball bat raised in his hands. I–"

"A baseball bat?" FJ interrupted.

"It did look like a baseball bat, but it turned out to be a broken piece of a two-by-two. As he limped toward me, he swung the two-by-two. In defensive mode, I raised my gun-arm to take the blunt of the blow across my forearm, and with my free hand, I stuck Mr. McBride with an uppercut, which laid him out. I hurriedly checked the inside of the shed but found nothing of interest. As most serial killers like to do, Mr. McBride had taken no trophies that I could see.

"It didn't take much for us to get Mr. McBride into the trunk of the Town Car. Then, Mr. Conrad called Mr. Bennett and asked him where he wanted the suspect. He gave us this address and met us here with a key to the padlock on the door. Mr. Johnston, that just about sums it up. Any more questions?"

FJ shook his head.
"Good. Now, are you ready to go in?"
FJ nodded.

Chapter 51

The setting sun was casting long shadows, and the building's interior was growing increasingly darker, making it more difficult to see. Luckily, someone had strung a single electric line through the building with bare lightbulbs, at intervals of ten feet. The floor was a maze of broken timbers, electrical conduit, rusting pipes, drywall, slabs of broken concrete; all coated in rat crap and pigeon poop. In places, FJ found it hard going and had to be lifted over obstacles. By the time the three reached the back section of the building, all three were covered in nastiness.

The chamber they found themselves in was a cavernous collection of large rusting boilers, vats, forges, presses, industrial grinders, tables and tables of discarded rusted hand tools, and a spider web of rails, with broken down ore carts. Unsold stacks of train castings lay abandoned here and there. FJ could hear water lapping against pilings close by, which told him, they were near the river. In a small, cleared area located in the center of a cavern of darkness, a single lightbulb shone on a single chair, upon which a bound man was slumped over. Standing over the man was Jim Bennett Sr.

"This is a surprise," FJ said. "I thought Conrad was talking about Jim Jr."

FJ knew both Bennett's, Jr. and Sr., from basketball games where Innocence cheered, and Randy had played. Franklin was a small town.

"Welcome, Mr. Johnston," Senior said. "If you were expecting Junior, then I'm sorry to have to disappoint you. Don't take this wrong. My son is a good man, but he doesn't have the balls to

255

attempt something like this."

"Junior ... Senior ... It doesn't really matter to me," FJ came back.

Senior smiled. "I'm sorry I didn't wait for you to begin my 'questioning.' But truthfully, you haven't missed a thing. He's a stubborn son-of-a-bitch. Watch."

Raising his hand, Senior slapped McBride across the top of his head, which caused McBride to jerk his head back, exposing his bloody face. FJ turned from the carnage and almost walked away. If not for the knowledge that here sat Innocence's killer, he would have.

"Wade McBride, first sergeant, service number RA29037864, date-of-birth 11-30-1994," McBride croaked through bloody lips.

"What's his problem?" FJ asked.

"That's what he says every time I ask him a question," Senior replied, wiping McBride's blood from his hands on a towel.

"It's a POW thing," Conrad explained. "If captured, the Geneva Conventions says a soldier is to give only his name, rank, service number, and date-of-birth. At some time, our friend here must have been a prisoner of war. He says he was born in 1994, so I would guess he was taken prisoner in either Iraq or Afghanistan. That would explain his murmurings in the shed."

"Mr. Johnston, would you like to ask Mr. McBride a question?" Senior asked, stepping aside, giving FJ plenty of room. FJ came in close. For two weeks, this is what he'd been longing for, what he'd been dreaming of. Making a fist, he raised his fist.

This is for Innocence.

Then he paused; his fist hanging in midair. He couldn't believe it. He couldn't bring himself to hurt this wretched man any more than he already was.

"Mr. Johnston, is something wrong?" Senior asked.

"No," FJ replied. "I've been waiting so long for this moment. I'm thinking of what kind of question I'm going to ask."

"There's no hurry," Senior laughed.

Wade raised his face to FJ. "Water, please," he whispered.

"What did he say?" Senior asked. "I couldn't understand

him."

"He asked for water," FJ replied.

"I bet he did. The damned want water in Hell too."

"What's the harm in giving him a drink?" FJ asked.

"Are you going soft? Remember what he did to your granddaughter. Remember what he did to my grandson. Hell, he raped and murdered all those people up north. He's a damn serial killer. Mr. Johnston, he doesn't deserve our pity."

"Did you kill my granddaughter?" FJ asked McBride.

"Wade McBride, first sergeant, service number RA29037864, date-of-birth 11-30-1994."

"Damnit," FJ screamed in Wade's face. "Did you murder my granddaughter?"

Through wild bloodshot eyes, McBride yelled back, "I am a murderer." FJ backed off.

"There! Did you not hear him?" Senior asked. "In any court of law, that's a confession."

"Who did you murder?" FJ asked softly.

McBride sat there staring off into space, like he was reliving an experience.

"Tell me, who did you murder?" FJ asked softly.

"Men. Women. Children," McBride sobbed, "and babies. I killed babies."

"There were no babies murdered," FJ said, looking at Senior, Monroe, and Conrad.

"None that we know about," Senior assured him. "Who knows where he killed them. He may have killed hundreds of people."

"Where did you kill babies?" FJ asked. "Focus, man. Where did you kill babies?"

"Wade McBride, first sergeant, service number RA29037864, date-of-birth 11-30-1994."

"Son-of-a-bitch," FJ exclaimed, turning away from McBride. FJ stood staring at his feet. Turning back to McBride, he said, in his deepest voice of authority he could muster, "First Sergeant, I order you to answer my question. Where did you kill babies?"

"Mazari Sharif, Sir."

"Where in the Hell is Mazari Sharif?" FJ asked those around him.

"Afghanistan," Monroe answered. "I spent a tour in Kabul. Mazari Sharif is north of there. Near the Uzbekistan border."

"If you say so," FJ confessed. Turning his attention back to McBride, he said, "First Sergeant, take your time answering this. Stay focused soldier. Did you, or did you not, kill people when you returned to the states?"

"No ... Sir ... Sergeant Major ... Sir."

"So, Mr. Johnston, you're now an officer," Conrad laughed.

"Do we have water?" FJ asked Monroe.

"What do you think you're doing?" Senior asked.

"I'm giving a thirsty man something to drink. Can't you see he's suffering from PTSD?"

"You don't know that."

"Sure I do, and I'll tell you something else, I don't think he killed our kids."

"That's bullshit," Senior yelled. "We have the killer right here. By God, he just confessed."

"He confessed to killing people in a town called Mazari Sharif," FJ admitted, "a place no one's ever heard of (Monroe raised his hand), except Monroe. He killed in the line of duty. That's what soldiers are trained to do. Sadly, there's collateral damage. Yes, men, women, children, and even babies are killed. That's the horrors of war, but that doesn't mean he killed those people up north. Nor does it mean, he killed our grandchildren."

Senior turned away and began to cry. It was deathly quiet, except for Senior's sobs. Each man was lost in their own thoughts.

"Water, please," broke the silence.

"He could still be the killer," Senior said, when he regained his composure.

"You're right," FJ agreed. "But, my gut says different."

"So, what do you think we should do with him?" Senior asked. "Turn him loose?"

"No. We need to turn him over to the cops. Agent K and J

can then collect their bounty. (Both men smiled) Let the police get to the bottom of all this."

"How are we going to explain the beating he received?" Senior asked.

"What beating?" Monroe answered. "He fell down a big pile of something trying to escape."

"I saw it happen," Conrad added, as he handed FJ a bottle of water, with the cap already off.

As carefully as he could, FJ gave Wade a few sips.

Wade whispered, "I've done some bad things overseas, but I don't know anything about your kids."

"So, what now?" Senior asked.

"I'll give you and Mr. Johnston a ride back to Franklin, while Mr. Conrad stays with Mr. McBride," Monroe proposed. "You will go on with your lives, as nothing has happened. You both will act surprised, when you hear the suspect has been captured. Mr. Bennett, you will pay us the reward money. As far as we're concerned, this meeting never happened."

"The reward money was if the murderer was captured," Senior said.

"The reward was offered for information leading to the arrest of the murderer. Mr. McBride could still be the murderer or could have information leading to the murderer. But you have something more important to worry about."

"What's that?"

"You better hope Mr. McBride doesn't remember any of this shit, and press kidnapping charges against you and Mr. Johnston. Remember this. Only Mr. Conrad and I can alibi both of you. I think the $100,000 is worth keeping your asses out of prison."

"Alibi me for what?" FJ stressed. "I don't have his blood on my hands. I'm just a bystander."

"Isn't that what Pontius Pilate said?" Conrad asked.

"Are you trying to blackmail me?" Senior asked.

"I have no idea what you mean," Monroe said. "We caught the man everyone was searching for. That should be enough. Besides, the money will just barely cover our expenses. (Conrad laughed) So, the question for you Mr. Bennett, are you going to pay us or not?"

Defeated, Senior nodded.

Chapter 52

FJ had been pacing the floor for two days. Monroe and Conrad told him and Senior, they would hold on to McBride for a couple of days, to let his wounds heal a little; the wounds he suffered when he fell down an embankment trying to escape. Nod. Nod. Wink. Wink. Then they would turn him over to the state police. FJ knew Wade's capture would filter down to Ray.

It would be the headline story in the *Franklin Favorite,* Franklin's weekly newspaper. It would be the headline story in every newspaper in western Kentucky. Hell, in the state. FJ could see it now on *Fox News– I-65 Serial Killer Captured.*

FJ wondered what kind of lie Monroe and Conrad would come up with. More important, what would McBride say? He'd have no reason to lie. Bennett Senior said they could use PTSD, as an excuse for McBride's delusions on the matter. *For God's sake, the man still thought himself a prisoner of war.* It would be his word against theirs, and who would people believe? That question ate at FJ. *Who would people believe?* It never occurred to FJ, until now, if people believe McBride, then he and Senior could be going to jail for a very long time.

Something else that ate at FJ was the knowledge McBride wasn't the murderer, at least that's what he thought. And if that was true, then who was the killer? Ray's gut had a way of being right, and it wouldn't take his gut long to come to the conclusion McBride was innocent. *Then what? Should I tell Ray everything? Probably should. Probably won't.* The killer is still out there. What will it take to apprehend the monster? At that moment, someone slammed on the door. FJ almost shit his pants.

261

"Oh. Hi, Betty," FJ said, holding the door open.

"Oh. Hi, Betty," Betty replied, stepping in. "Is that all I get? I'm glad to see you too, Dad."

"I'm sorry. I'm really glad to see you, Sweetie. What brings you out this way?"

"Can't a daughter drop by to see her dad without having an agenda?"

"Yes. Sure. I'm sorry. But what brings you out this morning?"

"Tom's mad at me, and I needed to talk to someone."

"What's Tom's problem."

"Dad, I told Tom I wanted to move. No, I told Tom we needed to move. I can't spend another day in that house. Everywhere I look, I see Innocence. Her fragrance hangs thick in the air. It nauseates me. I know that sounds silly, but it's true. Dad, I can't force myself to enter her room. I try, but something stops me at the threshold. My mouth gets dry. My head spins. My body seems to have a will of its own and just won't enter."

"Have you told Doctor Jennings all this?"

"The shrink?" Betty exclaimed. "Dad, I'm not crazy."

"I didn't say you were. Sweetie, you've been through a lot. Maybe, she could give you something for your anxiety."

And get hooked on pills? I've heard all the horror stories. That ain't going to happen to me. No, thank you. The best thing for Tom and I is to move."

"And if you move, your anxiety will just up and go away?"

"Maybe not, but it wouldn't hurt to find out."

"Maybe, you and Tom need to take a long vacation, and get away from all this."

"That's a good idea."

"Betty, if you want, I can call Tom."

"Would you, Dad?"

"Sure. Tom loves you. You know that (Betty nodded), and he wants what's best for you."

"I know that, Dad. Maybe I'm overreacting, but if you could give him a call?"

"Not a problem."

Betty leaned over and put her head on FJ's shoulder. "Dad, you're the only family I have."

"Are you forgetting about your Mom?"

"I meant, the only family here."

"I'm sorry about that."

"Are you?" she asked, sitting back up. "Why didn't you go to Nashville to see her off?"

"Is that what this is all about, me not going to the airport?"

"No, I really told Tom we needed to move, and he really is mad at me. But why didn't you go and see Mom off? I thought you and she were getting along."

"Betty, there's getting along, and then there's getting along. I would say, we were just getting along."

"Still, why didn't you go to the airport? We were all there. You would have been safe."

"Safe?"

"As in, safety in numbers."

FJ laughed.

"You still haven't answered the question."

"Betty, I don't have an answer."

"Could it be you didn't want to go through it again?"

FJ sat there, staring at her.

"Could it be you didn't want the pain of a second parting?"

FJ shook his head.

"While you were in the hospital, she sat with you. Did you ever thank her?"

FJ turned his head and stared at the widescreen, stared at the refrigerator, stared at the stains on the carpet, stared anywhere, but at Betty.

"Remember that day on the patio," Betty continued, "when she came outside to talk with you? She told me she apologized. Did you say anything to her?"

"Why are you doing this?" he asked.

"I want to hear it from you. Why weren't you at the airport? She was hurt. Is that what you wanted? To hurt her?"

"No," FJ confessed. "Everything you've said is true, but not the hurting her part. I was afraid of being hurt, being hurt again. I couldn't go through it again. I regret not going, but that's behind us now. You still have her. She's just a phone call away."

"I know. I'll call her every day."

"So, how's she doing?" FJ asked, hoping to change the subject.

"She's well. She's glad being back, and they're glad having her back. I may go out in a couple of weeks. It would be fun reliving that kind of life for a couple of days."

"And, you'd be getting away from all this for a couple of days," FJ added.

"And, I'd be getting away from all this for a couple of days," Betty agreed.

FJ's phone rang.

Chapter 53

"It's Ray," FJ said to Betty, pointing at his phone. He had seen Ray's name on Caller-ID.

"What's up, Ray?"

"I've got some news for you," Ray replied.

Oh crap, here it comes, FJ thought.

"Betty's here right now. Can it wait?" FJ asked, trying to stall.

"No, that's great. Betty needs to hear this, as well. Put your phone on speaker."

FJ smiled at Betty.

"You're on speaker Ray," FJ said. "Go ahead."

"Don't call me a gourd-head," Ray laughed. "You get it? Go ahead. Gourd-head. That joke never gets old."

"After hearing that joke from you a hundred-million times, it has gotten old," FJ assured him.

"Hey, Betty," Ray said, ignoring FJ.

"Hey, Ray. I liked your joke," Betty laughed.

FJ rolled his eyes.

"Thanks, Betty. Some people have a sense of humor," Ray laughed. "I got some news from Jenny Broxon. Do you guys remember her? She's the state cop from Frankfort."

"We remember her. What did she have to say?" FJ asked. *Like I don't already know. I think I'm going to puke. I hope I don't puke in front of Betty. I hope I don't puke on Betty. Has she ever seen me puke? Probably as many times as she's seen me fallen down drunk, which sadly is a lot.*

"They caught the homeless man," Ray replied.

There was silence.

"You guys still there? I said they caught the homeless man."

"We heard you, Ray," Betty said. "It's just hard to believe. Who caught him?"

"The men in black."

"Who?" Betty asked, confused.

"The two private investigators from Nashville, Monroe, and Conrad. Betty, they always wear black, just like the guys in the movie. Don't tell me you never saw the movie?"

"Yes, I've seen it," Betty answered. "How did they catch him? When did they catch him? Where did they catch him? Is he really the killer? Did he confess? Why did he do it? What happens to him now?"

"Slow down with all the questions. You're making my head spin."

"Okay. First question. How did they catch him?"

"That's a good question. Jenny gave me their number, so I called them. Let me tell you what they told me. A couple of days ago, they were at the rest area at the Kentucky-Tennessee state line. You see, they'd been checking out the towns up and down I-65. They had just stopped to take a pee and to get a snack from the machines, when one of them noticed a man at the back of the rest area, behind where the big rigs park, going through one of the dumpsters. They also noticed, the man had a limp and looked like he hadn't changed his clothes in months. How lucky was that?"

Real lucky, FJ thought. *So lucky, they need to buy a Powerball ticket.*

"The man must have seen them," Ray continued, "because before they knew it, he had climbed over the rest area fence and was heading across the *Kentucky Downs* racetrack. According to Monroe and Conrad, that's the investigator's names, *(You told us that already)* it was late in the day, and the racetrack was already closed to the public. Because of that, there was only a handful of track personnel around. Some were on mowers, cutting and grooming the turf. Some were exercising horses, while others were hauling manure in wagons to dump somewhere on the property. I'm sure you know; *Kentucky Downs* is a one of a kind racetrack.

It's a European-style course. (Ray couldn't see them, but both Betty and FJ were nodding) Its surface is all grass instead of dirt, and it is not an oval."

"Yes, Ray," FJ said flatly. "I've lost my 401K there many times."

Ray continued like he hadn't heard.

"So, they didn't catch him there?" FJ asked.

"Nope. So, this is where Conrad takes over with the story. Back at the track, Conrad sees the suspect running back along a service road, toward a big patch of woods, between the interstate and the racetrack. It turns out, the woods are located on a big rocky bluff. When they built the interstate, they went around the bluff, instead of plowing through it. I heard the cost to remove all that rock was more than relocating the road. Anyway, giving pursuit, the investigators, because of the suspect's limp, slowly gained on the man. Desperately trying to escape, the suspect, after making the woods, tried to run down the bluff through the woods, which turns out, was too steep, rocky, and woody; he slipped, or tripped and took a tumble, landing mostly on his face."

"That's amazing," Betty said.

"Yeah. I think so too," Ray added.

"The sound of your voice tells me you're not buying their story," FJ surmised.

"It doesn't add up," Ray said. "From Monroe's account, the only ones to see the suspect was the two investigators. No one else saw him running across the track, and there were men mowing, people exercising horses, and stable hands getting rid of horse shit. Surely, someone would have seen a man being chased, by two men in black. Dozens of men searched the stables and surrounding buildings. Again, according to Monroe's story, no one ever saw him. Only after they were about to give up, did one of the investigators see the man. Again, no one else sees him. And this tumble in the woods doesn't add up. How come only his face was injured? When people tumble down anything, most of the time, more than their faces get damaged.

"Monroe and Conrad, the investigators, *(Again Ray, we know*

267

their names and what they do for a living thought FJ.) took Wade McBride, the suspect, to the hospital, and they got him cleaned up. Monroe and Conrad called the state police, who called Jenny, who called Monroe and Conrad back. She told them to bring him here. Then Jenny called the station, and finally, Susan called me. Hell must have frozen over, because Susan had a fresh pot of coffee waiting when I arrived. I got to the office before Monroe and Conrad, so I called George Watson. Turns out, somewhere in the mix, Jenny had already called him, and he was on his way in. Jenny will be here sometime tomorrow. The long and short, the suspect is now in our jail."

"Did he confess?" Betty asked.

"No. The guy's a wacko. It's like he's a POW or something. The only thing he's saying is his name, rank, service number, and date-of-birth."

"Ray, do you think he did it?" Betty asked, hoping for closure.

"I don't know, Betty. Maybe. Logic says he did, but I don't know."

"Why did he do it?" Betty asked.

"Betty, he hasn't confessed," Ray said, "and I'm not sure he's the one we're after."

"Your gut thing, right?" Betty asked sarcastically. "You made that clear. But he was seen up in Park City coming out of a house, with a murdered person inside. Is that just a coincidence?"

"I don't believe in coincidences," Ray confessed. "Okay, he was seen leaving the house, but that doesn't mean he killed her. He's homeless. He's going to hang out in abandoned buildings. Betty, that alone doesn't make him a murderer."

"So, what now? You going to arrest him?"

"Arrest him for what? Again, there's no proof he's our killer. I can hold him a couple of days for being a vagrant. He's also a flight risk. For that, I might be able to hold him a while longer for questioning. He knows something, but getting inside his head is going to be a challenge."

"So, what are you going to do?"

"The first thing, I'm going to call the D.A. and make sure how long I can keep him. Then, I'm calling in a shrink."

"Ray, can I see him?" Betty asked.

"I'm not sure that would be helpful."

"What harm would there be? The station has one-way glass, doesn't it?"

"Sure. Doesn't everybody?"

"Then he won't see us."

"Us?"

"I assume Dad is coming," Betty replied, looking at FJ.

"How about it, FJ? You coming?" Ray asked.

"I guess."

"You guess?" Betty asked, questioning his hesitation. "Don't you want to see him?"

FJ took a long breath and slowly exhaled.

Chapter 54

Betty parked in the visitor's parking lot, in the back of the police station, next to a black Lincoln Town car.

Holy crap, FJ thought.

Betty got out of the car and walked around the front to FJ's side. He sat there, staring at the Town Car.

"Are you getting out?" she asked.

"Oh, yeah," he replied, opening the car door. He wished he had a Gin and Tonic. Make that a tall one.

"What's wrong, Dad?"

He wanted to tell her, that he didn't want to go in. He wanted to tell her to take him home. He wanted to tell her, somehow McBride would see him and spill the beans. Okay, maybe not the last part. It was finally beginning to sink in, that he could end up in jail for kidnapping.

"Nothing's wrong," he assured her, smiling. *That's a big lie.*

Ray met them at the back door and motioned them in.

"Here. Put these on and follow me over to interrogation," He said, handing each a visitor badge. Walking through a couple of hallways, they passed Susan getting herself a cup of coffee.

"Hi, Betty," Susan said.

"Hi, Susan. How are you doing?" Betty asked.

"I'm fine, sweetie. Hi, Frederick."

"Susan," Frederick nodded.

"Sugar, can you do me a favor?" Susan asked, looking down at Frederick.

"What's that," Frederick replied, nervously. You never knew what kind of favor Susan was going to ask. Once, she had asked

271

FJ to shoot her neighbor's dog for digging and pooping in her flowerbeds. It turns out, she was only kidding, but at first, it didn't seem that way.

"Can I take a selfie of me and you?" she asked.

"I guess," FJ replied, looking at Ray and Betty. "I don't have a problem with that."

"Susan, why do you want a selfie of you and FJ?" Ray asked suspiciously.

"Can't a friend take a picture of a friend?"

"And what are you planning on doing, with a picture of your friend?"

"I don't know what you mean."

"Susan."

"Okay. I was going to post it on Facebook."

"That's so sweet," Betty said.

"And?" Ray asked.

"And tell everybody, it's my friend and me."

"Your friend?"

"Yes. Me and my friend, Peter Dinklage."

"I don't have a problem with that," FJ chimed in.

"I didn't think you wanted your picture out there posing as the actor," Betty stated.

"But, it's not me claiming to be Peter Dinklage. It's Susan. And I don't have a problem with that."

"But, I do," Ray said, walking away. "No selfies today, Susan."

"You're a hard man, Sheriff. A hard man," Susan said, disappointed.

As they walked away, FJ looked back at Susan and mouthed, "Later."

Ray stopped outside a door with a sign that read, "Interrogation."

"Before we go in, I should tell you, there are several people waiting inside. George is here, of course. It's his case. Jim Bennett and his father are here, along with their lawyer Harold King. Mr. Monroe and Mr. Conrad are present," Ray said, reaching for the doorknob.

How am I supposed to act? FJ thought, as Ray opened the door. *I know I've met Jim Junior and Senior at Innocence's ballgames. I have no reason for ever having met the men in black. As far as the world's concerned, they're strangers to me. The thing for me to do is to keep my mouth shut and hope no one screws up.*

Ray motioned inside. "Ladies first." Betty went in. Taking a deep breath, FJ followed. The small room was extremely crowded. All the players were here. George nodded at Betty and FJ. They nodded back. A man Betty had never met walked over and took her by the hand. "Hello, I'm Ethan Monroe. This is my associate Phillip Conrad. We own a small private investigation agency in Nashville."

"You're the men who caught the killer," Betty stated.

"We're the men who caught a suspect in a murder. That's correct," Phillip Conrad corrected. "Whether he's a killer or not, is yet to be seen."

"I want to thank you, both of you," Betty said. Both smiled.

"You must be Frederick Johnston," Conrad said, holding out his hand to FJ. FJ nodded.

"Do you know Frederick?" Ray asked.

"Oh, we've never met. But, in our line of work, we need to know all those involved. We were told one of the victims had a grandfather, who was a little person."

"Dwarf," FJ corrected.

"I beg your pardon," Conrad said.

"I was born with dwarfism, so that makes me a dwarf."

"I'm sorry. Anyway, I'm glad to meet you. The Sheriff just introduced us to the Bennett's."

"Good day, Mr. Johnston," Jim Junior said. "I don't know if you remember me, but we've met at one of the kid's ballgames."

"I remember."

"I'm Randy's granddad, Jim Senior," Senior said, extending his hand, which FJ took. "I too met you at one of their games."

"I also remember you," FJ added. *That was easier than I thought.*

The two Bennett's and their lawyer nodded to Betty. She

remembered meeting the Bennett's at several games. She didn't recall the lawyer.

"Well, Sheriff," Jim Senior said, "now that we know one another, can we see the suspect?"

"Sure. You can see him. Remember, he can't see you."

Just like Law and Order, FJ thought. *Cool.*

Walking over, Ray pulled a cord and a blind raised, revealing the interrogation room. On the other side of the one-way glass, FJ could see McBride sitting on the opposite side of a metal table, with one hand cuffed to a metal ring in the table. On either side of McBride stood two state police officers, with their hands behind their backs.

Just like Law and Order.

Sitting on this side of the table, with her back to them, sat a women FJ had never met. He wondered if she was one of the Assistant District Attorneys.

Wade McBride looked like crap, not as bad as he looked in the warehouse, but still bad. Someone had tried to clean him up; whether it was the bounty hunters or the hospital, FJ didn't know.

"His face," FJ croaked. "He got that falling down a slippery slope?"

"It was more like falling off a fricking cliff," Monroe answered.

Yeah, but we know better, don't we? FJ thought, looking at Jim Senior.

"Who's the A.D.A.?" FJ asked.

"You even know what an A.D.A. is?" Ray asked.

"Hey, I've watched all four hundred and fifty-six episodes of *Law and Order*," FJ replied.

"Wow, and no, she's not an A.D.A.," Ray said. "She's Doctor Alice Payne. She's the shrink the state sent in to help. She's supposed to be one of the best."

"Has she gotten anything out of him?"

"Not yet, but she's only been here for half an hour. The only thing she's got is his name, rank, service number, and date-of-birth. I bet it takes hours to get anything useful."

As if she had heard him, Doctor Payne rose from her chair,

exited the viewing room, and softly closed the door behind her.

"That was quick," Ray said.

"We've only just begun," she said. "I–"

"Wasn't that a song by the Carpenters?" FJ asked, interrupting.

Ignoring FJ, Doctor Payne continued, "I need to take Mr. McBride down to Vanderbilt."

"Why Vanderbilt?" Ray asked.

"They have the best facility in this part of the country. Sheriff, what little time I've spent with your suspect, I can easily see he is suffering from PTSD, and most likely, TBI."

"TB who's it?" FJ asked.

"TBI. Traumatic Brain Injury. It's a disruption in the normal function of the brain. It can be caused by a bump, a blow, or jolt to the head, or by a penetrating head injury. More and more of the victims now-a-days, sadly, are infants. When I say sadly, I mean babies in abusive homes. Some of our service men and women who have been in an extreme explosion suffer from TBI."

"How can you tell if Wade McBride suffers from TBI?" Ray asked.

"We will perform an MRI on Mr. McBride. If he does have TBI, it will show up as black spots inside his brain."

"Is there any cure or treatment?"

"If there's severe damage, what's done is done. With rest and medicine, I believe your suspect should, could, come out of it enough to live a semi-normal life."

"Doctor, we have questions for him."

"Questions that you will be able to ask, in a couple of days."

"Doctor?"

"I'm sorry, Sheriff. If we push him too hard, I'm afraid of what could happen."

"What if you took it real slow?"

"Which is what I plan on doing."

"Doctor, he might be a serial killer, or he may have seen the killer. McBride could pick him out of a photo line-up."

"I've read his case file."

"The real killer could be getting away. Worse, he could be

killing someone right now. We don't want that."

"No, we don't. Sheriff, right this minute I don't know how bad Mr. McBride's condition is. If it's not too severe and with the proper medication, he might open up as early as tomorrow afternoon, but Sheriff, don't hold your breath."

"So, what do you recommend we do?"

"Go about your daily routines like Mr. McBride is not your number one suspect."

For a moment Ray just stood there, his eyes darting from Doctor Payne, to the men in black, to the Bennett's, to Harold King, to Betty and FJ, to Wade McBride, to George, and finally coming back to rest on Doctor Payne.

"You're right, Doc. I've made this whole thing way to complicated. I should throw out all the noise and chatter, and concentrate on the basic elements, just those things I know."

Chapter 55

FJ hadn't left his trailer since he left the police station two days ago. "Why not?" he asked his image, in the bathroom mirror.

"Because you're afraid someone will point their finger at you and tell the world you did it," his mirror image replied.

"But I didn't do it. I never laid a hand on him."

"Yeah. All McBride has to do is point his finger at you, and your ass is grass."

"Jesus, aren't you listening? I didn't do anything."

"I know that, but they don't. Didn't Monroe and Conrad tell you to keep a low profile? To keep to the story."

"What do you think I'm doing?"

"Hiding like a scared little bunny rabbit is not the same thing, as keeping a low profile."

FJ pitched himself a finger.

"And why did you send the girls away? They could have helped you forget your worries, for a few hours."

FJ pitched himself another finger.

Twenty or thirty minutes ago, FJ didn't remember, the two volleyball girls from Western had shown up at his door wanting to party. Never in his life had FJ ever passed up an opportunity to party with a beautiful girl more than half his age, let alone two beautiful girls more than half his age. But when he opened his door, he couldn't let them in. He didn't know why. He knew his spirit was willing, but he knew his body was weak. He was afraid he couldn't get it up, and that had never happened. He apologized, saying he had come down with something and he didn't want to infect them. With concern, their eyes suddenly grew bigger, larger.

277

"No. No. No, it's not some STD," he assured them. "Just a little urinary tract infection. I'll be fine in a couple of days."

He stood in the doorway, watching as their little red T-Bird pulled out of the driveway. No sooner had they pulled out, the black Lincoln Town car pulled in.

"Holy shit. What do they want?"

"Mr. Johnston," Monroe said, getting out of the Lincoln, "did we just see, what we just saw, leaving your domicile?"

"It depends on what you think you just saw?" FJ replied, turning back into the trailer.

"Two glorious angels driving away in a red T-Bird," Conrad said, stepping inside.

"You have good eyesight, Mr. Conrad," FJ agreed. "What brings you two out my way?"

"Just in the neighborhood."

Yeah. Right. FJ thought.

"Have a seat," FJ said, motioning toward the couch. FJ pulled a dining room chair around for himself.

"We were wondering how you were holding out," Monroe said, looking around the trailer.

"I'm fine," FJ replied.

"People in your situation have been known to freak out and do something they would later regret."

"My situation?"

"Come on, Mr. Johnston. I bet your insides are tied up in knots. You're afraid, and rightly so, that everything is going to come out. You're afraid of going to jail. Isn't that so?"

"Okay, I have thought of that. So, why are you here?"

"We're here to give you support. If you keep your cool, it will be our word against their suspect. By our word, I mean not only Mr. Conrad and myself, but also the Bennett's. We just came from Jim Junior's house. Luckily, his father was also there. We told them the same thing we're telling you. Keep cool and stick to the story."

"Speaking of the story," FJ said. "That's some whooper you came up with. How much did you have to pay the guys at the racetrack?"

"Pay them for what?" Monroe asked.

"For going along with your story."

"They 'went' along with the story, because that's what happened. Nowhere in the story do the searchers ever say they saw the suspect. Nowhere. Because they didn't. It was Mr. Conrad and myself who said we saw the limper crossing the racetrack and entering the paddock. It was Mr. Conrad who said he saw Mr. McBride leaving the track and entering the woods. Yes, we went there and went through all the movements in the story.

"You see, we had stopped at the rest area on our way back to Kentucky, to get ourselves and Mr. McBride some refreshments, before turning him over to the authorities. Mr. McBride was in the trunk at the time. While watching the activities at the track, Mr. Conrad came up with the story. It was brilliant, I might add. (Conrad smiled) So, we climbed the fence and played the rest by ear from there. Yesterday, I heard it from a friend of mine, who has a jockey friend, who said your sheriff called the racetrack and talked with the Racing Vet on duty that day. The Racing Vet backs our story. He has to of course, because that's what happened."

"You guys are good," FJ admitted, feeling better. "But what happens if McBride does remember?"

"Just stick to the story, Mr. Johnston. Just stick to the story."

"FYI, Ray doesn't believe your story," FJ said. "Too many holes."

"It doesn't matter, does it?" Monroe asked. "Just stick to the story."

***

Ray spent yesterday and today going over the events of Innocence's murder. He had put aside Randy's murder, the I-65 murders, the men in black, and Wade McBride. One thing at a time. Ray believed in the KISS theory–Keep It Simple Stupid. Work on one thing at a time. Ray felt if he solved Innocence's murder, it would also solve Randy's murder. They had to be connected. The evidence suggested that. How else could a strand of Innocence's hair end up in Randy's head wound? His gut told him the other murders weren't connected at all. They just couldn't be. If they were, he would never find the killer. It would become a cold case. Dave woke up from his afternoon nap, and Ray's phone rang.

For fifteen minutes, Ray sat there in silence, listening and staring down at the folders on his desk. When the caller had finished, Ray thanked her and said he'd get back. For a minute longer, he sat there staring down at the folders on his desk.

"Susan, is Deputy Glover still here?"

"Yes, he's getting me a cup of coffee."

"Could you and he please come in here?"

"Right Now?"

Ray didn't answer.

"On our way, Sheriff ... From the phone call and you just sitting there, something bad must have happened," Susan said, as she closed the door behind herself and Deputy Glover.

"You've been eavesdropping?"

"As always."

"Susan, I want you to print out two arrest warrants for me to sign. Deputy, I want you to deliver one of the warrants, while I deliver the other."

"Simultaneous, just like a sting operation," Glover said.

"Yeah, just like a sting operation."

"Should I take backup?"

"No. You don't need backup."

"Sheriff, whose names do you want me to put on the arrest warrants?" Susan asked.

"Jim Bennett Senior, and Milton Frederick Johnston."

Chapter 56

FJ answered the door on the first knock.

"Come on in Ray," FJ said, backing away from the door. "Do you bring good news or bad news?"

"When have I brought good news lately? No, FJ. Don't say another word, without your lawyer being present."

"What are you saying? Lawyer? I don't have a lawyer."

"Then the judge will appoint one for you. And FJ, no matter what you've seen on TV, the lawyer won't be free."

"What in the hell are you talking about? Lawyer? Judge?" *McBride must have remembered and spilled his guts. Stick to the story.*

"Milton Frederick Johnston, I'm arresting you for–"

Ray's phone dinged. It was a text from Susan.

"Sheriff, Glover just brought in Jim Bennett Senior. Mr. Bennett wants to call his lawyer."

Ray texted back, "Susan, let him call his lawyer. And, because he asked for his lawyer, you can't ask him any questions."

"FJ," Ray said, putting the phone back in his pocket, "I'm arresting you for–"

Ray's phone dinged again. It was another text from Susan.

"Does that mean, I can't ask him if he wants a cup of coffee?"

Ray texted back, "You can ask him if he wants a cup of coffee. You cannot ask any questions about the arrest warrant. Now, stop texting me."

"I'm sorry, FJ. Let me try this again. Milton Frederick Johnston, I'm arresting you for the kidnapping and torture of Mr. Wade McBride. You have the right to remain silent. Anything you say, can and will be used against you, in a court of law. You have the

281

right to an attorney. If you cannot afford an attorney, one will be–"

"I know the rest," FJ interrupted. "Ray, I know my rights."

"Are you sure? I don't want to screw this up. I've seen Lennie Briscoe and his partner, what's his name, screw up too many times."

"He had several partners, but the one I liked most was Mike Logan, and yes, I'm sure I understand my rights," FJ answered, holding out his hands.

"What?"

"Handcuffs."

"Are you going to try anything? (FJ shook his head) Then I think we're good. And, you don't have to ride in the back, no matter what you've seen on *Law and Order*. You can ride up front with me. Do you have anything to say for yourself?"

"I have the right to be silent."

Ray sighed. "Yes, my friend, you do."

The ride back into town was in silence.

Susan met Ray and FJ at the receiving section reserved for prisoners, with her cell phone in hand.

"And, what are you going to do with that?" Ray asked, indicating the phone.

"Do you how much money the tabloids will pay for a video of Peter Dinklage in handcuffs and being arrested?"

"First off," Ray said, taking her phone, "this is not Peter Dinklage, as you well know."

"But, the tabloids don't," she chimed in.

"Second. I want all this kept hush hush for now. I don't want to embarrass anyone, if I can keep from it. Third, if you look closely, you'll see, there are no handcuffs."

"Sugar, did you do it?" Susan asked FJ.

"I have the right to be silent," FJ replied.

"Hmmm. Sugar, I can see you being somebody's little prison bitch."

Staring at Susan with his mouth wide open, FJ was led by Ray to fingerprinting and booking.

"Susan's just pulling your chain," Ray said, trying to cheer up his friend. "But, when you're in prison, if you drop your bar of soap in the shower, don't bend over to pick it up."

"How's my client?" someone asked, coming up from behind. "I hope they're treating you well."

Ray and FJ didn't have to turn to the voice. They've heard it too much lately. It was Harold King.

"You're not my lawyer," FJ said.

"Do you have a lawyer?" Harold asked.

"No. But, I sure as hell can't afford you."

"Seeing that you and Mr. Bennett are being arrested for the same offence, I see no reason I can't represent both of you. You being pro bono, of course."

"Of course," Ray said. "And you wouldn't want their stories contradicting each other."

"My dear Sheriff, if they tell the truth and nothing but the truth, their stories won't contradict."

"If they tell the truth."

"So, Mr. Johnston, do you want me to be your counselor or not?"

"For free?" FJ asked.

"For free," Harold replied. FJ nodded.

"By the way counselor," Ray commented, "Monroe and Conrad have been arrested and are in route to Franklin, where they will be booked."

Harold raised an eyebrow.

"You know," Ray continued, "it may all come down to where the crimes were committed, if committed they were. According to the private dicks, Mr. McBride was captured and hence, the alleged kidnapping, at the rest area. That's in Kentucky. But where was he tortured? Was he taken to Tennessee, or was he tortured in Kentucky? Who has jurisdiction for which crime?"

"That doesn't matter to me," Harold said flatly. "I'm licensed in both states."

"It doesn't matter to me," Ray came back. "We'll let the courts fight that battle."

"Sheriff, is there no way we could all sit down and discuss this?" Harold asked.

"I'm working on it," Ray answered. "I've got a call in to Judge Chu. I want to see if we can get everyone together and sort things out, before this goes to trial."

"I wonder if they have lawyers," Harold said, walking away.

"Who?"

"Monroe and Conrad. I'll get back with you Sheriff, later today."

"I know you will," Ray said, rubbing his head.

Dave was tap-dancing to Elvis' *Jailhouse Rock,* on his temples.

"FJ, you'll be held here tonight and arraigned tomorrow morning. I'm sure Judge Chu will have it all figured out by then. Is there someone you want me to call?"

"Would you call Betty and tell her everything, and that I'm fine, and she doesn't have to come down here?"

"Will do. If you need anything, just tell Susan or one of the deputies."

Ray called Betty, and within the hour, Betty was at the police station.

Chapter 57

This is costing me precious time in solving the two murders, Ray thought as he unlocked FJ's and Jim's cell door, *but what's another week, when you've got nothing to go on?*

"Come on, guys. Let's get you arraigned."

Today, Judge Chu's courtroom was empty, except for Harold King, the stenographer, the judge's assistance, and the bailiff.

"Good morning, Frederick," the bailiff said, as they walked in. "How are you doing?"

"Good morning, Lee," FJ said back at him. "How am I doing? Just like the color of my jumpsuit, I'm just peachy, and you?"

"Doing well. My granddaughter lost her first tooth yesterday afternoon. Do you know how much the Tooth Fairy is giving for teeth nowadays? (FJ shook his head) Five dollars. Can you believe that? When I was little, I used to get a nickel."

"It's called having cheap parents," FJ said, looking around. "Just kidding, Lee. I'm a little nervous right now."

"I bet you are," Bailiff Lee said. "Frederick, I'm sorry you're here."

"Thanks, Lee. Me too."

"Jim, you and Frederick stand by me," Harold said, pointing to his side, "and let me do all the talking."

"All stand for the Honorable Judge Chu," Lee said, as the judge's chamber door opened.

"Be seated," Chu said, as she took her seat. "Christy, what have we here?"

A.D.A Christy Igleheart handed the docket sheet to the bailiff, who handed it to the judge. "Your Honor, we have two arrest

285

warrants for the kidnapping and torture of one Wade McBride. Seeing that both warrants are for the same crime, and both of the men accused have the same counsel, we're booking them together."

Judge Chu scanned the paperwork. "Harold, I take it you're representing both men?"

"Yes, Your Honor."

"How do you clients plead?"

"Both plead not guilty, Your Honor."

"Bail?" Judge Chu asked.

"We feel both men are not flight threats, Your Honor," A.D.A. Igleheart said. "Mr. Bennett is well known. His interests rest here in Franklin. The same is true of Mr. Johnston. We see no reason that they can't be released on their own ROR."

FJ raised an eyebrow.

"ROR, Mr. Johnston," his lawyer explained, "means, release on one's own recognizance. You won't have to return to jail before the trial, and bail money is not necessary. Correct, Your Honor?"

"Works for me," Judge Chu said. "Trial will be this time next week. I see no one else waiting in line, so good day to you all."

The judge rose and exited the room. The A.D.A. placed the signed docket sheet back in her briefcase and turned to leave.

"Christy, a moment of your time, please," Harold said.

"Yes, counselor."

"I was wondering if we could have a 'queen for a day?'"

"A queen for a day?" FJ asked. "Wasn't that a TV show back in the sixties?"

"I wouldn't know Mr. Johnston," The A.D.A confessed. "I wasn't alive back then. In legal terms, 'a queen for a day' is a proffer, allowing prosecutors and individuals under criminal investigation to tell the government about their knowledge of a crime, with the supposed assurance that their words will not be used against them in any later proceedings. Of course, any evidence collected could and would be used against them."

"What they said, could that be used to uncover evidence against them?" FJ asked.

"Yes. That's one of the dangers of a queen for a day."

286

"That's true, Mr. Johnston," Harold admitted, "but, if it's possible to get all the players together, my four clients and the victim for a sit down, we could hopefully sort things out and save the tax-payers the cost of a trial. Christy, I'm sure your boss would like that."

"What do you mean, your four clients?"

"Not only am I representing Mr. Johnston and Mr. Bennett, but I'm also the counsel for Mr. Monroe and Mr. Conrad."

"When did that happen?" the A.D.A. asked.

"Early this morning. So, can we have a queen for a day?"

"I see no reason why we couldn't. I'll have to okay it with the Judge, and Mr. McBride's doctor, to see if Mr. McBride is up to it."

"Would you please?"

"I'll get back with you this afternoon."

"Thanks Christy."

After the A.D.A. had left, Harold turned to his clients. "You're free to go. So, why don't I run you guys over to the jail and you can change out of those clothes and get your personal items. If that's okay with you, Sheriff."

"That's fine," Ray replied. "FJ, do you want me to run you home?"

"Thank you Sheriff, but I can run him home," Harold replied, before FJ could open his mouth. "I need to have a word with my client, and we can do that on the way to his house."

"I understand," Ray said, turning to leave.

"Thanks Ray," FJ said.

"FJ, if you need anything, call," Ray said.

"I will."

Chapter 58

Ray knocked on the Judge's chamber door, which was opened by the Bailiff.

"Good morning, Sheriff," he said.

"Good morning, Lee."

"Come on in. Everyone's here."

As Ray stepped into the room, he noticed everyone was present. The judge was sitting at her desk. Harold and his four clients were on the left side of the conference table. A.D.A. Christy Igleheart, along with Doctor Alice Payne and Wade McBride, sat on the other side.

"I'm sorry I'm late, Your Honor," Ray said as he walked over.

"You're not late Sheriff," Chu stated. "You're right on time. Why don't you take a seat at the end of the table? Would you like some coffee, water, or juice?"

"No, thank you, Your Honor."

"Very well. Then let's get this over with. Harold, according to Christy you wanted to have a queen for a day. (Harold nodded) Surely, you know how dangerous that can be. (Harold nodded) Very well. Why we couldn't wait till the trial, is beyond me."

"Your Honor, we could have indeed waited till trial," Harold explained, "but we were hoping, to avoid a trial."

"Go on," Chu said, taking a sip of her coffee.

"My clients feel–"

"Water," McBride interrupted, drawing everyone's attention.

"What was that?" Judge Chu asked.

"He wants a drink of water," Frederick answered, sliding off his chair and walking toward the Judge's bar.

289

"Frederick, you'll find a small frig under the bar," Chu said, pointing.

Frederick returned with a clear plastic bottle of water. Removing the cap, Frederick offered the bottle to McBride, who took the bottle with his right hand and grabbed Frederick with his left. Raising the bottle to his lips, he took a long pull.

"Thank you for giving me a drink of water," McBride said, looking Frederick directly in the eyes.

"You're welcome," Frederick replied. McBride released Frederick's arm.

"Your Honor, I have something I'd like to say," McBride said, looking at the Judge.

"Are you up for it?" Judge Chu asked.

"I am," McBride replied.

"Then, by all means, continue."

"I don't know this little person."

There was a low murmuring among those around the table.

"Dwarf," Frederick corrected.

McBride smiled.

"I don't know this dwarf, Your Honor."

"Are you sure, Mr. McBride?"

"I have never seen him before."

"But, you said—"

"This man has never done anything to me, except give me a drink of water," McBride said, holding up the plastic bottle.

"Are you sure, Mr. McBride?" Judge Chu asked, but looking at Doctor Payne.

"Your Honor," Doctor Payne said, "If I may?"

"Go ahead."

Ray wanted to say, "Gourd-head," but bit his lip.

"We tested Mr. McBride for TBI and found none. He is now back on his meds for PTSD. I would say, if Mr. McBride says Mr. Johnston isn't the man, then Mr. Johnston isn't the man."

Judge Chu nodded.

"Your Honor," McBride added. "When I was brought in, I'd been off my medications for months. Now that I am again stable,

I'm not sure there ever was a little person, I mean dwarf."

Judge Chu looked at every person around the room. "In that case, I don't see why the charges against Mr. Johnston can't be dropped. Does anyone object?"

There was only silence.

"Does the District Attorney's office object?"

"No, Your Honor. I don't see how we can."

"Very well. Mr. Johnston, the charges against you have been dropped. You're free to go, and I'm sorry for any inconvenience."

"Thank you, Your Honor," Frederick said, rising to leave.

Looking over at McBride, Frederick nodded. McBride nodded back.

As Ray and FJ were leaving, they heard Harold King say, "Your Honor, if Mr. McBride was confused about Mr. Johnston, could he also be confused about my other clients?"

"Well, Mr. McBride?" Judge Chu asked.

"No, Your Honor, I'm not confused about any of them."

"Then let's continue with our queen for a day."

That was all Ray and FJ heard as they shut the door behind them.

"So, sometime before today, you gave McBride a drink of water," Ray remarked, as they walked away.

"I did," FJ replied, taking a deep breath.

"I thought so. FJ, my friend, you're one lucky little shit."

"And, I have a big–"

"Enough," Ray interrupted. "FJ, there are things we need to talk about, things that should have been answered before now."

"I know, Ray. It's long overdue. Can we talk at your house?"

"I don't know why not."

"Over drinks?"

"It's awful early."

"Not if you just got out of jail."

"Agreed."

For the rest of the day, Ray and FJ spent their time alone, on Ray's patio, drinking and going over FJ's story.

Chapter 59

Since seven o'clock that morning, Ray had been parked in the student parking lot at the Franklin-Simpson High School. He had parked in the back, hopefully out of sight from any of the faculty. As students were walking into school, Ray would walk most of the way with them, and as they were walking, he would "accidently" bring up Innocence. *No harm in that,* he told himself. But that wasn't true, and he knew it. This was one of those "you could lose your badge and job" moments–talking with minors without their parents present. But it had been over three weeks, and Ray was spinning his wheels going nowhere in trying to solve her murder.

After talking with FJ yesterday, Ray decided to go back to his original idea; Innocence's death was a crime of passion, and the murderer had to have known both Innocence and Randy. Which means, it had to be someone both knew, and the likely "someone" was one of their classmates, coaches, or teachers. Two hours had now gone by and the likelihood of getting caught by a schoolteacher was increasing. *Reminds me of those days smoking in the boy's room.*

"Good morning," Ray said, as a young lady got out of her car with a backpack. "I'm Sheriff–"

"Harris. I know. I'm Wendy Logsdon. I was a friend of Innocence's."

"Have we met?" Ray asked.

"I've been over to her home several times. Mostly pool parties and her birthday."

"That's right," Ray said, smiling. "I remember you now. Listen, could I ask you some questions about Innocence, as you're walking in?"

"I don't have a problem," she replied.

"Wendy, I'm having trouble coming up with someone who can point me in the right direction."

"What do you mean, Sheriff?"

"Direction. Like whom killed Innocence."

"I'm sorry Sheriff, but I don't think I can help you with that."

"It's okay Wendy. Thanks," Ray said, turning back around toward his car. "I've been getting that all morning."

"Maybe you should talk with her BLF," Wendy called.

Ray stopped, wondering what he'd just heard. Turning back, he asked, "What did you just say?"

***

The driver of the blue Audi, hid by two rows of cars, watched as Ray talked with snotty-nose Wendy Logsdon. The driver had been spying on the Sheriff now for most of the past hour. The driver's only problem hiding over here this far away, was not hearing what was being said, but the driver knew it had to be about Innocence. *Wendy "snotty-nose" Logsdon doesn't know anything. You're just sucking wind, Sheriff.* Now the Sheriff was walking back to his car. *Why did you stop? What did she just say to you? What's she saying now?*

***

Ray thanked Wendy again and returned to his car. His mind was a little clearer, and Dave was taking a break. Putting the car in gear, Ray circled around to the visitor's parking lot. He needed to talk with principle Owen. Ray needed to set up another meeting. *But not now,* he reminded himself. *Later this afternoon, right before school ends for the day, and after I've put my ducks in a row.*

Chapter 60

Principle Owen was a man of his word, for everyone was in the gym as Ray requested. It was like the last time Ray requested a meeting. The coaches were sitting on the first few rows, followed by the Cheerleaders, with Ashley, Mary, and Janice among them, and then the basketball players. Ray could see Danny Harper. After a quick introduction, Principle Owen handed Ray the wireless mic.

"Well, here I am again," Ray said, holding the mic close to his mouth. "I want to thank you all for being here, and I promise I'll have you out of here before the buses run. I'm not here to ask you questions about the death of Innocence, or the beating of Mr. Johnston. If you've been living under a rock, then I guess you wouldn't know, but I'm sure most of you have already guessed why I'm here. I'm here about Randy Bennett. I don't have time today, so, tomorrow morning, I plan on asking most of you questions about Randy's death. (The students looked at each other) It will take place here at school. Plan on being here an hour and a half before classes begin. We'll meet here in the gym. Be sure to let your parents know, when you get home today. They'll need to get you here early. If your parents have a lawyer, then by all means, have him or her here as well. Okay, I want to take a few minutes to explain–"

Ray was interrupted by his phone.

"Hello," Ray said, not realizing he was still holding the mic close to his mouth. "FJ, I'm right in the middle of a meeting ... Really ... Incriminating evidence ... No. I can't do anything till I'm sure ... What did you find ...? What do you mean, not till I'm there?"

295

There were a few chuckles from the students. One student leaned over to a friend and whispered, "The old fart doesn't know we can hear him." Principle Owen heard and tried to take the mic from Rays' hand, but being caught up in his conversation, Ray pushed him away.

"Okay," Ray said, still holding the mic close. "I need to stop by the station first. I should be out at the MacGregor place in, say, forty or fifty minutes. Finally, this case could be turning around." Ray put the phone back in his pocket and turned his attention back to the students. He stood there a second trying to figure out what he was going to say next.

"I'm sorry, but something's come up, and I may have to postpone tomorrow's meeting. Principle Owen, we should probably go ahead and cancel it. (Owen nodded) I'll reschedule with Principle Owen, and he'll get back to you. Again, thank you all for coming." Ray handed the mic back. "Thank you, Principle Owen." It was three-thirty, and the dismissal bell went off.

Chapter 61

Ray squatted in a darkened corner, straining his eyes and ears, hoping what he was doing was the right thing; hoping his friend would not end up dead like Randy and Innocence. The late afternoon sunlight filtering through the cracks in the boarded-up window, made FJ look like a zebra with black and white stripes, with the black stripes being three times wider that the white. FJ stood in the middle of the living room like a staked-out goat waiting for a tiger, and Ray wondered what was going through FJ's mind.

Outside, the wind picked up making the house creak, crack, and moan, and it was playing tricks on Ray's mind. With every creak and crack, Ray knew someone was sneaking up on FJ from out of the darkest. With every moan, shadows were turning into monsters.

When the time comes, would I be able to tell the differences between shadows and monsters? If the time even comes.

Ray hoped the wild tale he just told at school, about FJ finding incriminating evidence, would smoke out the killer. As soon as the meeting at the school was over, Ray hightailed it to the MacGregor place. He parked the cruiser out back, behind the remains of the shed. Out of sight, out of mind.

Ray knew who the killer was, at least he thought he did, but something deep down inside wished he were wrong. It would take a criminal act, a smoking gun, to tie everything up. The bottom line–it would take a confession. Ray's legs were quickly starting to cramp from all the squatting. His bent spine and full bladder had become a duet, screaming for his attention. He was on the verge of calling everything off, when all hell broke loose.

The silence was broken by shuffling feet. With alternating streaks of light and dark from the windows, the scene reminded Ray of a disco's strobe light. With the light on, a person could be seen rapidly approaching from out of the dining room. Light off. Light on. The person was closer to FJ with raised hands holding something. Light off. Light on. The object in the person's hand was descending toward the back of FJ's head. Light off. There was a loud crack that resounded throughout the room. Light on. The person was standing there alone, and the person was too tall to be FJ. Light off.

Reaching up, Ray grabbed a corner of the wooden frame holding the boards covering a window. With a jerk, the frame and boards came tumbling down, filling the room with floating dust particles and intense sunlight. In the middle of the room stood Ashley McCoy with one hand shielding her eyes from the sunlight. The other hand was holding a baseball bat.

"Damn it Ashley," Ray said, jerking the bat out of her hands, "I knew it was you."

"How did you know?" she cried.

"At first I couldn't believe it. I had to be wrong. I must have gone over the evidence a dozen times in my head, and every time, the results always pointed in your direction.

"Innocence's death. Randy's death. Both killed the same way, the same place. They were just kids. Who, besides one of their peers, would want them dead? I couldn't think of a reason an adult, homeless or not, would want both of them dead? The evidence and my gut said, the killer must have known they were a couple, and they were having sex, and the killer was jealous. It had to be, because of the number of wounds in her back. That many wounds always point to crimes of passion. Whoever killed her must have loved her. Randy's death, on the other hand, had to be out of hate and revenge. Who loved her so much, and hated him that much? It came together when I was talking to Wendy Logsdon. I asked her if she knew anyone who would have a reason to kill either Innocence or Randy. She didn't, but she said I should talk to Innocence's BLF. It took me a moment, then it hit me, what she said. I asked her if she meant BFF, and she said no. She meant what she said, and I should talk to you Ashley, because you were Innocence's BLF, Best Lesbian Friend. I don't know if she meant it as a joke, but it made me think, maybe I was looking at everything all wrong. Who among Innocence's girlfriends was that close to her? You were. Who watched her every move? You did. Who imitated her–the way she dressed, her hair style, her mannerisms? You did. Who would be jealous of Randy? You would. Who told FJ a pack of lies about Randy and Innocence? Ashley, you did. Yes, FJ told me about all the shit you made up. Randy was a little turd, but Ashley, he wasn't a murderer."

A loud moan filled the room.

"FJ, you okay?" Ray asked.

"My head's killing me," FJ said, rising from the floor. "This damn helmet ain't worth shit."

"It's what we use for riot control," Ray assured him. "Not only does it cover your head, but the padding covers most of your neck and shoulders as well. Hell, it just saved you from getting your head split open."

"I guess it did at that. But next time, you get to wear it."

Both men turned their attention to Ashley. FJ, rubbing the back of his head, looked up at her, and said one word.

"Why?"

"I overheard you had evidence that could solve the case. If you did, then you had–"

"Damn it Ashley, I don't mean that," FJ interrupted. "I meant, why did you kill her?"

"She didn't love me."

"You're so full of crap," Ray spat. "You were her best friend. Of course, she loved you, but she could never love you in that way. She wasn't gay. As her closest friend, you should have respected that. As her true friend, you should have wanted what was best for her."

"I did want what was best for her. That's just it. I was best for her. Can't you see that? Don't you understand? But no, she could only love me as a friend, and that's not what I wanted. I wanted us to be more than friends. I wanted us to be lovers." Ashley chuckled. "It's funny. I used to wait for her after cheerleading practice, so that we could shower together. She never caught on."

"It's obvious you hated Randy, but to kill him?"

"I thought Innocence and Randy had broken up, and everything was cool. Maybe, just maybe, I could convince her, and she would love me after all. I used to sneak and read her diary. It told me they were back together. Can you believe that? She kept it a secret from her best friend, that they were back together."

"Do you have her diary?" Ray asked.

"It's at home. I couldn't bring myself to destroy it. She wrote it after all. But I couldn't let anyone else read it. It talked about them getting back together. It described the sex, and how wonderful it was, and how much they loved each other. I almost puked. It was also full of references about me being a lesbian, but Innocence wrote that it was alright. That is was cool having a lesbian as a friend. Like I was some kind of pet. You know the day you came over to her house, and I was up in her room going through her photos? (Ray nodded) That's when I took it. I hid it in one of the photo albums.

"The day before she died, I followed them out here. I watched them making love on the dining room table, and I hated her. God, how I hated her. Why Randy instead of me? Then it hit me. She was truly in love with him, and only him, and she would never be in love with me."

"But if you knew she didn't have the same feelings for you, why did you have to kill her?" FJ pleaded.

"She told me many times she would be my friend forever. What does that mean? Friends forever. I'll tell you what that means. Bullshit. Deep down, even then, there was a part of me that said, given time, I could change her mind. In her diary she wrote, she didn't love me as I loved her. Those words hurt me to the core. They had to be wrong. Didn't they? They could have been wrong. Right? I had to know. That's why I brought her out here."

"And if she couldn't love you the same way?" Ray asked.

"That's why I brought the bat. I know it's an old cliché, but if

I couldn't have her, no one else could."

"How did you get the bat out here without her becoming suspicious?"

"I skipped out of the next to last class and came out here, placing the bat in the dining room. It looked like it had been lying there forever.

"After school, I was supposed to go home. I was grounded, you know. But I called mom and told her I had something to do at school, that could help raise my grades and I needed to stay late. She was all in favor of that.

"I then told Innocence I had something important to tell her, but we needed to be alone, away from prying eyes and ears. She was so innocent, so gullible. After school, I followed her home so she could put her car in the garage."

"Weren't you afraid someone would see you?"

"I never thought of that. All I could think about was Innocence loving me, after I told her how I felt about her."

"But you just said, you knew how Innocence felt."

"A person can be wrong. I prayed I was wrong. I didn't know. Maybe there was still a small flicker of hope. I envisioned after telling her, Innocence and I would make love, laying on the table just like I saw her and Randy. So we came here, I lit a candle, and I poured out my heart to her. I tried to pull her close to kiss her, to seal our love, but she pushed me away. Do you believe that? The bitch pushed me away. That's when I lost it.

"She turned to run when she saw me grab the bat off the table, but it was too late. I hit her. I only hit her once, but I was so mad I put everything into it. I heard bones crushing, and Innocence fell. I kneeled, watching as her blood stained the hardwood floor.

"My plan was after we swore our love to one another, I was going to ask Innocence to exchange a lock of our hair, as a sign of our love. That's why I brought scissors. But with her dead, I saw no reason why I couldn't have a strand of her hair to remember her by. The strand is here in this locket around my neck, if you want to see it. (Ray shook his head)

"As I was cutting off the strand of hair, I felt a pain in the back of my head. I was lightheaded. I wanted to vomit. I know what it was. It was rage, and it engulfed me. I started stabbing. Over and over, I plunged the scissors. The room was full of the sound of my sobbing. And as I stabbed, my sobs became screams. Before I was done, the house was echoing with the howls of someone gone mad. The howls and moans slowly became a name ... Randy ... Randy ... Randy. And I knew it wasn't me that killed Innocence, it was Randy."

"Speaking of Randy, how did you do it?" Ray asked.

"I left a note on his car saying I had information the police would want to know. And, if he wanted it, he'd have to meet me out here. He came out here, and I killed him."

"Just like that?" Ray asked.

"Just like that."

"Clear this point up for me. Why did you tell Frederick that Randy tormented Innocence?"

"Innocence used to tell me her grandad had a temper, and he got drunk a lot. Hell, I read it in her diary. And when he got drunk, he did stupid, spur of the moment, things. (FJ frowned and turned his head) I knew how much he loved Innocence. So I thought if I could get him angry enough, he would get drunk and hurt Randy for me. When he failed, I knew it was up to me.

"Since the day she died, whenever I saw Randy, I thought of him as dead. That's all I could think about. He was dead to me. He was the reason she died. Not me. I loved her. He was the reason. He was the reason. He had to die. Plain and simple. It became a passion. It was the reason why I took a breath. It became the reason I lived. Surely, you understand. You loved her. You can't blame me. Randy didn't deserve her. I did. He caused this. I loved her more than anyone could. Innocence belonged to me and just me. It was only right. I wanted to touch her, taste her lips, and taste her body. I wanted that experience all to myself."

Ashley stood there wild eyed, staring off into space as if she was hearing her own screams floating through the deserted house. She didn't look like the same girl. Ray knew she was done talking.

With Ashley safely locked up in the back of the patrol car,

Ray and FJ stood there staring at the old house.

"I'll have a couple of guys come out and tow her Audi back into town," Ray said, staring at the house's broken windows.

"I think someone needs to burn it," FJ whispered. "Her car?"

"Hell no. I was talking about the MacGregor house, and I'm willing to supply the match."

"You wanted revenge for Innocence," Ray said. "Did you get it?"

FJ shook his head.

"We have Innocence's killer. That will have to do, but that's not the revenge I wanted, that I desired. That hunger is still deep down inside my gut. With time it will heal. You know, Ashley's hurting as much as me."

Ray nodded.

"She loved Innocence," Ray added, "but Innocence couldn't return the kind of love Ashley wanted. The kind of love Ashley needed or desired. With time, the anger and desire could become manageable. I pray it does for her sake."

With Ashley curled up in the backseat, Ray backed his cruiser out onto the highway. He was seriously tired from the adrenaline rush, but at least Dave was gone. Ray knew he wasn't coming back, and Ray would miss him, liked he'd miss a stick in the eye. Flames from the burning house danced above the treetops. It wouldn't be long, before someone noticed and reported it to the authorities. Thankfully, as old as it was, it would be nothing more than a pile of ashes long before they arrived.

"Ray, I've been wanting to ask you a question for a long time," Fj said, rubbing the back of his head.

"Go ahead," Ray said.

"Who mows your yard?"

Epilogue

Four months later

The three murders, the one in Munfordville, the one in Park City, and the one in Bowling Green, are officially classified as cold cases. Ray was right, when he said there was nothing that pointed to them being connected in any way. Wade McBride was no help. He had seen the dead body in the house and had panicked. He did not see who put her there.

Harold King got Wade McBride to drop the charges of kidnapping and torture, against his client Jim Bennett Senior and the two private dicks. But at a price. Fifteen million to be exact, as well as pre-paid PTSD therapy, under the umbrella of cognitive behavioral therapy. A month and a half into therapy, Wade started talking about his trauma, concentrating on where his fears were coming from.

Wade, now set for life, lives in a small trailer park in Key West, Florida. Every day you can find him sipping daiquiris at *Sloppy Joes*.

Late one rainy afternoon, Betty Hall received a phone call from the Los Angeles Police Department. They were sorry to have to report–her mother, Zoe Payne, was found dead under the Santa Monica Pier, of an apparent drug overdose. At 9:19 a.m. the next morning in Nashville, Tom, Mike, Stephanie, Margaret, and Charlotte watched as Betty, Ray, and FJ boarded American Airlines' flight 3036 bound for L.A. They were flying there to identify the body and bring Zoe home, to be buried beside Innocence.

About the Author

Kentucky has always been my home. I was born in Owensboro and raised in Daviess County. Life was simple back then. I grew up with outhouses, hand-pumps, and coal stoves. If you wanted hot water, you heated it on the stove. Both of my parents have passed on. I have a half-brother, Danny, but most of our younger lives he lived with his father, so we didn't get to see each other often. Looking back, sadly, it was like being an only child. My closest friends were the cows, chickens, pigs, goats, sheep, turkeys, geese, ducks, and horses my dad kept on our small farm. I hope I didn't leave anyone out. Farm animals can be so jealous. Our grocery store - mason jars of mom's canned vegetables and the occasional trip into town to the IGA.

My dad was a woodsman. You could give him a shotgun, a box of shells and a book of matches, and he could disappear into the forest for weeks. I used to hunt with him, but I was never the woodsman. I can't tell you how many deer, squirrels, rabbits, raccoons and ground hogs I've eaten.

My wife, Stephanie, and I have five kids (three boys and two girls) and eight grandchildren (five boys and three girls). All but one son live here in town. You should see Christmas day at our house.

I've had several jobs during my lifetime. When I was thirteen, I had a summer job. I was a soda-jerk at the Utica Junior High School playground. The school is now defunct. It is not my fault the school went defunct. As an adult, I started out as a janitor. Loved the work, but not the pay. Mapping came next. In other words, I was a draftsman who created maps from surveys. I did that for over twenty years. Mapping fulltime and going to Brescia College (It's now a University) at night, I got a BS in Computer Science. Career change. I was a Computer Analyst for over twenty years. There came a day when I realized I was the dinosaur of Computer Science. Technology had passed me by. So, I up and retired. That was in 2014, and I haven't missed working a day. Truth be known, I do miss the people I worked with. Notice, I've said nothing about writing. I could tell you a pretty good story, but putting it on paper was another thing. Stephanie, my wife, asked, "And why not?" I had no answer.

I should keep this short, so, I will tease you with two important events that happened in my life; two events that I haven't already discussed. When we meet each other, don't hesitate to ask me about them.

Monday, September 6, 1965, was a Labor Day, and I was out of school. On that day, I came in contact with a high voltage powerline. Seven thousand two hundred volts entered my hand and exited my head and my feet. That's not a typo. It was seven thousand two hundred volts. I was given up for dead for three days. There is a "rest of the story" as Paul Harvey used to say. Ask me about it when we meet.

The second event: September 17, 2017, I was ordained a Permanent Deacon in the Catholic Church. It keeps me busy these days. If you're not sure what a Permanent Deacon does, Goggle "Permanent Deacon of the Catholic Church."

There you have it. My life story summed up in 1000 words

or less. It sounds like a writing contest doesn't it. There's so much I left out. I could tell you about riding the rails, or the time I hung myself. But, those will have to wait until we meet.

www.ingramcontent.com/pod-product-compliance
Lightning Source LLC
Chambersburg PA
CBHW020942260626
47169CB00006B/1777